"COMMAND

Anything comi

"Affirmative," Riannon reported. "I've got another star moving on our six. They'll be within range in the next five minutes."

Rose focused on the fighting in front of him and watched as Hawg and an ambushing *Shadow Hawk* crumpled into the boulders. Coolant dripped like blood over the boulder that failed to provide cover for the fallen 'Mech. A flight of long-range missiles streaked past Rose, and he involuntarily flinched as they exploded behind him. He scanned for the attacker, but the firer had already ducked behind the protection of the boulders.

An enemy 'Mech popped up from cover and fired at Esmeralda. As the Clanner's shot slammed into the *Mad Cat*, it in turn was skewered by return fire from five different Black Thorn 'Mechs. The Clan 'Mech fell backward behind the boulders, but Rose knew the shots had been fatal.

"One Cat," said Hawg, "D.R.T." None of the Black Thorns responded to the cryptic announcement. After a moment of silence, Hawg came back on the channel. "Dead right there."

DISCOVER THE ADVENTURES
OF BATTLETECH

BATTLETECH®

D.R.T.

James D. Long

A ROC BOOK

ROC
Published by the Penguin Group
Penguin Books USA Inc., 375 Hudson Street,
New York, New York 10014, U.S.A.
Penguin Books Ltd, 27 Wrights Lane,
London W8 5TZ, England
Penguin Books Australia Ltd, Ringwood,
Victoria, Australia
Penguin Books Canada Ltd, 10 Alcorn Avenue,
Toronto, Ontario, Canada M4V 3B2
Penguin Books (N.Z.) Ltd, 182–190 Wairau Road,
Auckland 10, New Zealand

Penguin Books Ltd, Registered Offices:
Harmondsworth, Middlesex, England

Published by Roc, an imprint of Dutton Signet
a division of Penguin Books USA Inc.

First Printing, May, 1994
10 9 8 7 6 5 4 3 2 1

Series Editor: Donna Ippolito
Cover: Boris Vallejo
Interior illustrations: Rick Harris
Mechanical drawings: FASA Art Staff

 REGISTERED TRADEMARK—MARCA REGISTRADA

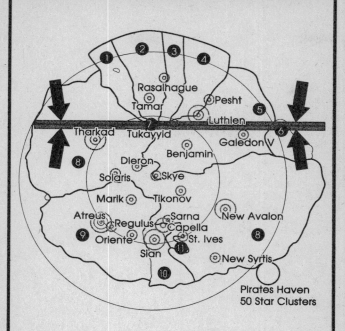

MAP OF THE SUCCESSOR STATES
CLAN TRUCE LINE

1 • Jade Falcon/Steel Viper, 2 • Wolf Clan, 3 • Ghost Bear,
4 • Smoke Jaguars - Nova Cats, 5 • Draconis Combine,
6 • Outworlds Alliance, 7 • Free Rasalhague Republic,
8 • Federated Commonwealth, 9 • Free Worlds League,
10 • Capellan Confederation, 11 • St. Ives Compact

Map Compiled by COMSTAR.
From information provided by the COMSTAR EXPLORER SERVICE
and the STAR LEAGUE ARCHIVES on Terra.

Prologue

It is the year 3057. Mankind inhabits the stars, but has taken his warlike nature with him. The thousands of human-occupied worlds of the Inner Sphere were once bound together in a glorious, prosperous Star League. With the fall of the League in 2781, a Dark Age descended as each of the five surviving star empires warred for dominion.

For almost three centuries, the five Successor Lords fought among themselves in the endless conflict that became known as the Succession Wars. Millions died and a few worlds changed hands, but for all the fighting and dying, little changed until 3049, when the fierce warriors known as the Clans invaded the Inner Sphere.

With their superior war machines and superhuman infantry, these warrior descendants of the legendary Aleksandr Kerensky's vanished Star League Army came to reclaim the Inner Sphere. For three years, the Clans were unstoppable, until the Com Guards battled and bested them on the world of Tukayyid. Their victory bought the Successor States a fifteen-year truce, paid for with countless lives.

Despite the truce, both sides continue to attempt daring raids and other dangerous actions in hopes of tipping the balance even before the day of reckoning fifteen years hence. Once more, the Inner Sphere trembles on the edge of apocalypse.

This time, no one may survive.

1

The high-pitched trill of laser fire was briefly accentuated by the sharp retort of a heavy pistol. Esmeralda continued her journey down the underground passage toward the double doors at the end of the hall. Pausing briefly at the doors, she could just make out a trio of male voices from within the room.

"Bah!" barked the biggest of the men as Esmeralda entered. "They'd never have us." He accentuated his point with a single pistol shot down the length of the firing room. Even though they were underground, the retort was no louder than it would have been under the clear blue sky. Their Borghesian employers had apparently gotten around to installing the additional layer of sound baffling that Captain Rose had requested. Esmeralda glanced down the firing range at the plastic target sheet. As usual, Hawg's aim with the oversized Sternsnacht was perfect. A single hole now gaped over the heart of the target, a shot that would have been an instant kill even against someone wearing light body armor.

"And I'd not have them, either, if it came to that." Jeremiah Rose looked over at Esmeralda and nodded briefly. Esmeralda touched her index finger to the side of her head, but said nothing. Rose arced an eyebrow in question, but didn't voice it. Instead he turned back toward the barrel-chested Hawg.

"You'd have a hard time convincing me anybody is crazier than Sun Tzu, but if there is someone, it's probably Aziz. She went 'round the bend even before I left the Com Guards, and we all know that's been a while." Though still speaking to Hawg, Rose had turned down-range and was holding his beloved laser at arm's length.

"From what I hear, the Word of Blake faction has found safe haven in the Free Worlds League. But that's not so surprising, given that Thomas Marik is a former ComStar adept." Rose aimed and pulled the trigger three times in rapid succession. The laser burned a single hole in the center of the target's forehead, but made not a sound. Esmeralda still marveled at the pistol even though she'd seen it fired often enough. It might look like any other weapon of its type, but it was obviously much more.

The well-won plastic grip was too smooth to have been worn away by a single user, even if the pistol had been fired daily. At first glance it looked like a Nakjama pistol, which, on the surface, was not particularly remarkable. Jeremiah Rose had, after all, been stationed in Luthien during his service with the Com Guards, and the Nakjama was the standard sidearm of Kurita MechWarriors.

Appearances, however, were deceiving. Subtle but important differences separated the pistol in Rose's hand from the Nakjama. Indeed, Rose had told them that the Nakjama was based on *his* pistol, not the other way around. For one thing, the barrel of this model was almost a millimeter wider in diameter. That meant a larger alignment crystal, which translated into more power. The range was also much greater—not that range was ever a factor with lasers. Most people, even MechWarriors, couldn't see as far as a laser pistol could shoot, and forget holding the pistol steady enough to hit a target at extreme range. What made the pistol special was what it didn't do.

Rose's laser made not a sound when fired. Esmeralda had listened carefully every time she'd been near its firing, and had heard neither the familiar hum of capacitors nor the distinctive trilling discharge. All that happened with Rose's pistol was silence and a brief flash of red light. The eye couldn't really register the flash of a laser, but the afterimage was briefly burned into the cornea, providing the illusion of sight.

Rose slowly lowered the pistol and turned back to Hawg. "Thomas Marik might still be in charge in the Free Worlds League, but we can't count on that lasting for the length of a contract. The next House we sign with has got to be able to provide some stability, and Marik still doesn't have that."

"But the League has been touched by the Clan invasion," argued Hawg.

Rose nodded. "True enough, but they've still had their share of problems, and the marriage of Isis Marik and Sun Tzu isn't going to make their realm any more stable."

"I concur," put in the third man, who'd been silent until now. Esmeralda noticed that Antioch Bell was frowning instead of wearing his usual grin as he rubbed his chin reflectively. "We shouldn't consider Marik as a potential employer unless we're willing to accept Sun Tzu as our potential commander—and if anything happened to Thomas, that's what he'd be. I personally don't believe he's as crazy as everyone seems to think, but it does look like he only uses people for his own ends. I'd hate to see the Black Thorns become just another one of his pawns."

Esmeralda nodded in unison with Rose and Hawg. She was glad House Marik was being ruled out as a potential employer.

"All right, then," continued Hawg. "I'll prove Mom didn't raise me a fool, and also eliminate St. Ives, Tikonov, and any other government along the Periphery. There's no way they can afford us, and they're not likely to be fighting the Clans anyway." Hawg raised the Sternsnacht and fired at the target. Rose's mark disappeared beneath the larger hole of the slug-thrower.

"Agreed," said Rose. "I founded the Black Thorns to fight the Clans, and that's what we're going to do. That leaves us with the Federated Commonwealth, who's currently signing the check, and the Draconis Combine." Rose nodded toward

Antioch Bell and glanced down the range. Bell shook himself loose from his thoughts and reached for his holster. Firing from the belt, he punched a hole in the target's right eye, his Sunbeam laser making the familiar noises Esmeralda associated with laser fire. When she looked from the target to Bell again, the pistol was already back in the holster.

"What about Rasalhague?" Hawg and Bell turned toward Esmeralda as she spoke. "They're not out of it yet, despite the losses they've suffered, and ComStar is backing their efforts."

"Right you are," said Bell, "but the leadership of Rasalhague is totally demoralized. The people are still willing to fight, but the rulers aren't willing to lead. Ever since their precious Prince Ragnar refused to be rescued from the Clans, they've been in a stupor."

"They might offer a high-risk garrison contract," Esmeralda said.

"You're both right," countered Rose. "We could probably get the work, but I don't think it would be work worth having. Any garrison duty, even high-risk, would pay too little. We've got to go on the offensive, and that means signing on with somebody who has the C-bills to take this fight to the Clans ..."

"And that means the F-C or Kurita," finished Hawg. "Both of them are on the rebound and ready to fight." Hawg fired twice down the range, matching Bell's shot with his first and opening a hole in the left eye with his second.

"You're assuming we can even get on with one of the Houses, Hawg," said Esmeralda. "What if we can't? We ought to be keeping our eyes open for another local contract like the one we're finishing now."

"Esmeralda's right again," said Rose. "We're riding some hot tech, but we can't assume that makes us marketable. The F-C or Kurita make the most sense, but neither one is ideal. I'd prefer the Kuritas, but that's personal taste."

"The Snakes? Why them? You're not still mad at the F-C for what they did to your family?" Bell sounded confused and somewhat hurt by Rose's rejection of the Federated Commonwealth. As a past member of the Federated Commonwealth Armed Forces, he retained more than a little pride in his former military. Rose titled his head and squinted slightly, an expression Esmeralda knew meant he was carefully considering his next words.

Jeremiah Rose had been born the eldest son of a MechWarrior member of the Northwind Highlanders, one of the oldest and most respected mercenary units in the Inner Sphere. In the debacle that was the War of 3039, the Highlanders, fighting for Prince Hanse Davion, had attacked several worlds along the Davion-Kurita border. It should have been a good plan, but Theodore Kurita's counterassault was even better; as a result the Combine succeeded in winning back some of the worlds they'd previously lost to Davion. Rose's mother was killed in the fighting, and Rose made no bones about the fact that he blamed Hanse Davion for his mother's death. His anger had created a rift between Rose and his father that eventually led the younger Rose to abandon the Highlanders and join Com Guard, the military arm of ComStar.

"No, it's got more to do with the politics of the situation," Rose said, but saw that Bell didn't seem convinced. "Here we've got the biggest threat the Inner Sphere has seen since Stephen Amaris practically sitting on our doorstep, and the Federated Commonwealth is still trying to decide if it likes being one big, happy family. The new boys are a perfect example."

Esmeralda knew Rose was referring to the Gray Death Legion. The members of that crack mercenary unit would probably have been furious to hear themselves being referred to so offhandedly, but Esmeralda already knew where Rose was going with his comment and agreed wholeheartedly.

"Ever notice how closely the Gray Death is tied to Tharkad and the Steiner family?" she said. "Maybe it's Victor Davion whose officially giving them their orders, but they still consider themselves a Steiner unit from the Lyran Commonwealth. That's where the Gray Death Legion began even before there *was* a Federated Commonwealth, and they're still tied to that past.

"And the F-C's far from being one big, happy family. Most of the ordinary people—and that includes people in the military—still think of themselves as being loyal to either Davion or Steiner. They work together and fight together, but they don't see eye-to-eye on many important things."

"Such as?" asked Bell.

"The Clans, for one," said Rose. "The Steiner side of the military has done a lot of the fighting and dying, and *all* the planets lost to the Clans have been on the Steiner side of the FedCom border. The Lyrans wonder why their Davion allies aren't helping more, while people on Davion worlds wonder why they have to help at all."

"It's a mess," Rose agreed quietly, his eyes turned downrange as he squeezed the trigger of his pistol. "The entire Inner Sphere is mired in a web of politics."

"Except Kurita," said Bell.

"No, Antioch, I suspect the Draconis Combine is as bad as the rest when it comes to playing politics, but they've got two important advantages the others lack." Rose didn't look at his friend as he spoke, but continued to send shot after silent shot down the firing range.

"First," he said, "except for what the Combine has lost to the Clans, they've maintained a fairly stable border. And the ordinary Kurita people stand behind Theodore Kurita in his efforts to beat back the Clan threat. I think we can safely assume that Teddy will continue to direct his entire war effort at stopping the Clans, not in looking for ways to attack the Federated Commonwealth.

"Second, the Kuritas have the most able military leader in the Inner Sphere. Theodore Kurita has proved that time and again. Unlike Victor Davion, who is still a boy, or Thomas Marik, who is, at best, a religious zealot, Teddy is a Mech-Warrior first, politician second. I think we can count on that."

"But the Snakes have a terrible reputation for how they treat mercenaries," put in Bell. Rose nodded and finally turned away from the firing range. In the time they'd been speaking, he'd fired two dozen times at the target outline, burning through the torso, head, and neck. He popped the energy cell from his pistol and replaced it with a fresh one from his belt before holstering the weapon.

"Quite true, but I think that attitude has changed, or, at least, is changing."

"Why?" asked Hawg.

"Well, ever since Wolf's Dragoons and the Kell Hounds helped save the entire planet of Luthien from a Clan invasion, the general population seems to look upon mercenaries as, well, less *un*acceptable. Teddy has never had a problem hiring mercs, and the reports from Outreach indicate that the Snakes are offering decent terms and the widest range of contracts."

Esmeralda cringed at the mention of Outreach, and Rose asked, "Something wrong?"

"That's the reason I came down here in the first place. I got so caught up in the discussion that I forgot to deliver a message from Ajax." Esmeraldo checked her chronometer. "Ria arrived on Outreach approximately thirty-six hours ago and has registered us with the Mercenary Review and Bonding Commission. She has started to look for available contracts, but is wondering if there's anything particular she needs to know."

Rose glanced around the room. With the exception of Ajax, the recon lance commander, and his sister Riannon Rose, who served as the executive officer of the Black Thorns, all the leaders of the mercenary unit were assembled in the firing room. It was true that the unit roster listed neither Hawg nor Bell as officers, but their experience and devotion to the Black Thorns had earned them a voice at impromptu meetings such as this one.

"Well, unless I've completely misunderstood our current discussion, we're looking for a chance to go on the offensive." He looked around the room at the trio of nodding heads. "She should probably start with the Draconis Combine, then go to the Federated Commonwealth." Rose checked the room again. Esmeralda and Hawg were already nodding agreement, with Bell joining in after a moment.

"Then it's settled. If Teddy will have us, he's the first choice. If he won't, we'll have to see what we can get."

"He'll have us," said Esmeralda.

"Oh, really?" asked Bell. "And how can you be so sure?"

"If everything we've heard about him is true, Theodore Kurita is too smart not to hire a unit as good as the Black Thorns."

2

Riannon Rose walked through the side streets of Harlech and marveled at the changes a year had brought. It was not that the city had changed so much—quite the contrary. It was she who had changed, and she liked the person she had become.

Looking back, she realized how much trust her brother had placed in her the first time she'd come here, just as he was doing today. Harlech was the capital of Outreach, homeworld of the famous mercenary unit Wolf's Dragoons. It also served as a mercenary marketplace where potential employers and mercenaries could find each other.

Ria glanced around her, more from habit than because there was any danger. Still, it made sense to be careful, and her brother always reminded her how many mistakes it took to kill a MechWarrior: one. Of course you could get killed even if you didn't make a mistake, she thought. You could get killed just because you were following orders, like Angus.

An extremely accurate—or lucky—blast from a Clan PPC had killed her cousin Angus and his 'Mech with a single shot in the fighting on Borghese. Ria shuddered unconsciously at the memory. There hadn't been much of Angus left to return to her uncle, but she'd made the trip back to

Northwind anyway. She hadn't wanted to do it, but Jeremiah had been adamant. As commanding officer of the Black Thorns, he'd have preferred to make the trip himself, but their contract with Borghese had made that impossible. As a result it was she who'd had to face her uncle and the rest of the family.

Just then her stomach began to rumble, reminding Ria of what had brought her outside in the first place. She glanced around again and ducked into a small restaurant, but what she'd thought at first was a second, inner door turned out to be a heavily muscled Elemental warrior on the way out. Without thinking, she stepped aside, her small body no match for the hulking brute in front of her. If the man noticed her at all, he gave no sign as he crouched low to be able to pass through the door.

Ria began to chastise herself for having so easily given ground. Would a real MechWarrior have retreated so quickly? She couldn't say, but decided to find out. Turning on her heel, she left the restaurant. Ten meters away the giant was making his way through the crowd, apparently oblivious to the throng of people around him.

Ria followed cautiously, maintaining the gap as she observed the man—if man was really the correct term. Elementals were Clansmen genetically engineered to be bigger, stronger, and faster than average humans, even Mech-Warriors. Trained from birth to fight in the special battle armor developed by the Clans, they were said to be unbeatable in single combat.

Ria had seen armored Elementals in films at the academy. Working in teams of five, they could quickly strip the armor off a BattleMech, then fire their lasers at the exposed components. On Borghese her brother's *Charger* had been almost overcome by just such armored infantry, but skill and luck had carried the day. Watching the replays of the battle from tapes made by the *Charger*'s external camera, she had marveled at the fearlessness of these individuals.

When the Elemental in front of her suddenly turned to his left, Ria briefly lost sight of him, but a quick trot put her around the corner and again on his trail. Back at the academy she would never have dreamed of tailing an Elemental. She could scarcely have imagined even having the opportunity, much less the desire, but here on Outreach anything seemed possible. Wolf's Dragoons had strong ties to the Clans even though the unit was no longer a part of the Clan military. At the academy Ria had been told that captured Clan warriors would usually swear allegiance to the Clan that captured them.

I guess that makes about as much sense as anything else about the Clans, she thought, studying the Elemental's back. Why waste a good soldier just because he's on the wrong side? And why be loyal to a side that obviously was inferior since it had been defeated in a battle?

Academy instructors had been very certain that the Clans fought with a carefully defined code of honor. That fact had been verified countless times on dozens of worlds, but most Inner Sphere MechWarriors had a tough time defining just what was "honorable" to a Clan warrior. Most of the time you were too busy trying not to get killed by the Clanners to have the luxury of trying to diagnose their motives, but on the few occasions when an Inner Sphere force had actually won an engagement and been able to take any prisoners, the captured Clan warriors seemed to be model P.O.W.s.

"Take this guy," Ria said aloud. She quickly bit her lip and looked around. Nobody had heard, or if they did, more likely nobody cared. People from dozens of different walks of life passed her along the way, each one with private worries or intents. Ria walked several paces with her eyes firmly on the ground. "Careless, careless, careless," she mumbled as she mentally kicked herself. When she finally looked up, the Elemental was nowhere in sight.

"Now where . . ." she began to say, but got no further before an unseen hand grabbed her shoulder and pulled her into an adjacent doorway. She reached for the fist and pushed back, throwing her weight the opposite way, but the effort was futile. With a muffled thump, she hit the hardwood door, jarring her free shoulder and sending a pain down her side. She tried to draw a breath, but a thick hand grabbed her other shoulder and spun her around. The Elemental shoved his forearm under her chin, choking off most of her air supply.

"I am right here. Now why are you following me?"

Ria looked up at her assailant. He was even bigger up close, with ice-blue eyes narrowed to slits as he stared down at her. His features were perfectly formed, beautiful in every detail, but on a larger scale than a normal person's. In answer, Ria kicked out with her left foot, aiming where his knee should have been.

She was rewarded with a solid strike. For a moment she thought she could feel the knee give way under the blow, but then nothing. The Elemental merely smiled at a kick that should have left him bawling on the floor. Even his teeth were perfect.

"The first one was free because I judge you to be new on Outreach, *quiaff*?" Although Ria lost most of the last half of his sentence, she knew enough to nod. Her blood was pounding so loudly in her ears that she could barely think.

"Never seen an Elemental up close," she rasped. At least not a live one, she tried to add, but she was out of air. The Elemental's forearm retreated slightly, and Ria took a lungful of air before the pressure returned. She reached for the man's arm with both hands, but her hands were too small to wrap around his giant biceps. She grabbed the front of his tunic instead.

"I fight for Wolf's Dragoons now. I remain a warrior despite my capture. I will not be followed and I will not be mocked." The perfect smile turned into a sneer. Ria saw his lips move, but most of his words were drowned out by her own rushing blood. The Elemental's free hand drew back as Ria's vision began to narrow. She wondered if she would pass out before the Elemental's fist knocked her out, but decided that was unlikely. He obviously knew what he was doing. She kicked out again, but her foot smacked him feebly on the thigh. If he felt the attack, he gave no notice. The man's smile returned, and Riannon closed her eyes in spite of herself.

When the blow did not come, she thought she might have passed out. Slowly opening her eyes as the pressure on her throat eased, she saw the Elemental begin to lean away from her. When he released her neck, she fell back into the door jamb and tried to re-inflate her lungs. Heaving gasps of air seemed to work best, so she sucked at it in loud gasps, resisting the temptation to lean forward. A small part of her mind told her the lungs needed to remain expanded, not contracted as they would be if she bent forward.

After several moments, her breathing started to return to normal, and Ria looked around for the Elemental. He was already fading away in the crowd, not even deigning to look back at her. Am I so little a threat, she wondered?

"How ya feelin'?" Ria rolled her head to the side and looked at the lanky redhead standing nearby. The woman was smiling from ear to ear as if she knew exactly how Ria was feeling.

"Feel like my 'Mech just stepped on me. How do you feel?"

"Me?" The redhead just smiled wider. "Why I feel just dandy." Riannon was beginning to think she didn't like this red-haired female when a third woman joined them.

"Can you move? If you can't, we'll help, but I think we'd best be on our way." Ria looked over at the new arrival and noticed that the holster to her pistol was undone. "He just rounded the corner, so he's out of sight, and I don't want to be around if he decides to come back. So, can you move?"

Ria didn't really consider before answering. "Yeah, I can move."

"Then let's be off."

Ria walked between the two women for several blocks, concentrating mostly on trying to breathe normally. By the time they'd reached the hotel district, she had most of her breath back.

"Thanks for the help. I guess I got careless," Ria offered.

"I guess," said the redhead. "Either that or you like your men really big." Ria flushed as the redhead winked.

"Don't let Kitten bother you, missy. She talks like that to everybody."

Kitten smiled even wider. "That's right, I do, and since I saved your hide back there, I was wondering if you would answer one little question?" Ria considered refusing, but didn't have time before Kitten continued. "You got any brothers?" Ria's eyes went wide for a moment, but Kitten just laughed.

"O.K., Kitten, that's enough. I think she's been through quite enough already. If you're all right, we'll be on our way," the other woman said to Ria, already turning to go.

Ria stopped her with a hand on the sleeve. "Wait a second. I do have a brother, but he's not on Outreach."

Kitten laughed and snapped her fingers. "Just my luck."

"But since Jeremiah's not around, let me buy you dinner. It's the least I can do."

Kitten didn't give her companion a chance to say no. "Free food? Well, maybe this is my lucky day. Where to?" When Ria suggested the Regalia, the restaurant at her own hotel just across the street, Kitten hooked an arm through Ria's elbow and left her companion to follow. "Sounds good to me. Let's get to it."

Neither Ria nor her guests were properly dressed for dinner, but she assumed that would not be a problem at this early hour. The hostess at the Regalia gave them only a slight glance of disapproval as she led them to a table. Waiters and busboys hovered around the women like battlefield scavengers, then went their separate ways once the food was ordered. The wine steward returned with a bottle from an unknown Davion vineyard and poured three glasses.

"To my rescuers, whoever they may be." Ria toasted each woman and sipped the white wine. "My name is Riannon Rose, but my friends call me Ria, as I hope you will. I am the executive officer of the Black Thorn mercenary unit, currently stationed on Borghese."

"That's near the Clan boarder, isn't it?" asked Kitten. Riannon nodded.

"Well, my name is Katherine Kittiallen, but everybody calls me Kitten, whether I like it or not. I pilot a *Panther*—as if being called Kitten isn't enough of a cat joke, but I currently"—Kitten made a great show of loosening her collar and pretending to be embarrassed—"am without benefit of employment." Ria smiled at the woman's antics and looked closely at her for the first time.

Kitten Kittiallen was long and lanky and almost totally lacking in feminine curves. Even her face was angular. But she always seemed to be smiling, which made her eyes glisten through half-closed lids. Her hair was deep red, a long, thick mass that shimmered in the lights of the restaurant.

"My name is Greta Podell, late of the Rasalhague Republic," said the other woman when Ria turned to her expectantly. "Like Kitten I am 'without benefit of employment,' Although I also find myself without a 'Mech." Ria studied Greta for a moment, but if the woman was embarrassed by the admission of being dispossessed, she didn't let it show. Most MechWarriors would be too ashamed to confess that they'd been shot out of their 'Mechs, especially to a complete stranger like Ria, but not Greta. "I've come to Outreach in hopes of joining a mercenary unit."

"As have I," said Kitten. Ria looked at the pair of women. Unlike Kitten, Greta was muscular, but rounded in all the right places. She could easily imagine Hawg and Badicus fighting over Greta had they been here in her place. She smiled at the thought. Even Greta's hair, which was black threaded with silver, seemed attractive rather than old.

"Well," said Ria as the waiters reappeared with the trays carrying their food, "I already have a unit, but I've come to Outreach in search of warriors." Neither Kitten nor Greta responded as the waiters hovered about serving them.

"My brother is commanding officer of the Black Thorns. We're only a demi-company now, but we've got several unassigned 'Mechs." Ria pretended not to notice the sudden fire in Greta's eyes as she went on. "I've been sent to Outreach to recruit new pilots and bring us up to company strength before Jeremiah arrives with the rest of the unit."

"You're going to do all the hiring?" asked Kitten through a mouthful of veal. "That's a pretty tall order."

Ria picked apart her game hen and considered. "True, but that's my job. I'm the XO of the unit. Logistics are my specialty, but Jeremiah sent me ahead to recruit. If I give the green light, he approves it and that's all there is to it."

"Why the rush?" asked Greta. "If he's going to be here in another couple of months, why not wait and let him make some of the decisions?"

"Time is money, Greta. We've got several high-maintenance 'Mechs in the unit already, and we can't afford to go very long without a contract. As it is, we're considering selling one off to help with the maintenance costs. If we want to avoid that, we need a contract quick."

"And the pilots to go with them, right, Ria?" asked Kitten.

"Right."

"So where do I sign up?" Kitten asked as she popped a final piece of meat into her mouth.

"Sign up? But you don't know a thing about us. Why would you sign up?"

"We know you," answered Greta, "or I guess I should say we know about the Black Thorns. You gave the Jade Falcons a black eye on Borghese a couple of months back, right?" Ria nodded silently. "Even if everything went your way—which it probably didn't—You've got to be a good unit to pull that off. The Black Thorns are good enough for us and for Leeza. The question is, are we good enough for you?"

Ria looked at the two women, still confused by the sudden turn of events. "Who's Leeza?"

"Leeza Rippiticue, our roommate," said Kitten. "The three of us split a room to cut overhead. We've been looking for a unit for almost four weeks, but still no luck. Leeza would have been with us this afternoon, but she had a simulator tryout with some yardbird outfit from the Periphery. Not that she'd take the offer, you understand. She just wanted the simulator time."

"By the way, what happened this afternoon? I thought I was about to become the poster child for reconstructive surgery," Ria laughed. Greta smiled and looked at Kitten, who seemed genuinely embarrassed.

"Well," said Kitten, "you seemed to be having some trouble, so I chucked a bit of steel at Mr. Tall, Rude, and Gorgeous."

"A knife?"

"Naw, it's more like a weighted stick. It sort of captures

people's attention, if you know what I mean, and in an emergency it can be used as a sap. Once I had his attention, Greta pulled her pistol and told him to hit the road. You know the rest."

"And nobody stopped to help?"

Greta shook her head. "The Elemental backed down pretty quick once I showed the pistol. He wasn't armed, and there was no way he could get to me or use you as a shield, so he just walked away."

Kitten leaned over to Ria. "I had my pistol pointed at his ear too, just in case he got cute, or cuter, if you catch my drift."

Ria nodded slowly, realizing her two rescuers had put themselves in considerable danger not only from the Elemental, but the city officials of Outreach, to save her.

"Ladies, again, my sincere thanks. Your actions prove you have what it takes to be members of the Black Thorns. If you'll forward your dossiers to my account at the Hiring Hall, I can begin the examination process. Have your friend Leeza send hers too if you're willing to vouch for her." Both women nodded and Ria settled back into her chair. "And I'll also see what I can do about getting all three of you some simulator time."

Greta lifted a glass. "I wouldn't have it any other way."

3

The next two weeks passed much too quickly for Ria. Long hours spent poring over MechWarrior dossiers and declassified intelligence reports kept her awake far into the night. She scheduled interviews, viewed simulation tests, and made frequent trips to the Mercenary Hiring Hall to check on new arrivals. Often she would look up from her hotel room desk to suddenly discover that it was near dawn. She slept when she could, but the hectic pace was beginning to wear her down.

Had any of the other Black Thorns been on Outreach, it would have been a great help to Ria. Not only because of the shared workload, but because the others would have been a sounding board for her ideas. But they weren't here, and so she felt it necessary to go over every mercenary dossier three times, only to decide the document needed one more pass before she could make a decision. The benefits seemed worth the additional effort, but the weary Ria often compounded her fatigue when she decided to check yet one more time just in case she had slept through an important detail.

Greta, Kitten, and their roommate Leeza were tentatively approved to join the unit. All that remained was Jeremiah's formal approval to make it official. Ria had also recruited another dispossessed pilot, Jamshid Al-Kalibi, hoping to put him into one of the Black Thorns' captured OmniMechs.

Even though acquiring the trio of female recruits had made her assignment easier, Ria considered Jamshid the prize of the new pilots. He was rail-thin and approximately the same height as Ria. His black hair was always perfectly in place, and he spoke in a whisper, each word uttered with just enough breath to reach the other person's ears. He answered each question with polite, yet firm replies.

At first Ria thought he was trying to con her into hiring him without a proper background check. If Jamshid was to be believed, he was qualified—at least on simulators—on every BattleMech produced in the Inner Sphere as well as on two Clan OmniMechs. Initially, she had dismissed his claims; after all, he was dispossessed, but a routine background check at the Hiring Hall confirmed his claims.

Jamshid had served as an instructor with the Fusiliers of Oriente for six years, teaching recruits the basics of piloting a BattleMech. His service jacket didn't give the reason for the split with the Fusiliers, but there was no evidence of ill feeling. Upon arrival on Outreach three months ago, Jamshid had begun simulator training on the two available OmniMech modules, the *Mad Cat* and the *Fenris*. Ria knew simulator qualification couldn't compare to actual field training, but Jamshid was head and shoulders above other recruits in critical knowledge.

The fact was not generally known, but the Black Thorns were one of the few Inner Sphere units possessed of Clan OmniMechs. Following their Pyrrhic victory over forces of Clan Jade Falcon on Borghese, the Black Thorns had scavenged the 'Mechs the defeated Falcons had left behind. Lacking the technical knowledge needed to salvage many of these marvels, the Black Thorns had been able to rescue only four of the 'Mechs and a small supply of spare parts.

Her brother Jeremiah piloted the eighty-five ton *Masakari Prime*. At least she assumed he was still piloting the OmniMech. The Black Thorns also had two *Mad Cat*s and a *Dasher*. The heavy *Mad Cat*s made a great pair. Ria knew Esmeralda already had her eye on one of them, would even be willing to give up her much heavier *Marauder II* for the opportunity to pilot one of the Omnis. If approved, Jamshid would pilot the other. It was the *Dasher* that was a problem.

The *Dasher* was the lightest OmniMech fielded by the Clans, at least as far as anyone in the Inner Sphere knew. It was faster than a *Locust*—which made the Omni blazingly fast—and that was without the MASC system engaged. When operating, the Myomer Accelerator Signal Circuitry set atop the *Dasher*'s engine acted like an old-fashioned turbo booster by increasing the strength of the electrical impulses to the *Dasher*'s legs. With assistance from MASC, the *Dasher* could reach speeds of greater than two hundred kilometers per hour. Ria knew she needed a special pilot to handle that kind of speed and not get the 'Mech shot out from under him before the MASC had a chance to remove the *Dasher* from harm's way.

She had the field of potential candidates narrowed down to two individuals. Once she made a choice, it would bring the Black Thorns up to full strength if Jeremiah approved. The Thorns would enter their next contract a full company, with seven battle-tested members and five combat veterans who were new to the unit. She simply needed to make the final selection.

A double rapping at the door of her hotel room told her the time for a decision was at hand. Straightening her uniform, she crossed the room, then threw open the door. Standing in the hall were two MechWarriors.

"Greetings, I am Lieutenant Rose." Ria smiled briefly and ushered the two warriors into the room. "I hope you will forgive my lack of formality, but I've found this room makes an excellent examination room." The two candidates glanced at each other, but kept their attention focused on Ria.

"Leftenant Donaldson, this is Yuri Dogdorvich. Mr. Dogdorvich, I don't believe you've ever held a rank in the armed forces, is that correct?" Both candidates stiffened at the words. Each knew this was a MechWarrior contract and that the only non-military MechWarriors were pirates. Donaldson's hand dropped to her holster, but she did not touch it.

Dogdorvich simply nodded. "You are well informed. My dossier was complete and well-prepared. How did you know it was a forgery?" he asked.

"Your bad luck, I guess. I've got a friend who used to be in the Lyran Guard. I called him and asked if he knew you or any of the references listed. Of course he knew all the references, but he also knew they were dead and he'd never heard of you, so I was pretty certain."

"I see," he replied. "Just bad luck then. I'd hate to think I'd spent my life's savings on a poorly constructed dossier." Dogdorvich frowned. "I suppose you'll have to tell the Dragoons?"

Ria shrugged. "That depends. I'm looking for a pilot." She turned to address Donaldson at the same time. "I know Donaldson's qualifications check out. What about yours, Dogdorvich?"

"The qualifications and kills are accurate. All I changed were the units involved and the names of the battles. I'm as good a pilot as I claim."

"I'm willing to pretend you're telling the truth for now," Ria said. "But I've got one problem. I only need one pilot and it's down to the two of you." She paused to study the two MechWarriors.

"Suppose I tell you the slot goes to the last pilot standing?" Donaldson cocked her head, thinking about the question. Dogdorvich dropped flat to the ground and reached out with both legs, one in front and one behind Donaldson. With a single scissor motion he knocked her to the floor, using the leverage and motion to stand upright once more. Donaldson reached for a chair on the way down, trying to avoid the inevitable, but she only succeeded in knocking over the heavy chair. Dogdorvich focused on Ria. Donaldson turned red and started to stand.

"Suppose I tell you the slot goes to the last pilot alive?" This time Donaldson did not hesitate. Rather than try to stand, she reached for her pistol, drawing the weapon across her body. Dogdorvich reached back between his shoulder blades and pulled an eight-inch stiletto, tip first. The laser-sharpened plastic was dull black and uniformly smooth. A perfect throwing weapon.

"Enough!" In the small room the sound of Ria's voice shocked both pilots into temporary inaction. By the time the effects of the command wore off, both realized the test was over.

"Leftenant Donaldson, thank you for your time. I apologize for the unorthodox interview process. That will be all."

The woman seemed ready to say something, but bit it back. Glaring at Dogdorvich, she turned on her heel and left the room. Dogdorvich kept his eyes on Ria, allowing the silence to build even after Donaldson was gone.

"You're quick," she said.

"Where I come from you have to be." He reached back with his left hand and returned the knife to its sheath. "Does this mean I'm in?"

"Time will tell for sure, but I'd say you've got a good start. I'll need a real dossier delivered here by eight tomorrow morning. The truth this time. We both know you were a pirate. If you want to be a mercenary, you've got the chance for a fresh start, but that means the truth from this point on." Ria looked Dogdorvich in the eyes despite the height difference. They were the same age, but there was something older in his face. Years of hard living, even by MechWarrior standards, had aged him beyond mere years.

"You'll have the report by eight sharp," he replied. "All the truth, if that's what you want." Dogdorvich turned to go, giving a ghost of a salute Ria knew was her only thank you.

"One more thing, Dogdorvich."

He stopped at the door, just as he was reaching for the knob. "Yuri, if you please. When I had friends, that's what they called me."

"Were you really a *Locust* pilot, Yuri?" He smiled for the first time, and Ria saw a sudden spark in his eyes she wouldn't have guessed was there.

"Yes, ma'am, I was. I still am. I just don't have a 'Mech right now."

"Would you ever consider piloting something else?" she

asked. Yuri rolled his head back and looked at the ceiling for a moment before answering.

"Yes, I guess I would consider it, but I'd have to call it the greatest waste of my life not to pilot a fast 'Mech. You know what I mean?" Yuri looked back down at Ria, holding her gaze with his eyes. "Something with more speed than armor. That's the 'Mech for me. I'd take an *UrbanMech* if I thought that's what it would take to get back into the hot seat, but I'd trade you a *Marauder* for a *Locust* any day."

"Oh, really?"

"Well, maybe not." He smiled and turned toward the door. "But I'd trade a *Shadow Hawk* for one. Even up." Still smiling, he opened the door.

Standing in the doorway, right hand poised to knock, stood an elderly man in a gray suit. Yuri paused in the doorway, face to face with the stranger. Ria looked around the other warrior's right side, wanting to see the reason for his sudden halt.

"Good afternoon," said the man. "I am looking for the Black Thorns. I am thinking, perhaps I have found them?"

4

Ria ignored Yuri's questioning look as he left the room. She ushered her guest inside and offered her hand.

"My name is ..."

"Riannon Rose, sister of Jeremiah Rose." The man ignored her offered hand for several moments, so Ria let it drop to her side. "I had heard the housekeeping staff was better than this." With a nod of his head, he indicated the overturned chair.

Ria shrugged. "Just an interview."

"I see," replied the man. Ria allowed him to walk around the room as he inspected pictures and peered through the partially closed drapes. He seemed perfectly at ease in the silence, but it was having quite the opposite effect on her.

"So, who are you and how do you know who I am?" Ria asked.

"You may call me Priam, although you can probably guess that is not my real name. I know you because it is my business to know everything about the people I may employ." Ria noticed the particular emphasis on the word 'may,' but she did not react. She had initially suspected that the man was a potential employer, as there was little chance of him being a MechWarrior.

His thin gray suit was neatly pressed, but slightly out of

date. Although perfectly acceptable for most meetings or events, the utilitarian cut and average quality marked the wearer as a minor functionary. Either that, or he wants to appear that way, Ria reminded herself. If he's a potential employer, he's probably also a skilled negotiator. Looking over at him, she was startled to find Priam staring at her.

"You were thinking?" he asked.

"You sound surprised," she responded.

"Touché." Priam smiled back at her. "I'll have to be careful of such a quick wit. What I meant to say was 'What are you thinking?' "

Ria considered for a moment, then decided on the truth. "Well, Priam, I was just thinking you're probably a contract negotiator. You're either very well placed or you have no clout at all."

"Why not something in the middle?" he interrupted.

Ria ignored the question. "You're probably not Periphery, because they're too self-conscious. There's no way you're Com Guard, because they always come in full gear. Word of Blake isn't hiring, the Federated Commonwealth always comes in pairs, Liao always comes in threes, and Kurita . . . Kurita always surprises."

"You seem to know the territory." Priam wandered away from the window and crossed to the room's wet bar. "Mind if I have some mineral water?"

"Allow me." Ria intercepted him at the bar and indicated one of the overstuffed chairs. Priam took his seat as she poured two glasses of bottled water. Setting both glasses on the end table, she reached for the overturned chair and set it upright. As Ria took her seat, the two were able to share the end table and still maintain a personal distance. Priam sipped his water and regarded Ria.

"You're right," she stated. "I do know the territory. Or maybe I should say I know the predators."

"You must be a fast learner," he laughed.

"I don't think so, Priam. I've been here for almost six weeks and all I've done in that time is work, sleep, and eat mercenaries. I've talked to countless candidates, read three times that many dossiers, viewed every bit of holo footage

I could find and talked to as many employers as would see me.

"Six weeks is a lot of time to do a job when there are no distractions."

Priam saluted her with his glass and sipped again. "As you say," he replied. "Still, there are many units here, smaller than your own, I might add, who have sent more personnel to accomplish the job you attempt alone."

"Well, I don't know about the alone part," she said, "but I am a little short-handed. Besides, I'm just laying the groundwork. Once the rest of the Black Thorns get here, they'll help with the work."

Priam took another sip and set down the glass. Steepling his fingers, he looked at Ria for several seconds before speaking.

"I am, as you surmise, a negotiator, but for whom I cannot say at the moment. I am empowered to offer an initial contract, but I have several questions first." Priam held up a hand as Ria started to speak. "I would not expect you to be able to accept a contract; however, I know you can convey my offer, should one follow, to your brother." Priam again steepled his fingers and paused. Ria nodded her understanding and Priam continued.

"First the hard part. The contract requires a unit no less than a company in strength. I understand you have offered several employment contracts, pending approval from your brother. Do the standing offers, when coupled with the current personnel, equal a full company?"

"The Black Thorns have six warriors on Borghese. Those and myself make seven. I have extended four offers, which I expect to be ratified. I anticipate extending the final offer tomorrow. If it is accepted, the Thorns will be twelve strong."

"The young man who left as I entered, is he the final pilot?"

Priam already seemed to know the answer, but Ria hesitated all the same in replying. It suddenly occurred to her that Priam was very subtle, having put her completely at ease. It wasn't that she had divulged any privileged information, but she realized that if she wasn't careful, the man's smooth manner might lead her to betray the Thorns. She reconsidered her answer, still watching Priam warily, but he seemed to understand her dilemma and filled the uncomfortable silence.

"No matter. Perhaps I should reconsider my approach. You are intelligent, but new to this process. I have, perhaps, underplayed my hand. Let me be as open as I can be to prevent any miscommunication between us, and ultimately, between my sponsors and your brother.

"First, what I already know. The Black Thorn contract with Borghese ends in three weeks. At that time the rest of the unit will board Captain McCloud's DropShip and return to Outreach, having turned over the defense of Borghese to a battalion from the Gray Death Legion. By the way, I would take it as the highest praise that Prince Victor has decided to replace your partial company with an entire battalion."

Ria tried not to react to Priam's compliment, but she could not help but feel proud. The changes in the political and military situation on Borghese were the real reason the Federated Commonwealth had decided to beef up the planet's defense, but there was, she hoped, some truth to the compliment.

"For the seven pilots currently on the roster," Priam continued, "you have an incredible twelve BattleMechs. The centerpiece of these are the four OmniMechs that the Black Thorns captured from the Jade Falcons. They are, I believe, a *Masakari*, two *Mad Cat*s, and a *Dasher*. The remaining eight include a *Charger, Banshee, Marauder II, Battlemaster, Warhammer, Shadow Hawk, Raven,* and, of course, your own *Phoenix Hawk*. The *Marauder* and the *Shadow Hawk* are currently up for sale."

He paused, but Ria merely reached for her glass. Let him think what he wanted. In truth, the two 'Mechs were up for sale to help defray the considerable maintenance expense for Omnis, but that was hardly the type of information a mercenary unit wanted made public.

Priam accepted the silent response. "Of the four offers you've made, two of the pilots already have their own

'Mechs, a *Mercury* and a *Panther,* I am told. That brings the unit's total to a staggering fourteen 'Mechs. Not bad for a new unit with less than a year's experience under its collective belt." Priam picked up his glass and silently saluted Ria before drinking.

He was right, Ria reflected. The Thorns had been luckier than most units and had doubled their total number of 'Mechs. The best news, however, was the actual 'Mechs themselves. The Black Thorns were very top-heavy, with a high ratio of heavy and assault class 'Mechs. Under most circumstances that would make the unit slow and cumbersome despite the power, but the four Clan OmniMechs gave the unit much more overall speed.

"Given the weight and capabilities of your 'Mechs," Priam went on, "your unit would be ideal for almost any company-sized operation. The only disadvantage—and it is critical—lies at the heart of your strength.

"With four OmniMechs and five conventional 'Mechs of more than sixty tons each, maintenance and spare parts will quickly present a problem. The Black Thorns will either have to sell a BattleMech to get the cash necessary to keep replacement parts flowing, or they will have to take a high-risk, high-pay contract immediately. Perhaps even a combination of both.

"Besides, the availability of parts and equipment is not necessarily enough. You would also need to acquire the knowledge necessary to repair the OmniMechs, since no technicians were captured on Borghese." Priam again permitted the silence to build.

He was absolutely right, and Ria knew it. Maintenance was a tremendous problem in dealing with the Omnis, not only in the field, but back at the base. The few Inner Sphere technicians who had even seen an OmniMech commanded outrageous prices and contract incentives. Even the worst among them was well outside what the Black Thorns could afford to pay.

"How am I doing so far?" Priam suddenly asked.

"Just fine, I guess. But I didn't realize you were asking questions. The unit's composition is common knowledge to all registered representatives of the Inner Sphere's Great Houses. The new hires you could have picked up easily enough by watching activity at the Hiring Hall. As far as maintenance, well, your analysis is as close to the truth as any. Again, it's common knowledge that it takes more to field a heavy 'Mech than a light one. OmniMechs are doubly tough at every weight class."

"Are all the 'Mechs operational?" Priam asked.

"Yes," Ria replied without thinking. In an era of diminished resources, many BattleMechs were forced into battle with broken components. That was one of the factors that made technicians so valuable. It was not unusual for a mercenary unit to have access to several 'Mechs, yet have only some of those 'Mechs available for combat at any one time.

"More water?" she said as Priam was about to speak. He reached for his glass, but Ria was already walking over to the bar.

"Will you continue to pilot your *Phoenix Hawk*?" he asked. She looked over her shoulder at him, but Priam was still looking straight ahead, talking to the air it seemed. Ria walked back to him and handed Priam his refilled glass.

"Does that matter for the contract?" she asked.

"No, not really. I was just wondering if you would stay with the 'Mech you know or move on to something else." Priam took a sip of his water and regarded Ria over the rim of the glass.

"Well, since it doesn't matter, I'm sticking with my *Phoenix Hawk*. With all the travel I've had to do, I haven't had the chance to work with another class. At least not yet. Maybe I'll have the opportunity to train with one of the other 'Mechs when we get to wherever we're going."

"Which brings us back to the purpose of my visit." Priam turned to squarely face Ria. "I offer a unique opportunity for the right unit. It is, in effect, two contracts in one. Each contract offers full pay and you are considered to be performing the first while fulfilling the second." Priam paused, but Ria decided to hear the entire proposal before commenting.

"The primary contract is for garrison duty. The length of the contract is one year, renewable upon the mutual consent of both parties. The supplemental contract varies and can be finalized at the time of your arrival at your new base." Again Priam paused and again Ria held her peace.

"Several points of the contract are nonnegotiable, and so experience has taught me it is better to cover these points in the first meeting. First, I may not discuss the supplemental contract with you, nor is it contingent upon the first. They are considered two concurrent contracts. Second, transportation may be provided by the mercenary unit, the Black Thorns in this case, but each DropShip or JumpShip will have a supplemental crew assigned by the employer. Third, there are no salvage rights for the garrison contract. Any equipment captured shall become the property of the employer. You are, of course, free to make whatever arrangements you are able to negotiate in the supplemental contract. Finally, all orders will be communicated to the mercenary unit via a liaison officer assigned by the employer." Priam eased back into the chair, giving Ria a chance to consider these points.

She sat for several moments trying to understand the implications of what Priam had said. Her mind seemed to scan over hundreds of possibilities and ramifications, but she had never heard of accepting concurrent contracts, especially from the same employer. The minutes flew by as she considered the vague offer. Although numerous questions came to mind, only two really mattered at this point.

"Are the Black Thorns guaranteed the supplemental contract if we accept the garrison contract?"

Priam leaned forward and set his empty glass on the table. "There are always supplemental contracts available, and they are, I believe, quite fair to both the employer and the mercenary. You have only to negotiate the unfulfilled contract you select."

"You say you are empowered to sign the garrison contract, correct?" Priam nodded. "Then I propose we send a message to my brother on Borghese. In the message we enclose the contract and the general information we've discussed. If he agrees to the deal, he can travel directly to the garrison world and avoid the additional expense of coming first to Outreach."

Priam looked shocked for a moment, then slowly smiled. "That would be acceptable if we can come to an agreement through hyperpulse communications."

Now Ria smiled too. The money the unit saved by avoiding the unnecessary trip would help the Thorns offset their maintenance expenses. If her brother trusted her enough to select the right recruits and deal with the garrison contract from this end, Ria could get the recruits to the garrison world and link up with the rest of the unit there.

"Priam, I think you should buy me dinner, since you're about to become my boss. Tomorrow we can send a message to Jeremiah and see what he thinks of your offer."

Priam rose slowly and gestured toward the door. "There is, I believe, a table reserved for us downstairs in the restaurant. It would be my pleasure to have you as my dinner companion this evening. Perhaps we can even send that message out later tonight."

5

Nadir Jump Point, Fort Loudin
Federated Commonwealth
28 November 3055

With a slight shudder, the JumpShip and its cargo unfolded
from itself and reappeared in normal space. Seemingly as
one, the passengers and crew released their collective breath
and returned to their duties.

"I'm just saying, I don't think this was the best plan I've
ever heard of, that's all." Antioch Bell crossed his arms and
looked down at Rose from his perch atop the bunk. Bell in
his bunk and Rose at his desk were both holding their places
with hands and feet firmly grasping nearby straps. As was
usual in space flight, there was no gravity. "We don't know
enough about what we're going to find."

"I agree with both points. This isn't the best plan, but it's
the best offer we got and that makes it the least worst plan."
Rose was on the verge of losing his patience with Antioch.
The discussion that had started some twenty-five light years
ago showed no signs of resolution, and the friction was beginning to wear Rose thin.

"Least worst? What does that mean?" asked Bell.

Rose rubbed his eyes and looked across the small cabin at
the opposite wall, keeping Bell just on the edge of his vision. "It means," said Rose, "exactly what you think it
means.

"Right now we're really short on good options. We've got

some of the most technically advanced gear this side of the Clan line. Damned impressive for a small unit like us, but we'll be forced to put most of the company in storage if we don't keep ahead of the maintenance curve with the OmniMechs." Rose held out a hand to forestall Bell.

"I know you understand the problems with the Omnis, but that's my point. We didn't have them when we signed the contract with Borghese, but now we do. A garrison contract, even a good one, won't pay the upkeep. That's why we need a good contract as soon as possible. The contract Priam is offering is only a garrison, but there's virtually no down-time. We won't be going ten or twelve months without a contract. We'll be out of pocket two months, three at the most. That makes it a least worst choice. Since there are no other good options available, given our requirements, we'll take the one that offers the fewest problems."

Rose finished and turned back to the status reports he'd been reading prior to the start of the discussion. Bell took the hint and floated off the bunk. Slapping the door release, he headed out into the small hallway.

"Hey, Antioch, one more thing." Bell stopped just outside the door without turning back. "Will you please round up the troops for a meeting in the level two mess room? I'd like to talk to everyone at the same time and brief them on what's been going on." Bell turned back toward his commander, surprised to see that Rose was smiling.

"The way I've got it figured, Antioch, if you're having such a problem with the situation, the rest of the crew must be running in circles trying to figure out what's going on. Let's put their fears to rest. How about fifteen minutes—and thanks."

"For what?" asked Bell, genuinely surprised.

"For helping me keep this whole thing in focus. We're a team and I have to make sure everybody knows that. Sure, I expect everyone to follow orders without question, but we both know I'll get better results if everybody understands the reasons for those orders."

Bell grinned and gave the shadow of a salute. "See you then. You want me to call Captain McCloud, or will you handle that? She probably ought to be there." Bell's grin became even wider as he skipped out the doorway. There was no way Rose was going to let him tell McCloud about the meeting. Talking to McCloud was one thing Jeremiah Rose always handled personally.

Waiting for the doorway to shut, Rose hit the intercom button and punched the bridge.

"McCloud."

"Good morning, Captain—or is it afternoon?" She laughed and Rose smiled even though he knew the *Bristol* had no visual intercom system.

"It's the middle of the night as far as I can tell," she said. "Why are you still up?"

"No rest for the wicked . . ."

". . . and the righteous don't need it," she finished. "Seriously, though, what's going on?"

"I've just called an impromptu meeting in the lower mess room. Thought you'd like to join us for a tactical update."

"Why do you military types always use such obscure terms? I assume 'tactical update' is the same as a status report?" she asked.

"It is," Rose replied.

"Well, then, why don't you just say so?"

"I just did," he said, smiling at her muffled cry of frustration. "Meeting starts in less than fifteen. See you then." He tried to sound cheerful just to twist McCloud's tail.

"I'll be there," she said. Rose reached for the intercom, catching something about "damn soldiers" before the connection went dead. He laughed in spite of himself.

McCloud still considered herself a civilian, even though she worked very closely with the Black Thorns. As the owner of a DropShip—or part owner, as she put it (the bankers owned most of the *Bristol*)—Rachel McCloud was much more concerned with the cargo she was carrying than the political situation surrounding it.

In this case the Black Thorns had hired the entire ship for the trip to their new base of operations. Although the Thorns wouldn't take up all the *Bristol*'s available space, Rose wanted to be sure McCloud was well-paid for the trip. He knew she needed the money.

In the Black Thorns' final battle with the Jade Falcons on Borghese, McCloud had been shot down while piloting a 'Mechbuster conventional fighter. Rachel had been lucky to survive the crash, but her wounds had landed her in the hospital for more than two months, and then several more months passed before she was able to take command of her DropShip. The loss of revenue from missed cargo runs had put McCloud in serious jeopardy of losing the *Bristol* to her creditors. Rose had helped her buy some time by hiring out the entire ship with the advance paid them by Priam, but she was still behind in the payments.

Rose had offered on several occasions to include McCloud and the *Bristol* in any contract the Black Thorns received, but McCloud always refused. She was a civilian, by choice as well as circumstance, and she did not want to be part of any fighting unit. Only the strong personal bond she shared with Rose kept her from leaving the Black Thorns after she'd recovered from her recent injuries. Rose hated to admit it, but part of the reason he'd accepted Priam's offer was the advance money. It had let him keep McCloud with the Black Thorns for another few months.

Rose picked up the last HPG message he'd received from Riannon and Priam and headed for the mess room. Finding himself the first to arrive, he triggered a cup of coffee into a dispenser bulb as the others gradually began to pile into the room. As he expected, most of the Thorns had been busy with various duties, so they came dressed in all manner of attire. Most wore simple duty uniforms, but Hawg and Esmeralda were wearing heavy coveralls, a sure sign they'd been working on one of the OmniMechs in the storage bays. When the last of Thorns arrived—and Rose considered McCloud a Black Thorn, no matter what she thought—he began the meeting.

"All right, troops, this is strictly informal, so if you've got anything on your mind, speak up. I wanted to have a brief, and I stress the word brief, meeting on our current status." Rose smiled at McCloud, who rolled her eyes at the private joke. "As you all know, we've been negotiating with an individual named Priam for a rather unusual mercenary contract. I can now tell you that the contact has been approved and guaranteed by the Mercenary Review and Bonding Commission. We're now under contract for garrison duty."

"We *just* received the sanction?" asked O'Shea. Badicus O'Shea was one of the most outspoken members of the unit, and so his question didn't surprise or rattle Rose.

"Officially, yes. Priam and I completed the agreement before we lifted off from Borghese. That's how we got the advance money and that's the reason I was willing to start this trip. It just took the Commission a while to decide if this was on the up and up. It seems that negotiating the contract through ComStar, then commencing the contract before receiving a sanction was a little out of the ordinary." Rose shrugged his shoulders. "Who knew? In any event we're legit as far as they're concerned.

"As of several minutes ago, we have arrived at the nadir jump point of Fort Loudin in the Federated Commonwealth. We'll be here a couple of days while the JumpShip recharges its batteries. Captain McCloud, anything to add?"

"Not really," she replied. "The JumpShip captain reports that he's not scheduled to pick up any other DropShips, and the sails are being deployed to recharge, so all is going well." McCloud shrugged. It was all going by the book, which meant there really wasn't anything to tell. Everyone in the room had spent plenty of time waiting aboard DropShips while the host JumpShip recharged its solar batteries so it could transport them to the next jump station. There might be slight variations in the actual routine, but the pattern of jump, recharge, jump never seemed to change.

"All right, then, here's something you don't know." Rose nodded to McCloud. As the DropShip captain, she was technically superior to Jeremiah Rose while he and his unit were aboard her ship. As a result, even though there were some things McCloud didn't know, she had been fully briefed on everything concerning the journey, including the destination and any special arrangements. "Our next jump will take us to Pilkhua in the Draconis Combine. From there, we make another series of jumps that will eventually bring us to the Kurita capital of Luthien." Rose paused to watch the expressions on the faces of his people.

"Yes, we've been hired by the Snakes, but I guess we shouldn't call them that anymore since they're the ones signing our paycheck." The Black Thorns' overall reaction was exactly what Rose had expected: silent acceptance. It didn't really matter to them who they served, just as long as they were treated fairly.

The Kuritas, whose symbol was the dragon, had not been popular among mercenaries for some time. It wasn't only that the late ruler of the Combine had issued a "death to mercenaries" order and had almost destroyed the legendary Wolf's Dragoons, but that the Kuritas were too unpredictable. In recent times, they'd viewed mercenaries as everything from murderers to a necessary evil to saviors. It was only within the last few years that the Combine had begun to permit mercenaries to even enter its space, let alone actively employ them.

"Does this mean we're going to garrison Luthien?" asked Ajax, though Rose was certain the Capellan already knew the answer to the question. Ajax usually spoke only when necessary, and even then his words were at a premium. Rose looked at the man for several seconds, but the Capellan just sat there with a blank expression on his face. Someday, thought Rose, I'll figure out what's going on inside your head. Then we'll see how you know so much.

"No, Ajax, we're not going to be stationed on Luthien." Rose looked around the room and let the silence build. All the warriors were doing their best to remain calm, but most were dying to know the exact nature of the new mission. Only McCloud seemed at ease, but, of course, she already knew the destination.

"The planet we've been hired to garrison is called Wolcott. Ever hear of it?"

"Jesus wept," said Badicus, looking as though he'd just been axed. The rest of the Thorns seemed equally surprised.

"No wonder the advance is so big," Badicus went on. "We'll never survive to collect the rest."

Rose laughed, but he could tell the rest of the Thorns were inclined to agree with Badicus. "Easy, people. It's not as bad as all that." Rose reached for another bulb of coffee and let the words sink in.

"It's true that Wolcott is in the Clan occupation zone, but the planet is strictly off limits for invasions. When the Clans couldn't take the world, they were forced to pass it by. According to their code of honor, they're not allowed to try to capture it again. That means that Teddy Kurita and the Draconis Combine Mustered Soldiery can still use it as a semisafe forward base of operations."

"Semisafe?" asked Esmeralda.

"Right. According to Priam, who turns out to be very well-placed in the Kurita high command, the Clans can't invade Wolcott, but they can besiege it and they can carry out raids. I admit I don't really understand how that's different from an attack, but I've been assured it is. According to the Clan honor code, they can make it very tough for Teddy and the boys to hold on to the planet, but they can't invade."

"That means a full blockade, right?" asked Esmeralda.

"That's the picture we got before we left Borghese," McCloud told her. "The Smoke Jaguars will attack anything that jumps into the system and will keep pounding until they either get too close to the planet or are driven off by DCMS defenders."

"That means the inbound run will be rough," said Rose. "Which is the reason we're heading for Luthien.

"Most of the Kurita effort to keep Wolcott supplied comes from Luthien. Snake—sorry, Kurita—JumpShips go from Luthien to Wolcott via a pirate point in the Wolcott system. The DropShips disengage and the JumpShip jumps out immediately. That means every JumpShip goes into Wolcott fully charged."

The Black Thorns were impressed and it showed. It was rare for a JumpShip to have the necessary energy storage cells to perform two successive jumps. The cost of equipping the Wolcott JumpShip fleet with that equipment must be straining the Combine treasury to its limits.

"We'll team up with Riannon and the new Black Thorns

on Luthien," said Rose. "We'll also receive some Kurita specialists to supplement the DropShip crew. They're trained for the Wolcott run and will handle some of the preparation." Rose knew better than to look at McCloud while delivering this news. Although she had already been informed that the specialists were a condition of the contract, she didn't like the idea of having other DropShip pilots underfoot on her ship. A fact she'd made very clear to Rose, several times.

"We jump to the Wolcott system, then burn our way to the planet. Once we land, we set up shop, and that's when the fun begins. While we're garrisoning Wolcott, we make a supplemental contract with the Kuritas." Rose paused to let that sink in. "Yeah, I thought that would raise a few eyebrows," he said.

"Here's how it works. We negotiate the supplemental contract with the local mercenary command. Although this one will not be sanctioned by the Mercenary Review and Bonding Commission, the Kuritas are trying to improve their reputation among mercs and will probably try to be as fair as possible. Of course, it will still be up to us to make sure we don't get the short end of any stick they hand us.

"And while we're on the supplemental contract—which might be anything from a raid to a recon—we're still considered to be serving the garrison contract. We don't receive double pay, but we'll be credited for the time. Now for the good part.

"Once we finish the supplemental contract, we're free to negotiate another and another. We don't have to go back to Outreach to work the deal. All funds and equipment will be processed from Wolcott, and once we serve the initial twelve months, we're not required to extend the garrison contract. We can simply negotiate supplemental contracts or leave, as we decide."

"There's got to be a catch," said Esmeralda.

"Of course," said Rose. "There are hundreds of ways we can end up losers on a job like this, but there's also incredible potential. If we're successful, we have a guaranteed string of contracts. So, what we've got to do is make sure we maximize the upside and cover our backs. That's going to take a lot of hard work on the trip to Luthien and more once we hit Wolcott."

Rose pressed his hands into the small of his back, which ached a little. Despite the lack of gravity, his back was slightly sore from the stress of the meeting. "Questions?" He let his gaze travel over each member of the Thorns and waited until he got a nod of the head before continuing. McCloud winked at him from her position in the back of the room, which nobody but Rose could see.

"That's it, then. I'll have duty assignments in twelve hours, people. You might want to get some rest between now and then, because sleep will be a precious commodity from that point on."

6

As expected, and quietly dreaded, the trip to Luthien was uneventful.

Per their contract, Rose and the rest of the Black Thorns were quartered aboard McCloud's DropShip as the JumpShip went from jump station to jump station in their voyage across the stars to Wolcott. The contract also prohibited them from talking with anyone outside the unit or the DropShip crew, which worried Rose even though he knew it was a necessary precaution, given their final posting. It was hardly a secret to the Clans that the Kuritas would be sending additional troops and supplies, but there was little need to broadcast exactly who they were. Rose trusted his unit to keep their destination a secret, but Priam wasn't convinced that trust was enough. As a result, the Black Thorns' only contract was with the DropShip crew and each other.

Priam had insisted on making all the arrangements for the contingent leaving from Outreach. In fact, the details were handled so quickly and efficiently that Ria began to wonder if she smelled a trap, but conversations with Priam eased her fears. The DropShip they'd be traveling on was a commercial vessel rather than on full-time assignment to the military. Normally, that would have meant several delays while the ship stopped to take on cargo or deliver supplies during the run; however, Priam, like Rose, had booked the entire DropShip for the trip to Luthien. From what Ria could see, the new recruits handled the journey even better than the vets because they had so much more to do. Not only did they have to learn about their new home among the Black Thorns, but most of them didn't even know each other.

When the *Bristol* arrived in the Luthien system, even McCloud, who had worked a number of busy jump points, was surprised to encounter all the activity and the increased security around the jump station. Luthien had survived one attack by the Clans, and the Kuritas were not about to chance their capital to half-measures. Hovering all around the jump point were armored DropShips just waiting to pounce on any arriving starship that did not instantly transmit the proper clearance codes.

The JumpShip's station-keeping thrusters jockeyed the starship into alignment with the system's sun as a pair of aerospace fighters swept past the *Bristol*'s viewports. Within an hour of their arrival, McCloud had freed the *Bristol* from the docking arms that attached the DropShip to the JumpShip during space travel. Here in deep space, McCloud used attitude thrusters that normally served to control the ship's descent during planetary landings to get the minimum thrust necessary to push the *Bristol* toward the nadir jump station.

Rose and several other Black Thorns watched the station loom longer and larger via the external camera-feed from the mess room. This station was one of the few surviving of its kind, housing a full complement of workers, scientists, and soldiers. The station could completely recharge a JumpShip's lithium battery in less than twenty-four hours instead of the fourteen days usually required.

All JumpShips were, of course, able to recharge their own batteries by deploying a solar sail. The sail collected solar energy and stored it in the ship's batteries for use during the jump from one star system to another. A jump through hyperspace was instantaneous, but it took most JumpShips a day or longer to deploy the solar sail. Once the sail was deployed, a JumpShip could recharge its batteries in ten to fourteen days, depending on the quality of the sail, the recharging system, the batteries themselves, and the sun providing the charge. When the batteries were full, the delicate sail had to be retracted again because it would never survive a jump unless folded away. It was all the recharging time that could make faster-than-light travel not very fast.

Space stations like the one at Luthien's nadir jump point were designed to provide a quick recharge to military vessels. Essentially a huge solar collector, the station drew continuous power from the system's sun and passed it to JumpShips as required. This station had been attacked several times over the course of the three hundred years known as the Succession Wars, but it had never fallen.

While other stations in the Inner Sphere were being destroyed or failing because of a lack of replacement parts, the Luthien station had become more and more important to the Draconis Combine. Aerospace fighters protected it in space, and elite Kurita infantry prowled the station's decks and outer hull, ever alert for saboteurs or attackers. From a distance the station was as glorious a construction as Rose had ever seen. As the distance diminished, however, the history of the station and the hard existence it had suffered were easy to see.

As the Black Thorns watched the station grow near, they felt the ship's gravity began to decrease. For most MechWarriors, that was one of the hardest things about space flight. The lack of gravity made everything difficult, especially for people not used to the condition. When the ship was under thrust, the acceleration provided gravity in varying degrees, depending on the thrust. But once the *Bristol*'s thrust was reduced, the apparent gravity decreased. Rose scanned the room for any cups still filled with liquid that could go flying, but the Thorns had all finished their beverages.

Gravity disappeared and Rose felt himself drift up. "Prepare to come about," came McCloud's voice over the address system. Rose swallowed and began helping the other Thorns adjust the equipment of the room.

Spherical DropShips like the *Bristol* posed several problems for the crew and passengers, and docking with the space station was the single problem Rose hated the most. The DropShip flew nose-first and would set down with the engines nearest the landing surface, which made perfect sense to him. The DropShip's docking collar, however, was near the engines. On a station with gravity, and therefore rotation, like the Luthien station, that meant the ship had to land tail-first. The spin of the station turned the entire ship upside down. That didn't matter to the ship—there not being much difference between the ceiling and the floor—but those inside had to adjust to their entire world being flip-flopped. Of course, the spacers could adapt without so much as the blink of an eye, but Rose knew even a brief stay at the station would be disorienting for most of his unit. The good thing was that the unit's BattleMechs were already stored safely away and locked down, having been loaded with this stop in mind.

Rose and the Thorns watched as the slowly spinning station grew to fill the entire screen. McCloud, meanwhile, was matching the movement of the DropShip with the spin of the station like a child chasing a merry-go-round. The docking collar slowly loomed into view and stabilized on the screen, but it was hard to detect any motion until the *Bristol*'s big docking collar nudged the side of the station. The *Bristol* was still faintly ringing from the impact when McCloud began broadcasting over the ship's address system.

"*Bristol* docked at Luthien nadir station. We're on downtime for the next few hours while the locals perform security checks. Senior staff is requested in the station briefing room at oh-seven-hundred for an initial debriefing on our mission and the trip to Wolcott.

"Rose, that means you, me, and one other person. All other personnel restricted to the *Bristol* until further notice.

"Riannon's ship is scheduled to arrive in fourteen hours. They'll be docked alongside us in Bay Rhoku. That's all for now and thanks for flying McCloud, the friendliest DropShip in the business."

Rose and the other Thorns grinned at the speaker and began to drift toward their duties. Arrival at any new destination meant there was work to be done, and none of the Thorns needed to be told what to do. Rose was still smiling when he met McCloud at the docking-bay doors three hours later.

"Just us?" McCloud asked when Rose appeared without an escort. He nodded while adjusting the collar of his dress uniform and shaking out his sleeves so they would hang smartly.

"I thought about asking Antioch to come, but he's getting the bays ready for Ria and company. Esmeralda and Ajax . . ." Rose paused, searching for words. "I don't know. They just didn't seem appropriate somehow." McCloud stepped closer and pulled down the front of Rose's jacket, straightening out the few wrinkles that remained. "No reflection on them, of course. I just thought we'd handle this together."

"Together. That's not a word I've heard in a while." McCloud stepped back and looked at Rose, smiling in approval.

"You're telling me? Antioch isn't bad as a roommate, but I much prefer the arrangement we had back on Borghese." Rose stepped toward McCloud, but she skipped out of reach.

"Don't blame me, big boy," she laughed. "Separate quarters were your idea, not mine. Besides, it's not like we've been complete strangers during the trip."

Rose shrugged. "I just thought it would be a good idea to keep the lines of command separate while we're on your ship."

McCloud raised a hand to stop a conversation she'd heard too many times before. "I know. I'm not asking for an explanation." She reached out and hit the airlock stud, sending the inner door up. "It made perfect sense at the time and I still agree with the reasons."

McCloud climbed up the ladder to the access hatch of the airlock and hit the stud on the other side. The inner door began closing as Rose climbed through. He wanted to say something, but he wasn't sure what it should be. Their on-again, off-again relationship had flourished following the Jade Falcons' rout off Borghese because Ria had virtually taken over the unit so Rose and McCloud could be together while she was recuperating. Once Rachel was out of the hospital, Rose had been all the more determined to stay with her. He continued to spend most of his precious free time with her, yet still felt he didn't know where the relationship was heading.

"Do you think I'm under-dressed?" McCloud's question brought Rose out of his reverie.

"Under-dressed? No, I don't think so." Unlike Rose, Rachel McCloud had no formal dress uniform. She normally wore spacer coveralls or very casual attire. Rose smiled to himself, thinking that the formal wear she did own would have raised every eye on the station, as well as the blood pressure of all the males.

"They're spacers themselves. They'll probably think I'm over-dressed."

Once the airlock finished its cycle, the station door opened to a view of a bare white ceiling. Climbing up to it, Rose and McCloud came face to face with two armored soldiers standing at attention; between them stood a small man in a nondescript brown uniform.

"Greetings, Captains Rose and McCloud. I am Uroshi. I will be your guide while you are on the Luthien nadir station. If you will please follow me, I will escort you to your meeting." With a nod the small man started down the hall, leaving the two guards and his charges to follow. Rose and McCloud looked at each other briefly, then set out after their guide, catching up with him in several strides.

"The station has no internal markings for direction," Uroshi began without preamble. "This is, unfortunately, a necessary safeguard in the event of an attack. As a guide, I have the honor of being one of the few individuals who actually knows my way around the entire station."

"What about those guards? How do they get around?" asked McCloud.

Uroshi smiled. "They know only their duty." Evidently that was answer enough. McCloud waited for more, but the small man continued on his way, passing door after nameless door, turning down corridors and passing through more identical junctions. Rose barely paid attention to where his feet were going, his mind was still partly on his brief conversation with Rachel. It had started him thinking about his future, especially his future with her.

His mind was still wandering when Uroshi suddenly stopped before one of the many nameless doors and reached for the handle to open it. Stepping aside, their guide let McCloud and Rose pass into the room, then closed the door behind them. Rose was not surprised that Uroshi didn't follow them in; he was only their guide.

The rectangular room was dominated by a plasteel table with several built-in chairs. Although the entire station was under near-normal gravity, the arrangement made it clear that the absence of gravity would not affect the room. Standing near the head of the table were two men in DCMS uniforms. From their insignia Rose knew each was a *chu-sa*, roughly equivalent to a light colonel in the Davion system. Great, he thought. Outranked again. With a serene smile, he bowed in formal greeting. McCloud followed his lead, but he knew she was winging it.

Each *chu-sa* bowed in return, neither as low as Rose, but Rose detected a measure of respect in their actions. "Greetings," said the one on the left, slowly smiling. "Your journey was pleasant, I trust." He indicated a seat near the head of the table.

Rose returned his smile. "I was in the hands of an excellent captain," he said, indicating McCloud with a wave of his hand. "Traveling with one of such ability is always pleasant." McCloud nodded at the compliment, but still said nothing. Following Rose, she sat next to him, across from the seats selected by the Kurita officers.

"I am *Chu-sa* Langley," said the one who'd spoken when they entered. "This is *Chu-sa* Vaynes. We have been assigned to coordinate your run to Wolcott." Warning lights went off in Rose's head, but he kept his face calm. Kurita colonels did not coordinate JumpShip travel, even to planets behind enemy lines. "As you have been recommended by Priam, I doubt there will be any problems in this situation. His recommendation carries significant weight and your reputation precedes you." Rose waited expectantly. There's a problem here, he thought, and I'm about to have it handed to me.

"You are familiar with the situation on Wolcott?" When Rose nodded, Langley went on smoothly, "The Smoke Jaguars hold both jump points, which means the approach to Wolcott can only occur at so-called pirate points. You are, of course, familiar with the term." Again Rose nodded.

Most hyperspace jumps occurred either well above or well below the orbital plane of the solar system, at either the nadir or the zenith of the system. The locations of a system's two "official" jump points were precisely fixed, again depending on the size of the sun. Pirate points were something else altogether.

Based on a complicated mathematical model of the solar system in question, pirate jump points could be anywhere in the system, depending on the current location of the different planets. Even at the best of times, these locations were not safe. The gravity of nearby planets could make even a slight error fatal. On Borghese, Clan supporters had used pirate points to leave the system and return with the Jade Falcon invaders.

"Due to the strong Smoke Jaguar presence, you will arrive at Wolcott at a pirate point." Rose understood the necessity, but that didn't mean he liked the idea. He'd never used one and doubted McCloud had either. "We've been using pirate points ever since the Clan invasion came this way. Timing and flawless performance of the jump and run to the planet are critical to the initial success of your mission."

"You mean we'll have to fight our way onto Wolcott," said Rose.

Langley nodded slowly. "As I said, we've been doing this for several months, but there are still risks involved. A specific pirate point only exists for a short period of time. Once that window is closed, the next point could be halfway across the system or further out in space."

Rose frowned and glanced at McCloud, who quickly jumped in to explain. "In layman's terms," she said, "a pirate point is defined by time as well as space. We're concerned about the point that opens up between Luthien and Wolcott at a specific point in time. Once that time is up, another point will open up, but in a completely different location."

"You can see the problem," continued Langley. "The Jaguars know we're coming, but the area of space is too big for them to patrol, and even they don't have the technology to detect incoming JumpShips. Still, the JumpShip is at considerable risk while in the system. The captain has to determine his exact arrival point in the system and compute a second jump out before he is discovered.

"That normally takes a matter of hours. During the compute time, the DropShips head away. Each makes for the planet by a different route, complete with course changes. That way, if a DropShip is discovered, the JumpShip cannot be directly traced. Outbound DropShips follow the same procedure back to the mother ship. Once the new ships are docked with the JumpShip, they make the jump out."

"Totally depleting their batteries," said Rose.

"That's right," said Langley. Both men silently acknowledged the danger of such an undertaking. If the ship should misjump, the entire vessel would be lost.

"Pretty high risk," commented Rose.

"Pretty high stakes, Captain Rose," said Langley. "That's why we've got all the security for inbound units. That's also why we've got two of the finest logistical experts in Kurita space working on two of the fastest computers in the Inner Sphere keeping up with the logistical demands of Wolcott." Rose could easily imagine the associated problems. He and Riannon had enough trouble just keeping the Black Thorns in supplies and equipment.

And that," said Langley, finally coming to the point, "is also the reason why the *Bristol* will have an Internal Security Force crew."

7

"The hell, you say!"

Rose grabbed McCloud by the arm as she jumped to her feet. She didn't even bother to look at him as she pulled her arm free.

"My ship, my crew. That's it. End of discussion." McCloud pointed an accusing finger at the two Combine officers, who seemed to take the outburst in stride. They sat calmly in their places, waiting for McCloud to calm down or at least stop shouting long enough to get a word in. Their refusal to react only fueled McCloud's anger, however, and it was several moments before she wound down enough to let anyone else in the room speak.

"I'm sorry you feel that way, Captain," said Langley. The way he stressed the word *Captain* left Rose with no room for doubt; they'd lost this battle before it had even begun. "You're right," he continued. "This is the end of the discussion, but you're wrong to assert that the *Bristol* will not carry a full complement of ISF agents to man the DropShip guns and to make sure the run to Wolcott goes as planned."

"You've got no right," she countered flatly, thumping the table for emphasis.

"We have every right," said Langley with a smile. "The Black Thorns signed a contract with the Draconis Combine government. That contract clearly states the terms of command. We were quite clear, up front, that there would be a military liaison. The entire Wolcott system is a military zone, and, therefore, under the control of the military presence there. When you jump into Wolcott, you are officially under military control. That means we have the right and responsibility to put your ship under our control with the people we see fit as crew members."

While Langley was speaking, Rose was trying to think of a way to salvage the situation. Unlike McCloud, he was not emotionally attached to the *Bristol,* nor was he offended at taking orders from a duly appointed military representative.

"Chu-sa," he said with as much of a smile as he could muster, "surely you're not taking command away from Captain McCloud." Rose was offering Langley a way out of the conflict and prayed the man would be good enough to take it. Langley never got the chance.

"Captain McCloud," said Vaynes, speaking for the first time since the meeting started, "please try to understand our position. Wolcott represents a significant military asset for the Draconis Combine. It is, perhaps, our only asset at the moment. We cannot allow Wolcott to fall, and that is why we are forced to take strong action."

Vaynes was right, thought Rose. Wolcott was deep in Clan-occupied space, and the Combine wasn't about to lose the planet through negligence. Although the Smoke Jaguars were honor-bound not to attack the planet, everything else in the system was fair game. If they could starve the defenders out, they would still end up capturing the planet and keeping their honor intact. McCloud started to counter Vaynes' argument, but the *chu-sa* forestalled her comment with a wave of his hand.

"Of course, Captain Rose, we would never take away a captain's ship or her right to fly it. We are only insisting upon the addition of several crew members, mostly gunners, for the trip inbound. Captain McCloud will have command, and all Internal Security Agents will report to her."

Rose knew that the Internal Security Force, or ISF, were an elite special forces arm of the Draconis Combine's intelligence operations. ISF agents were trained in a wide variety of roles, and this was certainly a task right up their alley. There was no doubt in Rose's mind that the ISF gunners would be good at their jobs.

"Who else will be coming aboard the *Bristol*, besides the gunners?" asked McCloud. It didn't take more than a glance at her for Rose to see how dearly the polite question was costing her. She still wasn't totally in control of her emotions, but was fighting to stay calm. Rose could see the vein in the side of her neck beginning to rise and hoped for a swift end to the meeting.

"In addition to the gunners, there will be one communications agent and one pilot. The ISF pilot will act as a second to the *Bristol*'s current pilot."

"Why is he needed? I don't have room for two pilots."

"The pilot we have in mind has made the Wolcott run fourteen times. He is something of a legend here on Luthien," said Langley. "His only job is to get you to the planet in case of trouble. If all goes according to schedule, he'll never need to lift a finger. Of course, he'll be there to provide assistance if it's needed."

"Don't bet on it," mumbled McCloud under breath. Rose decided it was time to step in again.

"Thank you, gentlemen, for your time and trouble." Rose stood and reached across the table, shaking each man's hand. "I'm sure there will be no problems from here on out."

"I understand that you'd like to get this over with as soon as possible, Captain," said Langley as he looked squarely between Rose and McCloud. "To that end, we've assigned priority status to the *Bristol* and her cargo." That caught Rose and McCloud off guard. Langley smiled.

"The rest of the Black Thorns will arrive on schedule and be transferred to the *Bristol* as soon as possible. Once the remainder of your BattleMechs are aboard, we'll transfer the ISF team and move you back into position aboard the next JumpShip bound for Wolcott."

"Flight stations and schedules?" asked McCloud.

"Those can all be handled through the station control room," said Langley.

"We make runs to Wolcott on a frequent basis," Vaynes told her, "but actually bringing a new 'Mech unit onto the surface isn't that common. When a new unit is bound for Wolcott, we try to make the trip as easy and swift as possible. Your run has been scheduled to take about five days, based on the arrival of the rest of the unit, the JumpShip, and the pirate point."

Rose nodded in appreciation. McCloud just stared at Vaynes as if trying to decide what purpose this additional information could have. While she was deciding, the door through which Rose and McCloud had entered slid open. Uroshi stepped just inside the door frame and bowed deeply to the four in the room.

"If it helps, Captain McCloud," offered Vaynes, "you're not the first ship captain to bridle at the demands of the Wolcott run." McCloud didn't bother to respond to the remark. She simply left the room in silence, leaving Rose to follow.

"I'll bet she holds a grudge longer than the rest of them," said Rose quietly as he left the room. Langley chuckled and Vaynes just shook his head. Any comment they had was lost in the sound of the closing door as Rose hurried to catch up with Uroshi and McCloud.

Rose decided not to say anything during the trip back to the *Bristol,* a choice apparently seconded by McCloud. Once past the airlock, Rose thought the tension would break, but he was wrong. It was obvious McCloud wasn't going to forget the meeting or the consequences of her decision to stay with the Black Thorns. As the interior door opened, she headed for the crew decks toward the top of the ship. Rose decided not to follow her and returned to the passenger levels near the ship's engines.

Despite the hurried launch time, there was surprisingly little for the Black Thorns to do. McCloud could handle all the DropShip maneuvering and the incoming commands from the station's traffic controllers. Rose was sure that all the flight information needed to get from the pirate point to the planet's surface had been downloaded to the *Bristol*'s computer for use on the run to the planet, but the equipment handled all those details.

In the end he decided to catch up on his sleep and advised the rest of the Black Thorns to do the same. After several hours of much-needed rest, Rose went down to the mess room for some coffee. He was still working on his first cup when Riannon and the new unit members arrived, creating a hubbub almost to the point of an uproar. Every one of the Black Thorns was trying to talk to her at once, each pressing for answers to his or her questions. Rose interrupted to insist on introductions being made all around.

Soon all the Black Thorns, both old and new, were clustered in the mess room, listening to Riannon tell stories of her time on Outreach. Rose quickly lost track of time and was startled to hear McCloud's voice over the address system. The *Bristol* would be leaving the station in ten minutes, and they still hadn't seen to the storage of the new BattleMechs. Rose quickly dispatched Hawg, Esmeralda, and Badicus to take care of it while Antioch and Ria showed the recruits their new quarters and caught up on last-minute tasks prior to leaving the station.

Rose made it to the airlock just as the inner doors were opening to admit the ISF crew. McCloud was obviously furious, but was managing to maintain a professional tone while talking to the ISF gunners and bridge crew. Rose accompanied the small group on their tour through the DropShip, but he didn't say much.

Since the ISF agents would only be aboard ship for a short time, McCloud wasn't inclined to make special arrangements for their comfort. Each gunner was assigned a berth near the weapon he would be manning. The bridge crew, which consisted of the communications technician and the backup pilot, was billeted in one of the storage cabins. Both McCloud and Rose would have preferred to have them stay in an actual cabin, but the two insisted that the storage room was as far from the bridge as they'd likely get. McCloud just shrugged and gave them their way.

During the tour, the *Bristol* began moving toward the JumpShip that would carry it to Wolcott. Rose considered staying on the bridge, but decided it would be better to join his own team. Leaving McCloud and the ISF agents to work out a truce as best they could, he returned to the lower decks to find that Ria and Esmeralda had everything under control. When all was finally in readiness for the jump, Rose called the entire unit to a meeting in the mess room.

The Black Thorns drifted into the mess in ones and twos, except for the recruits, who came as a group. Rose waited until everyone was seated and quiet before addressing the group.

"This will be short and sweet, so pay close attention." He looked out at the assembled faces and felt a sudden surge of excitement, a feeling he hadn't expected.

"We're heading for the JumpShip even as we speak. That's not news. What is news is the fact that we'll be jumping as soon as we're able." Several heads snapped up in surprise. "Wolcott is something of an armed camp, so we'll make the jump strapped into our 'Mechs. If the *Bristol* takes a hit, the BattleMechs will provide you with oxygen until you're either rescued or captured." Several of the veterans frowned. "I know that isn't a pleasant idea," Rose continued, "but it beats dying by a long shot, so when we break, saddle up.

"We're heading for a pirate point. The spacers know where, and we'll have to rely on them to get us to the planet. If the jump point goes well, I'll give the all-clear and we can stand down, but consider yourselves on alert. I want each of the new people paired with a veteran." Rose stopped and smiled at the new members. Several actually seemed offended by his remarks.

"Look, I know you're all veterans of some kind, but until we've had the chance to work together a little more, indulge me." Rose gave the thumbs-up to Riannon, and she nodded. He knew the pairing would be handled without problems. It was great to have her back with the unit.

"Once we're on the other side, we'll probably have more time to talk, so everything else can wait until then. Questions? No? I'll leave you to it then. Once I have more info, I'll pass it on."

As if on cue, McCloud's voice came over the room's speakers. "Attention all crew and passengers, this is the captain." Rose considered it a nice touch. With so many new people aboard the *Bristol,* McCloud needed to introduce herself. "The *Bristol* has just finished final docking maneuvers with the JumpShip *Ellyohippus,* and we're scheduled to jump in thirty-nine minutes." Rose checked his chronometer, as did most of the Black Thorns. It was straight out of basic training for all soldiers to know their time schedule, and Rose was glad to see that everybody was remembering the basics.

"I will announce the ten-minute countdown as normal. In the meantime, prepare for jump. Flight crew, man your jump stations."

Rose waited until the speaker popped off before facing his troops. "That means us too. Head for your 'Mechs and get ready for a hot jump, Black Thorns. We're heading into action."

8

The JumpShip *Ellyohippus* appeared in the Wolcott system with a slight shimmer. Emerging from the nothingness of hyperspace, the giant ship suddenly burst into existence. Most of the passengers and crew members had still not even fully registered the jump from Luthien to Wolcott before the captain of the *Ellyohippus* had set the *Bristol* free.

Rose felt a trickle of sweat run down his forehead and kept his full attention on his BattleMech's communication link. Deep in the hold of the *Bristol,* there was no chance of his scanners picking up an intruder in time to do anything, so there was only the waiting. He'd allowed the Thorns to open private comm channels among themselves, but they were not to talk on the company-wide band unless they had something of importance to report. Unlike the other BattleMechs, Rose's *Masakari* was connected directly to the bridge. He kept all his channels open, but did not broadcast. Instead he concentrated on listening.

Rose was no spacer, even though, as a MechWarrior, he'd spent considerable time being carried from place to place in starships. He had long ago learned that it took a special breed of individual to handle the loneliness of space. Rose liked, even cherished, his privacy, but space was simply too big and empty for him.

Despite all this, his previous experience and his special relationship with McCloud had given him the opportunity to learn a great deal about a DropShip's operations. It was that which made it possible for him to understand much of what was happening on the bridge even though he wasn't directly involved in the conversations. When one of the ISF agents inquired about the possibility of hostile forces in the area, McCloud made it very clear that she had detected absolutely none. Rose didn't have to be on the bridge to know exactly how McCloud looked as she informed the ISF gunner to mind his duty and leave her to her own.

Ten minutes passed as the *Bristol* slowly pulled away from the JumpShip. Already the captain of the *Ellyohippus* would be furiously computing the navigational path back to Luthien based on the ship's current location and time. Rose suspected that the Jumpship crew was working every bit as hard as their computers, but he could only guess at what must be going on on the deck of an interstellar ship.

At jump time plus twenty minutes the screens were still clear. Rose decided to give the all-clear a little early, as it was now obvious the Clans hadn't become aware of the JumpShip's presence in the system. His MechWarriors climbed out of their cockpits and drifted back to the mess room, which had now become the company's de facto head-quarters. Rose lingered slightly longer to inform McCloud of what he was doing. He was surprised when she asked him to come to the bridge as soon as possible.

Sliding down the ladder of his OmniMech, Rose thought about going to his cabin to change into some coveralls before continuing to the bridge, then changed his mind. His MechWarrior garb would help put him at ease in the unfamiliar environment of the bridge, and he was sure that the spacers would understand.

The fact that he was ill at ease on the bridge of the *Bristol* always struck Rose as odd. In other trips aboard other such ships, he'd been known to give various captains a severe dressing-down for one reason or another. With McCloud it was just the opposite. He was always ready to assume he was wrong when aboard the *Bristol*, at least on the bridge.

At first he thought it was because of his relationship with Rachel, the ship's captain. Eventually he decided that was only partially the reason.

Until meeting McCloud, Rose had not really trusted any of the DropShip captains with whom he'd traveled. Intellectually, he'd known they were competent, even exceptional, at their craft, but he wouldn't have trusted his life to one. At least none except McCloud. As a soldier, he realized that sentiment was the highest compliment he could pay another person, but Rachel had passed it off as one of his clumsier attempts to be romantic. He would never understand civilians.

Pausing at the door to the bridge, Rose ran a hand through his hair before stepping through. The large area seemed somehow smaller, then he realized it was because of the two ISF agents manning auxiliary consoles. With all the crew members, McCloud included, giving the two men an even wider berth, the ISF agents took up a good portion of the free space on the bridge. Rose crossed to McCloud and looked over her shoulder at the long-range scanner. Although she hadn't glanced up, it never occurred to him that she wouldn't know he was there.

"We just picked up two inbound objects on the edge of our scanning range," she said almost too casually.

"Clans?"

McCloud shook her head. "I don't think so, but I've got the gunners on stand-by. Chances are they're the two DropShips hitching a ride back to Luthien." Rose hadn't known there would be returning DropShips, but it made sense. Why waste the time and effort of a JumpShip returning empty?

"Glad to see you came with company," she added. Rose was confused until he followed McCloud's line of sight to the laser pistol on his left hip. The pistol was as much a part of his standard gear as his neurohelmet and cooling suit.

Rose frowned. "Expecting trouble?" He followed McCloud's glance toward the two ISF agents. By luck or planning, they were working side by side.

McCloud smiled. "Let's just say I like to cover my bets."

Rose smiled with her. "Lady, you only play when you know you can win." He watched for several minutes as the two objects on the screen came closer. Just as the crew member identified them as a pair of *Overlord* Class DropShips, however, the red light on the long-range scanner went off.

"What have you got?" asked McCloud. Rose could feel the tension level rise appreciably in the room, but McCloud seemed as calm as ever.

"Four inbound. From the thrust profile, they look like fighters," said the scanner operator.

"Have they spotted us yet?" asked McCloud. Rose had forgotten the possibility that they would not know the *Bristol* was present in the system. A DropShip could afford to mount better sensors than a fighter, but the sensor information wasn't always as useful because the ship was so often likely to be on a preset course. In deep space, however, it could buy a ship time in an emergency and make a real difference.

"No, not yet. Even with Clan tech, we've got a minute or two."

"Come to two-three-three and decrease speed."

Rose and McCloud stood and stared at the ISF pilot who had suddenly issued the command.

"Wait just one damn minute, mister. I give the orders around here," bellowed McCloud.

"We don't have time. We have to alter our course before they lock onto us. At our present heading, they'll vector back to the JumpShip."

"That true?" asked McCloud.

The scanner operator nodded. "They're closing on the two DropShips. At their present speed they'll have one high-speed pass on the DropShips, but by then they'll have seen the JumpShip."

"Will they be able to attack both?" asked McCloud.

The crew member hesitated. "I don't think so. They're coming in too fast, and the DropShips haven't made their final course change to the JumpShip. They'll have to take either or." The fighters had been accelerating constantly to catch up with the fleeing DropShips, but now their speed would be a hindrance during an actual attack. Moving at high velocity, the small ships didn't have the altitude thrusters necessary to change course quickly. By the time they came around for a second pass, the DropShip would be well out of the area. It sounded like the same thing was true for the JumpShip.

"Bring us around," the ISF agent repeated to the pilot.

"This is not our problem," insisted McCloud. "Whether we alter course or not, the fighters will still have a pass on the JumpShip."

"Maybe not. If the DropShips know the fighters are chasing them, they'll alter course away from the JumpShip," said the ISF pilot.

"That's suicide," said McCloud. "They'd never make it back to the JumpShip by the time it had to jump out."

"They'd still do it rather than risk the JumpShip. Now bring the ship around."

"Not a chance, mister," said McCloud. "Your heading will take us away from Wolcott. That could be fatal to us, even without engaging the Clans. By the time we're back on course, we might not have the fuel to make it to the planet."

Rose didn't even remember the ISF pilot's name, but the man suddenly had a very large part in his future. The conversation was quickly going over his head, but there was no doubt who he would back. Moving slowly, he undid the clasp on the holster.

The ISF agent carelessly waved McCloud's concerns away. "We're not as important as the JumpShip. That ship is one of only a handful equipped with lithium batteries. Its loss would be irreplaceable. If we have to sacrifice ourselves, so be it." As he spoke, the ISF pilot headed toward the pilot's chair. Rose knew now was the time to act. Moving toward the other man, he drew his laser with a single fluid motion.

"Not so fast," he told the pilot, who stopped short as Rose leveled the laser at his stomach. "Back up to your station." Rose waited for the man to move, resisting the urge to get closer and force him to do it. Having spent time on Luthien, he knew that all ISF agents, from assassins to waiters, were expert at hand-to-hand. Rose knew better than to come within arm's reach. The pilot faltered and Rose knew he'd won.

"Back over there," said Rose, indicating the free chair. The pilot, who moments ago had waved away the possibility of death by slow suffocation, retreated from the certainty of death by laser.

"You are usurping my command rights," complained the pilot.

McCloud laughed. "And I thought this was my ship."

"But this is my mission. I am here to make this very type of decision. That is why I'm on board."

"Then consider this mutiny," said McCloud evenly.

"Comm, warn the JumpShip that they might have company," she continued. "Navigation, we're going in just the way we planned." McCloud turned back to the scanner. "The fighters are not a threat to us; we're out of their operational window. We can probably expect more before this is all over, though." Rose kept his eyes on the two ISF agents as McCloud fell silent. He assumed she was watching the scanner, but he didn't take his eyes off the ISF men to check.

"The fighters should pick us up any second," said McCloud. Rose silently counted to ten, but McCloud offered no further information. "They're sticking to the two outbound ships."

"Can you still see the JumpShip on the long-range scanner?" asked Rose.

"No," said McCloud. "They're just out of range. Neither DropShip has made the final move toward the JumpShip, however, and their operational window is closing fast. Ahh, one is making the break."

"What about the fighters?" asked Rose. Even though he was taking no part in the battle, Rose wanted to believe that neither DropShip would risk sacrificing itself and its entire crew in a single, high-speed attack on the JumpShip.

"They're staying with the first ship," reported McCloud.

"Looks like the second ship will make it to the JumpShip on time."

"What about the first?" asked Rose.

McCloud let out a long sigh. "Lost them. We're out of scanner range."

Rose let the gun drop and silently slid it back into the holster. "Was there still time?" he asked, turning toward McCloud.

She shrugged. "Probably. Maybe. Maybe not. Who knows?" She tried to smile and mostly succeeded.

"Nav, lay us our course. Prepare for first course correction per original flight plan."

Rose left the bridge and went back to his cabin, failing completely to put the fate of the DropShip out of his mind.

9

McCloud spent the next three days living on the bridge of the *Bristol*, but there were no other fighter encounters. Evidently their pirate point was well enough away from the main Clan body that it was only lightly patrolled. The two departing DropShips were either very unlucky, or else they had made some mistake that gave the Clan aerospace fighters a shot at them.

The ISF agents meanwhile treated the crew of the DropShip and the Black Thorns like lepers, and the feeling was mutual. The agents decided there was nothing more they could do with the crew of the *Bristol*, so they continued to perform their duties side by side with the other crew members, confident of a day of reckoning when the ship finally arrived on Wolcott.

By the time the *Bristol* reached the protective umbrella of the Wolcott-based Kurita aerospace fighters, Rose was sure McCloud was about to drop dead on her feet. The fighters under whose protection they entered were a squadron of *Shilone* mediums; as expected, the ISF crew immediately began to broadcast the events surrounding the *Bristol*'s arrival insystem. Rose was halfway convinced that the planetary command would have a squad of armed BattleMechs on the tarmac to greet them as the DropShip touched down, but nothing out of the ordinary happened when they landed.

As was customary when arriving at a new duty station, Rose walked his command out of the DropShip aboard their BattleMechs. The sight of a 'Mech was surely nothing unusual at the Wolcott Spaceport, but to Rose's intense satisfaction, the Black Thorns turned every head in the area. He smiled behind the faceplate of his neurohelmet. The Black Thorns might be small, but they were well-equipped.

Rose was in the lead in his *Masakari,* the OmniMech that had been the pick of the booty taken from the Jade Falcons fleeing Borghese. One reason the Clans were so deadly in combat was that they used modular weapons technology that allowed them to reconfigure their Omnis with new weapon arrays in less than two hours. Though the *Masakari* was a prize, the Black Thorns had not captured enough spare parts to vary his *Masakari Prime* to any other configuration.

The *Masakari* was roughly humanoid in shape, but its shoulders were positioned well above the head, giving the eighty-five ton machine a hunchback appearance. The 'Mech's main weapons were twin PPCs mounted where it would otherwise have had hands, plus a long-range missile launcher able to fire ten missiles in under three seconds. The launcher was placed over the 'Mech's head, and Rose had almost had a heart attack when a missile flight went screaming over the cockpit during his initial test firing back on Borghese. By now he was used to the noise and smoke, but was still baffled about why the designers had put the launcher so close to the 'Mech's head.

Directly behind Rose came Antioch Bell in his *Banshee.* The *Banshee* was a common design, but Bell's was completely outfitted with new technology that gave it a new profile and upgraded capabilities. As the commander's bodyguard, Bell stayed near Rose, but not close enough to hinder Rose's movement. On the battlefield Bell would be responsible for watching Rose's back and keeping him protected while Rose looked after the rest of the unit. Bell had already saved Rose's life once, and the veterans in the unit knew he would risk his life to do the same again.

Next off the DropShip were a pair of *Mad Cat*s, two more captured Jade Falcon OmniMechs that were perfect duplicates. Though the 'Mech weighed seventy-five tons, its long, ostrich-like legs easily kept pace with 'Mechs half its weight because of power supplied by the Clan extra-light fusion engine. The compact body of the *Mad Cat* sported two overly long arms, each ending in a heavy weapon mount instead of a hand. Each mount carried a Clan-built extended-range large laser and extended-range medium laser wrapped in a special sheath designed to wick away some of the tremendous heat created when firing the weapons. Mounted on each shoulder was a twenty-rack long-range missile launcher, which were nearly identical to the ones on the *Catapult*. Esmeralda piloted the first *Mad Cat* and kept a watchful eye on her partner, Jamshid. Although this was the first time he had actually piloted the 'Mech, he was handling the Omni with finesse.

Badicus O'Shea, Hawg, and Ajax appeared from a second cargo door and moved around the DropShip to join the leading Black Thorns. O'Shea was at the controls of Esmeralda's *Warhammer,* which seemed to actually strut under the big man's control. That's great for the grandstand, thought Rose, but let's hope that's as far as it goes. O'Shea had never handled such a large 'Mech, and Rose wondered if the additional firepower might go to his head. He decided that a quick and private chat was in order once they got settled. Hawg and Ajax followed O'Shea in a *Battlemaster* and a *Raven,* respectively.

The *Raven* looked more like a child's toy than a war machine when sandwiched between the two other 'Mechs. In contrast to its companions, the *Raven* was built for reconnaissance missions rather than slugfests, which gave it something of a fragile appearance. The job of recon pilot was one of the most dangerous on the battlefields of the Inner Sphere. The pilot had to get close enough to identify the enemy, but be able to get away before being destroyed. Rose knew Ajax was as good, maybe better, than any other recon pilot he'd ever seen.

Riannon was at the head of the final group of 'Mechs

coming from the ship's other cargo bays. She tried to take the lead in her *Phoenix Hawk,* but the recruits had never worked together before and they looked more like a mob than a formation as they joined the rest of the Thorns. Rose could hear Ria trying to give orders, but tactics and battle-field direction weren't really her strong suit. After silently watching several failed attempts to establish order, Rose turned the group over to Esmeralda and asked Riannon to monitor the comm channels.

Esmeralda, assisted by O'Shea, whipped the recruits into something of a line in short order. That was her specialty. Esmeralda had been the leader of O'Shea's old lance on the Solaris game world where she and Rose had first met. She had even been Rose's commander in one of the 'Mech duels he had fought there. During his time on Solaris, Rose had discovered that Esmeralda was not only a shrewd tactician but an excellent leader. Once the Black Thorns got to Borghese, she'd also shown herself to be a good teacher. Es-meralda had been responsible for training the local militia during their contract, a task she had handled without super-vision.

Ria was the unit's communications specialist and execu-tive officer. Although new to combat, she was a logistical genius. Her ability to juggle several things at one time kept the unit supplied when at base and informed when in the field. She also looked after the countless details necessary for running the Black Thorns and keeping them combat-ready. Despite his years of experience, Rose knew he couldn't have done half as well.

Each of the other members were also called upon to per-form as necessary, depending on the duty. All were required to learn about BattleMechs and field repairs, and each MechWarrior was tutored in several skills by others. It was not unusual for student and teacher roles to be reversed sev-eral times in the course of the day's duties.

A Kurita staff car appeared from between two of the spaceport buildings. As Rose watched them approach, Ria informed him that the staff car contained their duty officer. Whoever rode in back would officially welcome the Black

Thorns to Wolcott. Without waiting for Rose to contact him, the driver picked up the pace and headed for the main gates of the port. There was little Rose could do but signal the rest of the team to follow.

The car led Rose and the rest of the Thorns out of the spaceport to a billet provided as part of their contract. The facility was just over twenty kilometers away from the port, on the edge of one of Wolcott's many swamps. Their new home had once been a manufacturing center, but the interior had been destroyed during the fighting for the planet. Rather than rebuild on a world behind enemy lines, the owners had simply moved on to a fresh start elsewhere.

The compound was secured by a steel mesh fence. There was also a three-story watch tower in one corner, but it had obviously not seen use since the place had been converted to military use. Dominating the compound was a huge warehouse. Though it had once encompassed more than thirty acres under one roof, almost half the structure had been destroyed and subsequently carried away. There were no walls, but the roof seemed solid and was well supported by red iron I-beams. It would shelter the 'Mechs and their pilots from the worst of any weather.

Along the north side of the warehouse were the remains of the factory complex. Entering the compound, Rose could only guess what might have been produced here before the Clan invaders reduced the factory to a pile of twisted rubble. Most of the structure remained where it had fallen six years before, forgotten or ignored by the people using the compound.

Next to the remains of the factory, in the northeastern corner of the compound, was the barracks. Built on the site of the factory's former offices, the gray ferrocrete structures were as dull and lifeless as every barracks Rose had ever seen. Function over form had always been the rule of the military, and the Thorns' new home was no exception.

As they had still not finalized the lance assignments, Rose led them into the compound and to the warehouse without orders. The compound had apparently been used for a company billet before, as 'Mech bays had been marked on the floor, providing a clear system for quartering the 'Mechs. Rose took the 1-1 position. Bell took the 1-3 position, leaving the 1-2 position for Ria when she arrived. As the leader of the second lance, Esmeralda took the 2-1 position. Positions 2-2 and 2-3 were quickly filled by O'Shea and Hawg, respectively. Ajax settled into 3-1, and the recruits finally came to rest in the nearest open bay. As 'Mechs were powered down and secured, the pilots began gathering at the feet of Ria's *Phoenix Hawk,* where Rose and Bell were talking.

Rose let the entire company assemble, taking his time and chatting with each pilot as he or she appeared. Although the initial assembly had not gone as expected, each Black Thorn had quickly fallen into line and the trip to the compound had been efficient, if not always perfect.

"Not bad at all, people," said Rose as Ria climbed down from her 'Mech to join them. "We've still got some work to do, but at least we didn't embarrass ourselves or the unit on the way here." There were murmured laughs from some pilots who knew that they had indeed embarrassed themselves.

"We're going to have a busy couple of days, but since everybody is nice and rested after all that free time in space, the hard work should be just the thing to whip us into shape." There were groans all around. From the time they'd boarded the DropShip, most of the veteran members had been working nonstop on everything from 'Mech repair and maintenance to tactical drills and simulator practice. Rose knew the recruits had worked just as hard, but perhaps without the same sense of direction.

"First order of business is to secure the compound. Ajax, take two volunteers and start on that. It needs to be done by nightfall. You'll have to wait to store your gear, but you'll get first pick of the bunks. Looks like you'll be up late tonight."

Ajax smiled softly and nodded. Glancing around at the assembled Thorns, he pointed to Yuri and Kitten. "I'll take these two to help me."

"Ahh, we do love volunteers," said O'Shea.

Rose smiled at the ancient military joke, then went on. "Ria, take two and set up the command post. You can store your gear first, but we need to be up and operational as soon as possible." Riannon nodded and selected Leeza and Greta.

"Antioch," continued Rose, "I'd like for you and Jamshid to set up quarters for the DropShip crew. After the fiasco on Borghese, I don't want them unprotected." There were grim nods from all the veterans. The Thorns had been much closer to the spaceport on Borghese, but they'd still arrived too late to prevent the *Bristol* from being hijacked. Rose was determined not to let anything like that happen again.

"McCloud square with that?" asked Esmeralda.

Rose started to nod, then shrugged. "She agreed to the idea, but I don't know how long it will last. She's still not officially a member of this unit, and she doesn't like the idea of being so close. If we give her a reason, she'll pack up and move out with her crew. That's why I want to make sure the spacers are taken care of."

"We could use the tech and dependents' quarters in the north half of the barracks," Ria suggested, which seemed like a good idea to Rose. Most mercenary units, even ones as small as the Thorns, traveled with a number of additional personnel who were noncombatants. If the unit was lucky, techs made up the largest portion of that number, but it could also include families, servants, and other miscellaneous support personnel. The Black Thorns only had themselves.

At a nod from Hawg, Rose turned to see the staff officer approaching the cluster of Black Thorns. "Looks like it's time to report for duty," murmured Rose. The approaching figure looked old and overweight, and by the way he moved his legs, as though it hurt not only his legs but his whole body. Rose decided to relieve the man of some of his difficulty by walking forward to greet him. The staff car and driver were still parked by the main gate.

"Captain Jeremiah Rose, reporting for duty, sir," said Rose when the two drew close. The portly man nodded and waved at Rose. There was no way the gesture could be called a salute.

"Glad to have you here, Captain Rose," the man replied without feeling. He handed Rose a worn plastic satchel and waited for Rose to look inside before continuing. "Here are the keys to the compound and a standard operational briefing of the current situation here on Wolcott. Nothing especially new, except now it's all official. You're officially a part of the Mustered Soldiery."

"Thank—," Rose began.

"Save it. This is a formality and one I don't especially like. You're now in charge of the base and the property therein. In the unlikely event that Wolcott is attacked before you formally report, you'll find all the proper frequencies in the satchel. I hope you have the good sense to destroy all the printed material after you've read it." Rose nodded, but the man didn't even pause to note his answer.

He continued to drone on for several minutes, but Rose had quit listening. The man was obviously from the old school of the Combine military, which considered mercenaries to be nothing more than cannon fodder. You didn't have to treat fodder with respect.

"Questions?" the man said when he finally finished his speech.

"Just one," said Rose. "We've got most of our equipment stored on the *Bristol*. We'll need transport to get the gear to the compound."

The man waved the question away. "Of course. You'll find the proper frequencies to the motor pool in the satchel. Is that all?"

Rose considered for a moment, then nodded. The man returned Rose's nod and turned away without speaking. Rose watched him go, then, with a slow shake of his head, returned to the Black Thorns.

"Looks like we're in good with the locals," observed Hawg.

"Ah, just like old times," laughed O'Shea.

"Well, let's hope it's not that bad," said Rose. "Badicus, you and Ria arrange for transportation of our gear. Then see about getting some people out here to help with the compound. Cooks, a couple of sentries for the gate and compound when we're away, and a driver should cover it."

"It would be a pleasure," said O'Shea with a deep bow. "Perhaps we could use a maid as well?"

"And let you grow soft and lazy?" said Rose. "I don't think so." Hawg poked O'Shea in the ribs, and Rose thought he saw something pass between the two men. Hawg was grinning like a madman, but so was O'Shea. Rose knew they were up to something, but decided to let it drop.

"Esmeralda, that leaves you and me to draw up the duty schedule and contact the locals," said Rose. Esmeralda nodded once. "Questions?"

"What about the scuffle with the ISF boys aboard the *Bristol*?" asked Hawg. "Still no word?"

Rose shook his head. The local command had had more than three days to respond to the ISF reports and his and McCloud's counter-reports. He'd tried to find out more prior to touch-down, but whoever was in charge of mercenary relations was keeping quiet on the whole affair. Although the incident had been logged, no one seemed to know what the outcome might be.

"We'll have to wait that one out," said Rose. "Tomorrow we officially report for duty. Maybe we'll learn something then.

"Anything else?" Rose looked around the cluster of warriors. They were like a pack of hounds eager for the hunt. Even the boring assignments he'd given them would be tackled with relish.

"Fine," he said. "Then it's time to hit the deck. Ese, grab your gear and follow me."

10

Mercenary Garrison District
Wolcott, Draconis Combine
20 February 3057

As it turned out, Rose did not leave the compound on the next day, or the next, or even the next. Once Ajax had swept the perimeter, the entire company was needed to set up the barracks, which had suffered woefully at the hands of previous occupants. O'Shea hired several laborers to help with the grunt work, but the technical skills of the Black Thorns were necessary to get all the compound facilities on-line.

Rose took an equally active role in the preparations. Once Ria had rigged up the communications center to operate on supplemental power from Ajax's *Raven,* Rose reported to the mercenary liaison office that the unit would be delayed several days before formal reporting. Rose had expected resistance, but instead received a polite extension of three days to complete any preparations necessary. Totally bewildered, Rose handed the receiver back to Riannon. When he'd been stationed on Luthien, the Kuritas had treated mercenaries as if they were socially and intellectually inferior to convicted felons. By comparison, this seemed like the red-carpet treatment.

Thanking god for small favors, Rose fell to work with gusto. He was alternately furious and amused by the unit's findings, or situations, as Ria liked to call them. The electricity to the barracks was restored by Yuri and Leeza, who came back from their work covered with silt and dripping swamp water. The power remained dependable, however, so Rose decided not to ask. Just after dark, a small convoy dispatched by McCloud arrived from the spaceport with the bulk of the Thorns' heavy gear. Shortly after two in the morning Rose ordered everyone to bed.

Hawg obeyed, but sneaked out as soon as he heard Rose closing the door to his quarters. With the help of Esmeralda, he spent most of the first night on base repairing the compound's plumbing system. Although they weren't able to clear the sewage system, the base did have clean water when the rest of the unit stumbled out of their racks the next morning. Rose was happy to have the fresh water, but decided to keep the two late-night workers on full duty all the next day. Disobeying orders still merited punishment.

Rose spent the entire day working on the perimeter of the compound with Ajax. With the help of Jamshid and Riannon in the comm center, the four managed to install the unit's new security system. After the attack on their base on Borghese, Rose had invested considerable unit money on a defensive system for the base. The system went with the Black Thorns when they left Borghese. As night fell, Ria was able to monitor the entire compound with audio and visual sensors. The passive system was concealed among the rubble, but the active defenses were in plain view. Ajax figured the obvious mines would deter casual crime.

When Rose and Ajax returned for the evening meal, they found the whole barracks back in shape. O'Shea had either conned or bribed a city utility worker into repairing the sewage system. The barracks were completely habitable, if not pristine, and Yuri had managed to restore power to the 'Mech warehouse. Over dinner, Ria, who had stayed at the communications center all day, filled everyone in on the latest happenings on Wolcott. After dinner the company began to unpack the remaining Black Thorn equipment. Several of the recruits seemed surprised to discover how much material it took to keep the Black Thorns in the field. It was a feeling shared by most civilians and many regular army veterans.

Most army units would rely on their parent command to

supply them with the basics needed to fight and live. Company commanders went to the battalion, and battalion commanders went to the regiment, on up the line until the proper forms were secured and the equipment was delivered. The Black Thorns did not have that luxury. They had to rely on themselves for all essentials.

Even the greenest pilots knew that meant food, clothing, and supplies for the 'Mechs, but most did not count all the incidentals. Just operating the compound was a drain on resources. In addition to the basics, the Black Thorns had to look to themselves for security, first aid, 'Mech repair and maintenance equipment, ammunition, spare parts and backup equipment, internal security, training, and a whole host of other things that Rose always counted on Riannon to remind him about.

Rose and the rest of the company spent the next day unpacking equipment in the warehouse. Esmeralda and Hawg selected the site for the repair center, and the rest of the Thorns put themselves at their disposal to set up a small maintenance facility. Although the Thorns would never be able to perform major repairs, this would at least give them a place to perform maintenance and minor field repairs by the end of the day. Dinner that night was a repeat of the first, except for Ria's announcement that she had secured a practice area just east of the compound where the unit could perform small-scale maneuvers. Rose assigned Esmeralda to lead the company on a shake-down exercise the next day while he and Jamshid reported to the mercenary liaison. He received several questioning looks from the Thorns at his choice of a second, but no one said anything.

By the time most of the unit was up the next morning, Rose and Jamshid were gone, each traveling to the liaison office in his 'Mech. The rest of the Thorns entered the practice swamp with powered-down weapons and training programs running on all computer systems. Although the system wasn't as good as the one used by Wolf's Dragoons, the Black Thorns had used it successfully for training on Borghese. Esmeralda led the Thorns into the swamp and set them up for a perimeter sweep. Fifteen minutes into the drill, the first Black Thorn 'Mech was killed.

It was Rose who fired the shot, his *Masakari* rising from a depression in the muck, hitting Greta's *Charger* with all four PPCs. All four shots struck the center torso, the computer slicing off sheets of armor as the combined attacks bored into the 'Mech's heart, carving through the engine and gyro in a single wave. Greta's computer told the rest of the Thorns she was dead even before most of the unit had time to register the attack.

Although Esmeralda hadn't known about Rose's surprise attack, she had assumed one would take place when Rose selected Jamshid to accompany him. The two of them in their OmniMechs would make excellent sparring partners for the other Thorns. As Greta died, Esmeralda fired on Rose, scoring a hit with one large laser and a scattering of missiles. But when she saw Jamshid rise from the water to her right, she knew she'd been had.

In turning to fire, Esmeralda had exposed her 'Mech's back to Jamshid, who was firing every weapon his *Mad Cat* had. The range wasn't ideal, but he managed to hit with almost everything. One large laser drilled a hole into the *Mad Cat*'s back, ruining all the armor over the right torso while the other skewered the 'Mech's right leg. More laser fire stabbed at Esmeralda until both flights of missiles came roaring in. Her computer system showed five of the long-range missiles exploding around the laser hole in the right torso. One missile set off a secondary explosion, igniting her entire long-range missile load on the right side.

With a flash, the right side of the 'Mech disappeared in a haze of computer-generated smoke. The cellular ammunition storage system held, however, confining the blast to the right torso. The *Mad Cat*'s right arm and right-side weapons went dead with the destruction of the 'Mech's torso, the heat scale spiking as the extra-light engine components in the destroyed torso section failed. Although the Clan technology kept her from being an immediate casualty, Esmeralda knew she was out of the fight.

The end took longer than it should have, but there was no

doubt about the outcome. Rose and Jamshid fought without regard to their own safety. The remaining Black Thorns closed in on all sides, but the duo stood toe-to-toe with the rest of the company and traded shot for shot. When Rose finally called an end to the exercise, he and Jamshid were both dead, but so were Esmeralda, Greta, Kitten, Ajax, Badicus, Leeza, and Riannon.

"Let's try it again, people," said Rose over the company-wide communication channel. "Ajax, lead them back to base and wait twenty minutes, then come back out. Esmeralda, you stay with Jamshid and me." The battles continued throughout the day with steadily improving results. Although the Black Thorns always lost 'Mechs in the encounters, they began to fight more and more like a team as the day went on. At dusk Rose led them back to the compound to find that the DropShip crew had arrived while they were gone.

Dinner that night with McCloud and the DropShip crew was spirited, but Rose kept everyone focused on the events of the day. Even the DropShip crew remained after dinner to hear the retelling of the events in the field. Most MechWarriors weren't prone to talk about combat, but the simulation didn't seem to fall under the same aegis and the warriors were quick to share their successes and failures with the spacers. It was hours later that Rose finally rose to retire.

Before leaving the table, he addressed the whole group. "Tomorrow, Captain McCloud and I will be reporting to the liaison office. Jamshid, in view of your outstanding performance earlier today, I'd like for you to accompany us." The slight man smiled and nodded an enthusiastic yes. "Esmeralda, you have the command. Let's try another set of exercises, but better keep sharp, we might be waiting for you again." With a nod of his head, Rose left the mess and returned to his room. He was not entirely surprised when McCloud joined him several minutes later.

"All settled?" he asked, glancing up from his small desk. McCloud shrugged, a familiar gesture when she was on the ground. In space she was unquestioned leader, but on land she often seemed unsure of herself.

"Problems?"

McCloud shook her head and crossed to the bed, where she threw herself down. Rose turned around at the desk and regarded her sprawled on the bed.

"You know," she said, "the only thing I ever miss about being planetside is the room. You've got more wasted space in this room than I've got on the entire DropShip." Rose laughed. "It's true. All this room and you don't have to do anything with it."

"The extra space is nice," Rose agreed, "but close can be fun too." He got up from the chair and slid onto the bed with McCloud. She surprised him by sitting up just as he was lying down. Rose rolled his eyes, a gesture he was sure McCloud would have found offensive if she'd seen it.

"Something on your mind?" he asked, rolling over to sit next to her on the edge of the bed.

"Yes," she said, patting the bed. "What are we going to do?"

Rose rubbed his jaw, pondering how to answer the question. Stalling for time was all he could think of. "Do? What do you mean do?"

"I mean, where am I going to quarter while we're stuck on this planet?"

"Oh." Rose had already considered the options and knew what he wanted, but he wasn't sure how McCloud would react. Several quiet moments passed before he decided to follow his heart rather than his head. "You should stay here, with me."

Several more moments passed before McCloud responded. "That's what I'd like." Rose relaxed internally. He could seldom second-guess McCloud, but it looked like this time he'd hit the nail on the head.

"There would have to be some rules, however." Or maybe not, he thought. "First," she continued, "my crew is strictly under my control. They signed on with me, not the Black Thorns. I'm the one who has to be accountable to and responsible for them. Agreed?"

It certainly made sense to Rose. His only direct knowledge of spacers came from McCloud. Hell, he thought, I don't even know half their names. To me they're just the crew. "Agreed," he said simply.

"Next, the *Bristol* is not a part of the Black Thorns. I've pretty much admitted to myself that you've got me hooked, but that's on a strictly personal level. There are places I'd follow you that I'd never take the *Bristol*."

Rose was suddenly uncomfortable with the confession. He knew how he felt about McCloud, but he'd rarely heard her return the sentiment, at least not in a conversation such as this. He wanted to make a joke to relieve his own discomfort, but realized the discussion was too important to McCloud, and him, to make light of it that way.

"What do you have in mind?" was all he could think to ask.

"I'm a big girl now. Nobody has tried to play mommy to me in over ten years and I like it that way. I'm in serious financial trouble because of the accident on Borghese. Even with the trip here, I'm in real danger of losing the *Bristol* to my creditors. I could run, but that's hardly the type of life I want for myself or my crew.

"The Black Thorns have been good to me, but I want something understood. I'm not military. I never was and I never will be. As hard as it is for some people to understand, I don't like getting shot at and I don't like having soldiers on the crew decks."

"But you've hauled 'Mechs before," interrupted Rose.

"Hauled, yes, but I've never been in anything close to a battle. Even my three pirate encounters were little more than hostile words exchanged at a distance. Those Clan fighters were the closest I've come to combat in all my years as a captain."

"But you handled it perfectly," countered Rose.

McCloud snorted, and Rose was surprised to see tears spring to her eyes. "After you left, I went back to my quarters and cried for almost an hour."

Rose was shocked. He stared at McCloud in disbelief. It wasn't her reaction that took him aback. Hadn't he been reduced to the same state after the destruction of his command on Tukayyid? What infuriated him was the fact that she hadn't called on him to help her through it.

"Why didn't you tell me? Why didn't you ask for help?" Rose jumped from the bed, suddenly restless.

"No way, Jeremiah. No way. There is absolutely zero chance I'd let someone else see me like that aboard my own ship."

"Then why tell me now?" he asked in a rising voice.

"Because now we aren't on the *Bristol*," she shouted in return. Rose locked her with an intense gaze, trying to look beyond the tears and his own frustration. McCloud held his gaze with equal intensity, and neither one moved as they regarded one another. Rose wasn't sure how long the moment lasted, but with sudden clarity he knew the reason she hadn't called on him. The understanding of that single action spread like a cool wind through him as he realized things about himself and McCloud that he had never been able to comprehend before. He wasn't sure he could put it into words, but in his heart he knew and that was all that mattered.

He took her hand and smiled. "I understand. Your ship, your command, your decision."

McCloud closed her eyes, flushing tears from the corners. "When I'm caught up financially, I'll pay back the money the Black Thorns have invested in the *Bristol*. You have to agree to that."

Rose smiled and nodded. "Done." It was the easiest thing he'd ever agreed to. "Anything else?"

"Yes," she smiled as the tension in the room evaporated, "you can help me move in. Then we'll really christen our new home."

11

Mercenary Garrison District
Wolcott, Draconis Combine
28 February 3057

Rose called for a car early the next morning and rode to the liaison office in high spirits. If Jamshid, sandwiched between Rose and McCloud in the back seat, noticed, he didn't mention it to his commander. McCloud also chose to keep quiet and spent most of the ride staring out the side window.

The car dropped them in front of the building, where the trio paused briefly to straighten their field uniforms before ascending the broad marble stairs. Despite the early hour, the plaza was crowded with warriors in an array of clashing uniforms. Most were busily pursuing personal interests, but several lounged along the fringes of the plaza, eyeing everyone with equal attention. Rose was inclined to think that they were security, but it was also just as likely they were exactly what they seemed: warriors looking for a home.

Upon entering the lobby, Rose thought it looked more like something out of a corporate headquarters than a military installation. There was even an information booth facing the main doors. Rose announced himself and his destination to a polite woman behind the counter, and waited patiently for her to clear him through. He was surprised when she indicated a set of stairs just visible through a narrow archway to the right. He'd expected tighter security.

McCloud shrugged and Jamshid offered his usual smile,

so Rose led the way to the stairs. Three flights later, they came to a single steel door set opposite the top step of the landing. Jamshid opened the door for Rose and McCloud, then followed them in. In the hallway beyond stood a small woman clutching a bundle of papers to her chest.

"Captain Rose," she said with a shy smile, "I am *Chu-i* Reiza Myoto." She bowed as low as the papers would allow, then nervously stuck out her right hand. The papers threatened to spill all over the floor, but she managed to prevent that by quickly retracting the offered hand. She smiled and shifted the papers to one shoulder, again offering her hand. Rose took it quickly and shook once before letting go. Her hand was warm and slightly sweaty, but the strength of the grip surprised him.

"*Chu-i* Myoto, may I present Captain McCloud of the DropShip *Bristol* and MechWarrior Jamshid Al-Kalibi." Myoto bowed to each in turn, then indicated the expanse of hallway beyond with her right hand before the papers once more threatened to spill.

"If you will please follow me, I will escort you to a meeting with *Tai-sa* Zimmer and his staff." Rose hitched his stride in midstep at the mention of the name Zimmer, but continued on. McCloud looked at him in surprise, but Rose shook the unasked question away. "I have your briefing papers here," continued Myoto. "The binding was not ready, and I thought them too important to wait."

"Thank you, *Chu-i.* Jamshid, since they are meant for us, would you please help her with them?" Jamshid rushed to take the lion's share of the papers, leaving Myoto only the top dozen sheets. Again she bowed, and Jamshid returned the gesture by reflex.

"Zimmer . . . " said Rose. "That wouldn't be Adrian Zimmer, would it?"

"Why, yes," said Myoto, surprised that Rose knew the *tai-sa.* "He is the head of the mercenary liaison department of the DCMS on Wolcott. He is ultimately the commander of all the mercenaries here."

Rose ground his teeth in frustration. "Working with

Zimmer," he said almost to himself, "and I swore never again."

"Captain?" asked Myoto.

"Nothing, *Chu-i*. The *tai-sa* and I are old acquaintances." Rose worked on loosening the cramp in his jaw as Myoto indicated an open door on the left side of the hallway. The door opened into a room already occupied by two men and a woman.

"Rosie!" The largest of the three came bounding across the room, right hand extended. As Rose reached for it, the man pulled him against his expansive chest in a sudden bear hug. "Rosie, I knew you'd come back to me."

Rose endured the greeting in silence and waited until Zimmer let him loose before responding. "Zimmer," he said coolly, "it's been a long time. How's the eye?"

Zimmer touched the side of his face. "Gods! It's terrible. The damn thing is never in proper focus, and I get some massive headaches. And until the medics can get that problem solved, they can't even cover up the artificial cheekbone with synthetic skin."

"Good!"

"Pardon," said Zimmer with a suddenly intense stare.

"I see you've brought food," said Rose with half-smile. "Will this be a long meeting?"

"No," returned Zimmer, his eyes suddenly narrowed. "Just my little way of welcoming you back. And who do we have here?"

"*Tai-sa* Zimmer, may I present Captain McCloud, commander of the DropShip *Bristol*." McCloud stuck out her hand, which Zimmer took and raised to his lips. Just as he bent to kiss it, McCloud pulled her hand away.

"Pleased to meet you, *Tai-sa* Zimmer."

"Oh, now, that won't do. My friends call me Pauly-o."

"What friends?" asked Rose with a smile.

Zimmer turned on Rose and glared. "Still holding a grudge, Rose? I thought time healed all wounds."

"Wounds, yes," agreed Rose. "Deaths, no. I'm afraid time can never erase those."

"We all lost friends on Tukayyid, Rosie," countered

Zimmer. "You've got no right to think you're the only one."
The big man took a step toward Rose and seemed ready to
fight. Rose kept silent, but McCloud saw him curl his feet
inward, a sure sign he too was ready to fight. Zimmer suddenly smiled and relaxed. "You know, Rosie, I've never understood why you don't like me."

"Got an hour?" asked Rose.

Zimmer smiled at the comment, but he was obviously
back in control. No matter that this man enjoyed the sleep of
the innocent, Rose blamed Zimmer and those like him for
the destruction of his command on Tukayyid. Tucked away
safely in the rear they sat back and handed down orders
while Rose and his men fought and died following those orders. Zimmer was one of a handful of superior officers Rose
had prayed never to see again.

A voice that dripped honey interrupted Rose's thoughts.
"Perhaps you could introduce us, *Tai-sa*," said the unnamed
woman as she crossed the room. Her voice didn't much affect Rose, but it stopped Zimmer cold.

Watching her, Rose wondered if he'd ever seen such a
beautiful woman. Her long black hair was silky and shimmered in the light of the meeting room. She had classic ori-
ental features, with a slightly rounded face and
almond-shaped eyes that seemed to promise answers to unasked questions. Her regulation DCMS uniform fit too perfectly not to have received the attention of an excellent
tailor.

"Rosie, this is *Tai-i* Siriwan Toshirov. She is my chief of
staff. The man behind her is *Tai-i* Joseph Patti. He handles
all mission assignments and contract negotiations for company contracts and below.

"That's what you're running now, right, Rosie? A company?"

Rose nodded cooly and kept his attention on Zimmer.
Toshirov was clearly a distraction, and Rose was determined
not to let her presence cloud his thinking. He silently
thanked God he'd undergone his revelation with McCloud
last night. It gave him a certain amount of armor against distractions like Toshirov.

"I suggest we get down to business," said Zimmer. He moved toward the table, grabbing a pastry on the way to the head chair. Leaning back in the chair, he downed the pastry in two huge bites, dusting powdered sugar off his fingers as he watched the Black Thorns take their seats.

"As I said, Patti usually takes charge of meetings like this, but since you and I go back so far, Rosie, I thought I'd handle this one personally." Zimmer smiled, and Rose felt a shiver run up his spine. Zimmer was again in control of his destiny. "We're old buddies, Rosie, so we can cut straight to the good stuff. Here's the deal.

"The Combine runs this planet with a lenient hand. They don't really like mercenaries—and that, of course, means you—but they've realized they're a necessary evil." Zimmer paused to make sure Rose heard the word "evil". "That's where I come in. I work for Kurita and you work for me." Rose started to object, but Zimmer waved him away.

"I know, I know. That's not the way it works on paper, but that's how it's done in practice. We've got a unique situation here, one that calls for the ability to handle problems creatively as they arise."

Rose knew just what Zimmer meant. When they'd both been members of the Com Guards, Zimmer had been involved in more operations than any two people. He always had something going on, and always managed to keep a step ahead of his enemies. Creative thinking and complete lack of conscience were Zimmer's specialties.

"What you've got now," continued Zimmer, "is a standard garrison duty contract. You and I both know the pay for that kind of thing will force you to sell one of your precious OmniMechs before the contract is over just to keep the other three running." Zimmer leaned forward onto the table.

"Unless you want to sell one now. I could put you in touch with somebody from Procurement. They'd make you a nice offer, even on the *Dasher*."

Rose ground his teeth and shook his head. He didn't trust his voice to answer.

"Oh, well, no matter. The fact is, unless you take a contract with us, you'll be forced to sell anyway. Either that or the company store."

The "company store" was a term feared and hated by every mercenary in the Inner Sphere and a potential problem for the Black Thorns. Most employers were willing to let mercenaries purchase goods and supplies on credit backed by their contract, but a merc unit could quickly run up more expenses than they could cover with their contract. A major battle, for example, could put a unit in debt to the employer for years just to cover the cost of repairing 'Mechs damaged in a single battle.

The problem could be compounded by an unscrupulous employer. Since a mercenary unit's assignments came from their employer, they could be sent light years away from the parts they needed. The employer could eventually supply the mercenary, but at a greatly inflated cost. Purchasing equipment, supplies, and technical expertise from the employer all fell under the title "company store," a practice which often turned struggling mercenary units into virtual house units of their employer. Once that happened, the merc unit might retain its own name, but it was at the beck and call of the employer just like any other regular army unit.

"So all that brings us to Wolcott," said Zimmer, "and the unique opportunities which abound here. Patti, what is your most lucrative contract at the moment?"

"Operation White Knight, sir. It's a rescue mission on the fringe of our operation area. It's been open for three months with no takers."

"And why is that, Patti?" asked Zimmer, never taking his eyes off Rose.

"The target is protected by an entire galaxy of Smoke Jaguars, sir. It's suicide unless the Clanners lower their defenses."

"Thank you for that astute comment, Patti. What does it pay?" asked Zimmer.

"Pay grade Alpha-prime, sir," gulped Patti in reply.

"Which means, Rosie, you get to name your price. Name the price and I get to accept or reject. And you know the best part? The part that keeps that particular contract from being filled?" Rose shook his head, even though he suspected the answer. "The best part is I've got a dozen more just like that one.

'We send mercs on missions nearly every week from this planet: raids, recons, even a minor assault or two. Garrison troops just pack up and leave for a couple of months, then come limping back. At least the lucky ones are still able to limp. They spend their contract money on repairs and off they go on another. It's like a goddamn revolving door."

Rose nodded. From the reports he'd seen by Priam, that was exactly what Wolcott offered. Mercenaries ran a string of high-risk, high-pay contracts back-to-back from Wolcott, supplemented by garrison duty.

"You guys operate independently of the Mercenary Review and Bonding Commission for all non-garrison missions," observed Rose. "How do I know I'll get paid when I get back?"

Zimmer smiled, but it was Toshirov who answered. "The money is placed in your name in a bank on Outreach. The money is listed as a deposit, which can't be touched for the length of the contract." She smiled, too, taking her cue from Zimmer. "Once the contract is over, the money reverts solely to you."

"No strings?" asked Rose.

Zimmer laughed. "None needed, Rosie. It's real simple. If you make it back to Wolcott, you've probably earned half the payment. Each contract has a primary and a secondary objective. Provide proof of completion of the primary and you get the whole thing. Finish the secondary and you get two-thirds."

"What if I don't make it back?" asked Rose.

"Well, that's the down side," said Zimmer with a smile, indicating he didn't think it was down side at all. "You don't come back and the Combine keeps the whole thing."

"What about an insurance clause?" asked Rose.

"No such thing on Wolcott, Rosie. Oh, that reminds me ... there's no such thing as an advance, either."

"Sounds too good to be true," commented McCloud.

"It is at first glance," said Toshirov, "but once you examine it, you'll see that the contracts offer us some real advantages. If you make it back at all, the Draconis Combine will benefit even if you don't fulfill either mission objective. If you don't come back, we're out some incidental cost, but that's small change compared to a standard contract."

"What's to keep you from pulling the contract money once we jump into Clan space?" asked Rose.

"Good thinking, Rosie," replied Zimmer. "The first time we jerk a merc unit around is the last time we get any more of you out here. Wolcott has to rely on its solid reputation. Theodore Kurita himself has issued that directive, and nobody here wants to take the risk of ticking him off.

"So what do you say?" Zimmer smiled. He already knew the answer, but wanted to hear it out loud.

"We're in," said Rose.

"I knew it all along, Rosie. You're a real thrill-seeker."

"Patti, see that Captain Rosie receives a copy of all outstanding contracts and preliminary reports as appropriate."

Patti indicated the forgotten Myoto. "*Tai-i* Myoto has all the pertinent information, sir," said Patti.

"Myoto, I almost forgot about you. Please excuse me," Zimmer said, then turned back to Rose. "Rosie, I'm sure you remember a small point of the contract which indicated that command of your unit passed through a liaison officer?" Rose closed his eyes, praying that he wasn't about to hear what he feared might be the next words. "Myoto is that very officer. Treat her nice, Rosie, because this is her first assignment." Rose cringed and Zimmer barked in laughter.

"Once you've selected a contract for bidding, contact Patti and he'll set everything up." Zimmer turned to Patti. "Whatever they ask, Patti, give it to them. No questions asked." Zimmer turned to Rose, but continued to address Patti. "After all, we're old friends."

Rose stood, followed immediately by Jamshid and McCloud. Bowing slightly to the Combine officers, he headed for the door with Myoto, McCloud, and Jamshid in tow. Just as he was about to open it, Zimmer called out to him.

"Take your time selecting, Rosie. Maintenance is getting cheaper by the week." Zimmer was still laughing when Jamshid closed the door.

= 12 =

Mercenary Garrison District
Wolcott, Draconis Combine
1 March 3057

While the rest of the company worked around the base and continued their practice sessions, Rose concentrated on the selection of a supplemental mission. If the task was difficult, it was because he had way too much information instead of the usual lack of it. In many cases the reports named the Clan opponents right down to the individual star, which was the standard Clan fighting unit roughly equivalent to an Inner Sphere lance.

Rose had protested vehemently when Myoto appeared the morning after this meeting with Zimmer at the controls of a Kurita *Grand Dragon* heavy BattleMech. While Myoto waited patiently in her 'Mech, Rose contacted the liaison office to ask why she was at his compound and why she'd insisted on bringing her 'Mech along with her. Ranting and raving did no good and neither did polite requests to have her 'Mech quartered in the Kurita compound. After over an hour of "conversation" with the liaison office, Rose was finally forced to accept Myoto's posting with the Black Thorns.

It wasn't so much personally or professionally that Rose objected to the assignment of Myoto. She was competent enough, even if slightly clumsy, and the reports she had gathered for the Black Thorns were certainly complete.

Rose's objection had to do with having a liasion officer so close to his unit. He had accepted the idea of the liaison, had even looked forward to it in an odd sort of way. After all, the liaison officers he'd known as a member of the Com Guards had always seemed to be a little unusual. Usually they were individuals at the end of their military careers who were only interested in finishing their service with honor. Occasionally, he'd met a young firebrand or a disgraced warrior assigned to a problem mercenary unit, but that was the exception. It took a person of experience and/or talent to stand between an employer and a mercenary unit, unless the employer wanted that mercenary unit dead.

But even with that, it wasn't usually too hard for a mercenary unit to get away with some things. There was always a black market for spare parts, which every merc unit in the Inner Sphere relied upon to keep their 'Mechs in shape. Parts that couldn't be had from the employer at any price could often be obtained from the market. Of course, dealing with the black market was a strict violation of most contacts since it encouraged thievery. With Myoto in his back yard, Rose and Riannon were going to have to work overtime on logistics.

Rose knew Myoto had every right to be quartered at his compound, but he had never really considered it a possibility. Most liaison officers preferred their own compounds, which were, as a rule, better furnished and more comfortable. Even by the standards of the military, Rose knew that Myoto's posting to the Black Thorn base was a cut in lifestyle. Hell, he'd taken a cut from their quarters on Borghese.

Myoto certainly wasn't old nor did she display any of the characteristics of a rising star, so Rose put her down as a misfit. She should have been at the peak of her career, but most individuals didn't consider liaison work to be an outstanding career move, especially those in service to the Draconis Combine.

Rose signaled to O'Shea to let Myoto in at the gate. While Antioch Bell led her around to the warehouse, Rose contemplated what to do. With Myoto actually in the compound, he would have to rethink his strategy for dealing with the Combine military and Zimmer, who he refused to think of as Colonel or even *Tai-sa* Zimmer. The man was a coward and a snake, someone who would surely cause problems before this was over; Rose knew it in his bones. There was little he could do about that at the moment, however. Sighing heavily, he resigned himself to his fate and went to greet Myoto and apologize for the delay.

Rose worked out with the rest of the unit three times over the next week, supplementing the lance commander's information with his own analysis. Myoto proved to be an excellent pilot, but one of the worst gunners Rose had ever seen at the controls of a heavy 'Mech. If they had the time and she was willing, the Black Thorns would have to correct that before she went into battle.

One week after his original meeting with Zimmer, Rose was back in Patti's office, one thin folder in his hand and a grim smile on his face. It was a smile shared by Patti.

"I've selected a mission," said Rose, handing Patti the folder.

The thin man took the folder and read the name across the top, whistling slowly as he opened it up. "Nothing shy about you, is there, Rose?" he said as he thumbed through the folder, then tossed the folder onto his desk.

"The intelligence estimates in that report are accurate and up-to-date as far as we know, so I don't think there's anything else I need to give you."

"I know. *Chu-i* Myoto provided me with new reports last night as I was making my final decision. She has proved quite skillful in that area." Rose paused for a moment, suddenly struck by an idea. "Tell me, just who is *Chu-i* Reiza Myoto?"

Patti looked up from his desk where he was filing out an unnamed form. "What, she hasn't told you?" Patti rubbed his chin and considered the thought. "That's interesting." He suddenly shook his head and wagged a finger at Rose. "If she didn't tell, then neither will I." Patti chuckled to himself and continued writing. Rose sat in silence and watched while the man filled out the form and slid it across the desk toward him.

"This is a preliminary contract. It indicates that both sides are acting in good faith and are entering the contract of their own free will. Somewhere in there it also says what each party, that's the Black Thorns and the Draconis Combine, will and will not do. It further provides the rate of remuneration, salvage rights, command rights, transportation, et cetera." Patti leaned back and pulled a pipe from the side drawer as Rose read in silence.

Rose was halfway through the first of two pages by the time Patti got the pipe going. "As you're a close personal friend of my illustrious commander," Patti said, "there is little room for negotiation. You're getting our best deal up front; I might as well tell you there will be no negotiation. I can give you the names of several other company commanders to verify that, but I doubt they'll willingly tell you how much they made, so you'll pretty much have to take my word for it."

Rose suddenly leaned forward and looked up from the contract. Patti stared at him, completely bored with the entire process. "I gather you've read the part about remuneration. It is rather excessive."

Rose leaned back and considered the statement. Excessive barely covered it. The contract would pay almost four times the amount they'd been paid on Borghese, and would be complete in four months. In addition, the Black Thorns retained all rights to any salvage they managed to acquire while on the mission.

Rose looked back at Patti, but the man was staring up at the ceiling. He'd obviously seen the same reaction countless times, but wasn't completely used to it. Rose read on.

The advance money was terrible, but Zimmer and Priam had both warned him of that. The Thorns could borrow up to thirty-five percent of the contract's value, but the interest rate was twenty-two percent, so Rose prayed he would never be forced to do so. He continued reading, covering the front half of the contract and turning the page over.

"You don't like Zimmer much, do you, Captain?" said Patti. Rose snorted and continued reading. "Any specific reason?"

Rose nodded. "He got a lot of good people killed on Tukayyid."

Patti shook his head. "Like I said, nothing shy about you, is there?"

"Just the truth," countered Rose.

"But the Com Guards won."

Rose stopped reading and set the contract down. He paused a moment before looking into Patti's eyes. When he spoke, it was very slowly.

"Won the war, but we lost one hell of a lot of battles. It was all-out war. No quarter asked or given. In most cases, if you weren't still standing at the end of the fight, it was because you were dead. Zimmer was one of the people pulling the strings. He called the shots on most battles I was in."

"But you're a warrior, Captain. You're supposed to fight," replied Patti.

"Fight, yes. Get butchered, no." Rose paused, caught in a memory. When he spoke again, his eyes had a distant look. "You want to know one of Zimmer's best plans? His masterful tactical scheme?" Rose's voice dripped sarcasm. Patti nodded briefly.

"The mobile wall. Simple tactic really. Just stand in the Clans' way and let them pound you to snail snot. Get blasted, then fall back. Get blasted, then fall back. Eventually the Clans got careless and advanced too quickly. Hell, they probably thought they were having a great time. They over-committed, and other Guard units cut them off from their supplies. Big bloody victory. Of course, most of the pilots assigned to be punching bags weren't around to celebrate."

Rose paused and silently dared Patti to speak, but the man said nothing. Rose picked up the contract and stared at it for several long minutes before he began reading again. He was just about to conclude that this was the best contract he'd ever heard of when he stopped short.

"Now wait just one goddamn minute." Rose threw the contract onto Patti's desk and jumped to his feet. "I've already got a DropShip and a crew. I don't want or need Combine transportation."

Patti leaned forward, placing his pipe in a special holder to his left. He didn't even look at Rose as he pushed the contract back toward him.

"As I said, this is not negotiable."

"Then I'm out. The Black Thorns are out. I'll reconsider the open contracts and get back with you later this week." Rose turned to go.

"The transportation clause on any contract we present you will be the same as this one, Rose. You're stuck with Kurita transportation, whether you like it or not."

Rose stopped at the door and turned back. He knew he would be forced to accept a supplemental contract. Both he and Patti, as well as Zimmer, knew that the Thorns needed the extra money to keep the unit afloat financially. But not being allowed to work with McCloud was something he'd never considered.

"Why can't I work with McCloud?" asked Rose. Patti's face suddenly relaxed and he reached for his pipe. He looked like an old soldier forced to do his duty even if he didn't like it. If Rose hadn't seen the trick before, he'd surely have fallen for it this time.

"It has nothing to do with me or even Zimmer. The plain truth is that Captain McCloud has not been cleared for operation in Clan space. She can still make the jump from Wolcott to any Combine system, but she's not allowed to transport combat troops on any mission."

"Then get her cleared for combat," demanded Rose.

Patti shook his head. "Can't be done," he said flatly. "That little stunt she pulled inbound cost her dearly. The Internal Security Forces blacklisted her when she refused the ISF pilot's order to correct her course. I don't think even an order from Theodore Kurita himself could get her cleared."

"But there was nothing she could do," Rose insisted. "Her decision not to change course couldn't have affected the Clan aerospace fighters in any way." Rose knew there was no point in arguing with Patti, but he had to try.

"I know, Rose. As it was, there was no harm done. The JumpShip got away clean, as did one of the DropShips."

"And the other?" asked Rose, already knowing the answer.

Patti shook his head. "The Clan fighters figured the one that made the break was the decoy, so they stuck with the lead ship. Once the fighters were out of range of the JumpShip, the DropShip captain slowed to engage. All six Clan fighters were destroyed, but so was the DropShip."

Patti continued to shake his head. "That's the price of this invasion. McCloud has been condemned by the ISF, not because of the outcome, but because of her refusal to follow the orders of the ISF agent. I shouldn't have to tell you that chain of command is inviolate, Captain Rose."

Rose nodded and accepted defeat. He knew McCloud would be furious. She'd never wanted to go into combat in the first place, but now that she would be barred from it, he knew it would hurt her more than anything she'd encountered in the time he'd known her.

"All right, *Tai-i,* I'll take the contract." Rose reached over and signed the final page. A part of him felt like he was betraying McCloud, but as commander of the Black Thorns he couldn't allow that part of him to place the unit in jeopardy. This contract, or another one like it, was vital to the unit's survival, and he couldn't ignore that fact.

"Excellent, Captain Rose," said Patti, who was trying not to look superior but failing miserably.

Rose knew this contract would be the envy of any mercenary in the Inner Sphere, but he still felt like he'd just lost one of the most important battles of his life. The worst part was knowing he couldn't have done anything to prevent the loss.

Patti took the contract and placed in his desk. "The final papers will be drawn up and the appropriate funds transferred to the account on Outreach per your meeting with *Tai-sa* Zimmer last week."

"We'll want to start training immediately," said Rose.

"I would expect nothing less from a man in your position," said Patti. "I'll see that complete intelligence reports are delivered as soon as the final contracts are signed. Will there be anything else?"

"When will we start training with the new DropShip crew?" asked Rose. Although he still felt crushed, a small part of his brain continued to function as the Thorns' commander.

"Two, maybe three weeks." Patti consulted several logs and nodded. "The contract calls for a combat drop of the entire company. Myoto can handle all the arrangements for flight clearance and landing. I expect that will give you time for any special arrangements needed." Patti continued to smile, and Rose was filled with a desire to flee the room. Instead, he forced himself to rise slowly and shake Patti's hand.

"I'll be in touch," said Rose as he turned to go.

Patti waited another five minutes after Rose had gone, then picked up the phone and tapped in a number.

A deep voice answered on the other end. "Zimmer. What have you got, Patti?"

"Rose, sir. He's selected a contract and been informed about McCloud."

"How'd he take it?" asked Zimmer.

"Like a PPC to the head, sir. He never saw it coming and didn't know how to react when it came."

Zimmer didn't answer immediately, and Patti could almost hear him thinking. "What about money?"

Patti felt a sudden knot of fear. "I gave him the entire amount, sir."

"Good. He'll earn it by the time he's through." There was another brief moment of silence on the phone, and Patti could feel his forehead break into a sweat.

"He doesn't like you much, sir," Patti offered. "He blames you for what happened to his men on Tukayyid."

"I figured as much," Zimmer said, as much to himself as to Patti. "That's not my problem, however. As long as he does his job, he can hate the ground I walk on, for all I care." Then the line went dead in Patti's ear.

Patti took a moment to compose himself, then reached into his desk for a red folder. Only one thing left to do, select a DropShip and a captain for the Black Thorns. Once that was done, he would get out from between his commander and the mercenary. Patti took the first profile in the list. He nodded approval and placed the sheet in the folder with Rose's contract. As far as Patti was concerned, that closed the entire mission.

13

Rose sat back in his chair in the mess room of the Black Thorn compound and watched the other members of the company fall into the room. Unlike previous meetings here, there was very little talking and absolutely no laughter. MechWarriors and crew members simply filed into the room, then sat down and waited.

Rose looked over at McCloud, who smiled but looked worn and tired. She'd insisted on being present at the meeting, along with her entire crew, though Rose had only agreed to please her. He returned her smile, but his eyes had gone back to surveying the room.

Rose had returned from the meeting with Patti on the previous day, but rather than call an immediate meeting, he'd gone straight to McCloud and then to their cabin. Nobody had disturbed them until dinner, which Rose refused for the two of them. With Esmeralda maintaining the duty roster and Riannon continuing to monitor the communications channels, Rose was not absolutely needed, but his behavior was strange nonetheless. The next day he'd participated in the morning training, but had said he would not discuss the outcome of his meeting with Patti until later in the day. As time passed, the unit's normally high morale began to falter.

Though all the Black Thorns understood the situation on

Wolcott, the only ones who knew exactly what was going to happen were Rose, Riannon, Bell, and the two lance commanders. Rose had, of course, sought out the opinions of the company's leadership, but the final contract decision had been his alone. Seeing him return from the meeting in a dour mood, all the Thorns had begun to assume the worst, and their expressions were various shades of pessimism as they entered the room. Riannon was, as usual, the last to arrive. She took the chair nearest the door and continued to monitor the communications center with a wireless earphone. When Rose saw that she was settled in, he stood up and began to speak.

"As you all know, I have been involved in selecting a supplemental contract for the unit while we are here on Wolcott. Some of you have contributed to that process and I'd like to thank you for your opinions and input. Well, the decision has been made.

"Yesterday I signed a preliminary contract on behalf of the Black Thorns to undertake Operation Green Dagger." Rose paused and let his gaze play over the silent group. "I assure you that, colorful as the name sounds, that is not the reason I chose the mission." Rose noticed a few smiles, but most of the warriors still looked concerned.

"This mission is fairly straightforward. We've accepted a contract to raid a Clan-held factory on Courcheval. Though the Combine's first choice would be to get the factory back, they'll settle for denying it to the Clans." Rose began pacing the room. "And that's where we come in.

"We'll enter the system from a pirate point behind the Clan system defenders. I know that's a concept hard for ground-pounders to understand, but I'm told it can be done. In any event, we arrive behind them and slip toward the planet. The JumpShip waits until we return, cleverly hiding from the evil Clans." A few more smiles. That was a good sign.

"The Black Thorns will make a combat drop near the facility. Once on the ground, we'll shoot and stomp everything in sight. What isn't nailed down, we'll carry away."

"And if it can be ripped up, it isn't nailed down."

Rose turned and looked at Hawg. As usual, he was the first one to come around. Rose smiled and nodded. "Exactly," he said.

"In the meantime, the DropShip will land at a destroyed factory several hundred kilometers away. The place probably won't be defended because the factory has been almost totally gutted. By traveling under the radar net, the DropShip will be able to disguise its position to some degree. The debris of the factory should further hide the landing.

"The Black Thorns on the ground will head toward the DropShip in a serpentine manner to minimize the chance of the ship being detected." Rose began to walk around the room, giving part of the mission to each MechWarrior individually. That made it seem like he was talking to the various members of the unit personally—just one of the things Rose did instinctively that helped to build the team. By now he was back in the center of the room.

"Once we're safely on the DropShip, it lifts off and heads back to the cleverly concealed JumpShip. We link up, and it's another thrilling ride home to Wolcott." Rose put his hands on his hips and smiled.

"The essence of simplicity," he said. "But the whole operation will obviously require split-second timing on the part of all involved, and that means we've got to be in peak form when we ship out."

"It's a good thing we've got McCloud," said O'Shea. Rose rolled his head back and looked at the ceiling before turning to the man. "Wait a minute. We don't have McCloud?" the big man asked.

"Something tells me that's the sand in the lubricant," said Hawg to Greta. Rose scowled at Hawg, but McCloud stood and drew everyone's attention.

"O'Shea is right. The *Bristol* will not be part of this mission. After all my bitching about not wanting to be in the military, I finally decide I'll do it and the Snakes say they don't want me." She hung her head in shame for a moment, then looked back at the group.

"It seems I've stepped on a few toes during our brief stay here on Wolcott. Because of that, I've been denied clearance for flying combat missions." Rose could hear the strain in her voice, but hoped that was only because he knew McCloud so well. Her statements to her crew and the Thorns were costing her dearly, but she continued to speak.

"I wish there was some other way to do this, but you'll be using another DropShip for this contract. The *Bristol* will be making runs back into Combine space while you're gone." McCloud sat down abruptly. Rose had heard her voice start to break as she spoke the last few words.

He picked up where she'd left off. "The *Bristol* is not leaving us, at least not on a permanent basis. We've all got bills to pay, and spacers are no different in that regard. The *Bristol* and her crew will still be based here on Wolcott, but they'll be living their own schedule for a while."

Sudden silence filled the room as Rose quit speaking. Even though the captain and crew of the *Bristol* weren't really going anywhere, the veteran Thorns felt like they'd just lost a close friend. McCloud had never officially signed up with the Thorns, but every warrior in the unit considered her and her crew a part of their family.

Rose allowed his people to collect their thoughts for a moment, then went on. "At any rate, we'll be assigned a new DropShip and crew in a few weeks. Then we'll have a couple of months to train, both on the ground and with the ship. I shouldn't have to tell you that isn't much time, but I'll do it anyway—it isn't much time." Rose let his voice rise, capturing the full attention of every warrior in the room.

"Starting tomorrow we'll devote ourselves to training for this particular mission. It just so happens I've got the lance roster constructed, so we'll be fighting and moving by lances from now on. I know we've been rather informal about leadership up to this point, but that changes effective immediately." Rose looked around the room and was happy to see everyone was giving him their full attention. "All warriors report to your lance commander immediately following this meeting.

"Recon lance under the command of Lieutenant Ajax. Yuri, you'll take command of the *Dasher*. Treat her right.

Leeza, you've got your own *Mercury* so the recon lance shouldn't be much of a surprise to you. Good luck. Kitten, you and your *Panther* round out the lance. Ajax, you've got nothing but unmolded clay to work with."

"I shall be an artist," Ajax responded without a trace of a smile.

Rose continued. "The recon lance is designed for speed, but they're not short on firepower. The *Panther* and the *Dasher* make sure of that. Keep in mind, however, that the primary job of these 'Mechs is to locate the enemy and tell the other two lances where to find them.

"That leads me to the battle lance under the command of Esmeralda. Hawg and O'Shea, you'll keep your original postings with the *Battlemaster* and the *Warhammer*. Let's remember why we're out there, all right?" Rose looked at all three members of the battle lance, but made sure O'Shea understood the seriousness of his position. He was happy to see the man nodding solemnly. "Joining you will be Greta in the *Charger*."

Rose turned to Greta. "That used to be my ride, so treat her nice."

"I'll treat her as my very own," said Greta.

"I'd rather you treat her like she belonged to your commanding officer," Rose rebutted with a smile and a wink. The look on her face showed she didn't know it was a joke until Hawg lightly elbowed her.

"That leaves the command lance for everybody else. I still get to be the leader and Antioch Bell still gets to make sure I stay alive long enough to enjoy the position. Riannon will handle the communication work, and that leaves Jamshid as our newest member. He'll be piloting the second *Mad Cat*." Jamshid looked as though he would burst with pride at the new posting. Rose couldn't help but return the sentiment.

"Any questions?" he asked, glancing around the room.

"Just one," said Esmeralda. "If it isn't breaking security, which of the Clans are we going against?"

Rose considered the question for a moment. "Well, I don't think I'm letting anything slip if I tell you we'll be up against the Nova Cats."

"Ha!" barked Yuri from across the room, turning suddenly sheepish under Rose's stare. "Oops. Sorry, sir."

"Did you win money, son?" asked Rose.

Yuri smiled and shook his head. "No, sir, something better. Now I've got somebody to make my bed for the next week." Rose looked on in surprise as everybody turned toward Esmeralda, who just shrugged and held up her hands.

"I even got odds. One month versus one week. Should have known better." Esmeralda looked totally forlorn, but the veterans knew better than to buy the act. They knew Yuri would receive a payback, probably before the end of the week. Rose could only stand there shaking his head.

"That's all. Everybody out of the room. I can't stand to hear any more. Gambling in a mercenary unit. I'll be a laughing stock." Rose waved the other Thorns away in mock remorse, amused to see Yuri receiving a considerable amount of good-natured attention. Within seconds only Rose and McCloud remained.

"I think that went well," he said, crossing the room to sit down next to her. She nodded, but didn't speak for several moments.

"I've been thinking about it, and I believe I now know what I have to do." McCloud was very solemn, a stark contrast to the cheerful group that had just left the room.

"And that is?" prodded Rose.

"I have to find a contract to transport a company back to Luthien or someplace. Something I'm cleared to do." The very words dripped contempt.

"You could wait a couple of weeks. That way we'd have some ground time together."

McCloud smiled. "Not likely. Now that you've got a mission, you'll throw yourself into it. Up early, back to bed late, and too tired to do anything but sleep."

Rose sat straighter. "Never. I'm never that tired."

McCloud smiled and leaned into him, forcing Rose to put his arm around her shoulder to keep his balance. "Well, I guess we'll have to see about that, but I know I can't afford to wait much longer for a contract run. Without the money for transporting the Thorns, I'm going to be short on the next payment if I don't turn up something quick." Rose wanted to say something clever or something that would make it all better, but McCloud had stated the problem very clearly. She needed the work and she needed it right away.

"All right," he said, accepting the idea of McCloud's imminent departure. "I understand you have obligations that don't include me, but give me some time. I was just getting used to having you around, and I don't think I'm ready to have you gone." Rose felt his chest tighten. If Rachel was going to make a trip to Luthien, she would have to run the Smoke Jaguar blockade. Patti had already told him that was not a simple—or safe—thing to do.

"Don't worry," she said, as if reading his mind. "I'm not through with you." She laid a hand on his arm. "I'll be back before you leave on this Green Dagger thing."

"I'll count on it," he said. Rose was still wrestling with the new idea of McCloud being in danger and him unable to help. He'd already had to contemplate the prospect of losing her several times in the past and had found it almost unbearable. The idea of McCloud actually dying scared the hell out of him.

"Let go to bed," she said standing slowly. "Can they live without you for the rest of the night?"

Rose nodded and also stood up. "The lance commanders will handle everybody but Jamshid, and Antioch will take him." He smiled. "Looks like I'm free for the evening."

"Then let's not waste it." She turned and headed back to their room, leaving Rose with only one option: follow her and make sure the night was put to good use.

14

Mercenary Garrison District
Wolcott, Draconis Combine
15 March 3057

The next two weeks passed in little more than a blur of training for all the Black Thorns, but especially for Rose. Every day the company, which now included Myoto, marched into the swamp for a full day of training. When they arrived back at the compound, the poor performers for the day were detailed to hose down all the BattleMechs before reporting for duty. While the rest of the company was engaged with their duties, Rose would plan the next day's activities and work with Riannon on the unit's supply requirements.

Ria was great with the actual numbers, but didn't have the experience to predict what types of supplies would be necessary beyond the basics. Now that Rose knew the mission they'd be undertaking, he began looking for specific pieces of gear and ordnance. Once he'd determined what he wanted, Ria would make all the necessary arrangements for items to arrive in a timely manner.

After the dinner hour Rose usually spent time with specific members of the company, depending on the day's activities. He particularly enjoyed the company of Bell and Hawg, but also made a point of socializing with the other members of the company during his leisure hours to make sure he got to know everyone. The evenings Rose always spent with McCloud. Occasionally they'd invite Esmeralda or one or more of the recruits, but mostly they spent their time alone, which was just the way Rose wanted it.

McCloud passed her days looking for a contract, and Rose wasn't surprised when she announced to him one night that she'd accepted a job to transport a BattleMech company returning to Pesht. Rose lay awake the entire night staring at the darkened ceiling and listening to McCloud sleeping softly beside him. Although she hadn't said it, Rose knew the acceptance of a contract meant that from now on she would live on the *Bristol* until it was time to lift-off.

He considered asking her to remain with him, but he knew what the answer would be and didn't want to hear it out loud. He also considered telling her how he felt and his hopes for their relationship, but the words failed him once again. In the end he settled for helping her pack up her gear and then seeing her off to the spaceport. They'd see each other again before lift-off, but by then she'd be firmly in her captain persona, giving him little opportunity to talk about the things that really mattered.

Later that morning Rose got a call from the spaceport. At first he'd thought it was McCloud, but the message was from their new DropShip captain, Sinclair Danes. Rose was invited to meet with the captain to discuss the specifics of training and their upcoming mission. Rose wasn't sure whether to be offended by Danes' request that he come to the spaceport instead of Danes coming to the compound, but in the end he decided it didn't matter. He dropped out of the daily practice session and went to the spaceport alone.

Rose was so lost in his thoughts on the way over that the driver had to jolt his daydreaming passenger back to the present before he realized the ride was over. As the car pulled away, Rose studied the DropShip in which he and the Black Thorns would travel to and from their mission. He wasn't sure whether to laugh or cry.

The DropShip was the same class as the *Bristol*, but all similarities ended there. The nameless ship sat on its four legs, but leaned severely to the north. Rose could see that the struts on the northern leg were buckled badly. Most of the components to the leg doors had been removed—or shot away, Rose thought—and three technicians were performing repairs on the damage. He could also see that several of the giant armor plates had been recently replaced, but the leg still need several more new ones.

As Rose walked toward the main cargo door, he continued inspecting the DropShip, now able to see the scars from small-arms fire around the frame of the cargo door. The bottom set of hinges were slightly askew, and the entire ramp was marred by blistered paint and burnt couplings. It could have been a fuel fire, thought Rose, but more likely the damage was the result of a homemade grenade. He smiled to himself. It looked like Danes had had his share of warm departures.

Climbing up the ramp, Rose continued to see the after-effects of small-arms fire and the indication of repair work. It was impossible to tell just how recent some of the repairs were, but it looked as though every visible part of the ship had been worked on at least once. When he actually got into the cargo bay, he saw that the damage was almost as heavy on the inside as the outside.

The bay was empty except for two men standing amid a pile of junk. Rose couldn't hear a word, but from their faces and gestures, the conversation was obviously heated. As he got closer, the smaller of the two threw up his hands in disgust and stalked off toward the cargo door. He brushed past Rose without so much as a glance.

The other man had his back to Rose, but turned around just as the mercenary was about to speak. In a flash Rose knew that this was the captain of the DropShip that would him and his men to Courcheval.

The man was Rose's height, but much thinner in the hips and waist. He had broad shoulders, but not Rose's broadness of chest. Rather than the standard coveralls Rose associated with all DropShip crews, the man wore black work pants and a red shirt open to the waist. He studied Rose for a moment, pulling gently on his thin mustache. Then he smiled and began to pick his way down through the unstable debris. With a jump to cover the last meter, the man arrived alongside Rose. He ran one hand through his curly brown hair and, with another smile, extended the other to Rose.

"Sinclair Danes. You must be Jeremiah Rose." His grasp was firm, but not at all the kind of petty test of strength Rose might have expected. After a simple shake, he withdrew his hand. "I'm so very pleased to meet you." Rose was surprised; the greeting seemed sincere.

"I hope that wasn't trouble," said Rose, indicating the man disappearing down the ramp.

Danes laughed. "Nothing of the sort. That was my first mate. He just quit on me." Rose's heart sank, but Danes only smiled the wider. "Just as well, I suppose. The man had no class."

Danes wrapped an arm around Rose's shoulders and gently turned him toward the interior door to the ship. "Why don't we take a look around?" Rose just nodded. "You're new to Wolcott, aren't you? No need to worry, I've been here since the start of this whole bloody business." Danes clapped Rose's shoulder good-naturedly. "I can't remember the number of times I've made the run past the Jaguars.

"Say, mind if I smoke? Nasty habit, but I'm afraid it's a weakness." Danes nudged Rose in the side. "One of many, I'm afraid. He pulled a long brown cigarette from a shoulder pocket that looked like it had been designed to hold just such an item. Flicking an old-fashioned lighter, Danes lit up in a cloud of blue smoke.

"Nothing like it, I'm afraid. Care for one?" Rose shook his head. "They say it'll kill me, but who wants to live forever?"

Rose decided to keep his opinion to himself and concentrated on enduring the tour of Danes' ship. It was every bit as bad as he'd feared. Danes introduced him to several crew members, whose names Rose promptly forgot. Several spaceport technicians scuttled around lending their help to the variety of repairs that seemed to be happening everywhere on the ship. Danes talked on and on about the ship, the Clans, the Kuritas, and anything else that came to his mind. Rose decided he wasn't supposed to interrupt the monologue, so he kept quiet. All he could think of was that the minute he got out of here, he must contact Patti immediately about getting a new captain, of that there was no doubt.

Rose was just about to make a break for the cargo doors, which had to be nearby, when Danes grabbed him by the elbow and gently pushed him through a doorway. At first Rose thought it was another serviceway, but after a short hallway they came to another door. Following Danes through the door, he realized this one led to a stateroom. Danes closed the door behind them, then flicked on a red light as he approached the bar.

"Gods, but I'm dry." Danes poured two tumblers of amber liquid and passed one to Rose. "Too early?" he asked. Rose considered, but decided it was close enough to lunch to accept. He took the glass, but paused when Danes raised his slightly.

"To comrades in arms," the other man said solemnly. At first Rose thought the toast was meant for him, but looking at Danes, he realized it was meant for someone far away and probably long since gone. Rose repeated the toast and sipped the liquid. Scotch. Maybe Danes wasn't so bad after all.

"You could have helped me out, you know," said Danes between sips. Rose could only look confused. "I mean, I had to carry the entire conversation. Not that I couldn't, you understand, but it is hard on the throat." Danes took another sip.

"Excuse me?" said Rose. "I thought you were very happy talking to yourself."

"Pah," said Danes, waving the comment away. "That was for the ground crew. Most of them either work for the ISF or report to the liaison office. It's hard to tell who to trust, so I don't trust any of them."

"But you trust me," said Rose.

Danes considered the statement. "I have to, at least a little. You certainly proved you're a patient man and I like that in a person. Patience is such a rewarding attribute, don't you think?" Rose nodded and sipped again. The scotch was quite good and totally out of place in this room.

"So, where are we?" asked Rose with a wave of his glass.

He pointed to the red light. "Connected to some type of white noise generator?"

Danes nodded. "You're good," he smiled. "I like to think of this as the conference room. It's actually listed as a storage room, but what's in a name? It's one of several places on the ship where we can talk in private when on the ground. After working with *Tai-sa* Zimmer, I've found secrecy has its advantages."

"I concur," Rose said with a grimace. "So why the meeting? We could have talked at the Black Thorn compound and saved all this charade."

Danes shook his head and set down his half-full glass. "I wanted to see how you operate away from your element. Get a measure of the leader I'll be working with." Rose nodded.

"Of course, it's still too early to tell," Danes added quickly, "but I'd say you've got promise."

"Thanks for the vote of confidence."

"That vote is still pending. First let's see how you handle a little old-fashioned honesty," said Danes.

"Is this the part where you tell me I'm not standing in a beat-up old DropShip on its last leg?" Rose allowed himself to feel slightly relieved. Maybe things were looking up.

Danes laughed and reached for his glass, downing the contents in a single swallow. "Oh no, Captain Rose, you're standing on what may pass for the worst excuse for a DropShip this side of the Tukayyid line, and I don't speak those words lightly. I am quite a judge of a ship's caliber."

Rose cringed and drained his glass. He waited until he was sure his breath was back before trying to speak. "That bad?"

Danes nodded. "Most of the armor is shot away, and there are significant power distribution problems to several of the components. The engine is solid, but it could stand an overhaul. Some of the systems are currently running on backup, but I hope to have all the mains back on-line by the end of the week."

"Can she even fly?"

Danes considered the question before answering. "If she had to, yes, but I'd like to have thirty or forty days on the ground before I take her back up. If I had my wish, I'd take another month to run tests and calibrations before she takes passengers."

"That doesn't leave me much time to train," replied Rose.

Danes pulled on his thin mustache and nodded. "No. Of course I'll push the schedule as much as possible, but I'll need the first month just to put the ship back within safety limits." Rose was frustrated and it showed. Danes shrugged. "Sorry, but that's the best I can do on short notice."

"Short notice? I've known about this mission for two weeks."

Danes stroked his chin and stared at his black boots. "I didn't find out until yesterday when we landed."

Rose sighed and rubbed his eyes. This was not working out the way he expected. "I thought you spacers were supposed to take pride in your ships, like MechWarriors and their BattleMechs. I'd never let my 'Mech . . ."

"Sir!" Danes snapped, cutting Rose short. "This abomination is not my ship. No, let me rephrase that. This was not my ship until very recently. I would never allow a vessel under my care to fall into such a state of disrepair."

Rose realized he'd overstepped himself. Danes had shown too much style for this to be his ship, but Rose had missed the obvious. Apologies were definitely in order, but Rose wasn't sure they'd be accepted.

"I'm sorry, Captain Danes. I spoke without thinking. You're right, of course. This ship could not possibly have been under your command for long. I regret my hasty words."

"Apology accepted, Captain. Let's say no more about it. Truth to tell, I'm overly touchy about the subject myself." Danes smiled and Rose responded in kind. He wanted to know what had happened to Danes' original ship and how he'd come into possession of another so soon, but to ask that in their current situation would be out of the question. Rose decided to stick to the mission.

"Have you seen the contract?" asked Rose, to which Dane nodded assent. "The contract is for only four months, which gives us a very tight schedule."

"I agree," said Danes. "The mission is scheduled for two weeks, including system travel at the target. With another two weeks for travel to the jump point here at Wolcott, that leaves us three months."

"Right, but we'll probably want a two-week cushion—and two weeks are already gone. That puts us right in the middle of your testing period."

"Damn," muttered Danes, and Rose had to agree with the sentiment. "I'll just have to see what I can do, that's all. We can cut some corners, but not many. If I can have the ship ready in six weeks, will that give you enough time?"

"Not really, but I'll take it and smile. I'd like to give the company one combat drop before the mission and some training on loading and fire support if the take-off is hot."

"I'll do my best, then," Danes told him. "Six weeks. Sooner if I can manage it." Danes headed for the red light, flicking it back off as he went to the door.

"By the way," said Rose, "does the ship have a name? My people will want to know."

Danes paused and slowly nodded. "She's called the *Tracy K*," he said.

"Nice name. Does it mean anything special?" Rose asked.

Danes' eyes began to mist slightly as he stared at Rose. "Not a thing," he replied in a tight voice. "Why do you ask?"

15

Rose returned from the daily training session one afternoon and discovered McCloud waiting for him in the communications center. He didn't have to be told why she was there. Her presence was enough. They talked about the Black Thorns in general and the prospects for the upcoming mission, both of them trying to postpone coming to the obvious purpose of her visit.

McCloud knew Danes, but by reputation only. He was something of a drifter, even more ill at ease on the ground than she was, which spoke volumes to Rose about Danes' character. Rumors hinted that Danes was a pirate, but no one had ever been able to prove it. He was still wanted in Steiner space for questioning about several raids, but McCloud doubted Danes would ever return to Steiner space, warrants or not.

"His wife was also a DropShip captain," said McCloud as Rose slipped into his uniform for dinner. "They operated as a team, working for several Lyran regiments until the arrival of the Clans. From what I gather, Danes decided that hauling for the army was too dangerous, but his wife continued short-haul work for one of the Lyran Guard units. I'm not sure which one."

Rose stuffed a foot into his boot and looked over at

McCloud. "Her name wouldn't have been Tracy, would it?"

"I don't think so," McCloud said after a moment's thought. "I think it was Kelly, or Kimmie, or something like that." Rose stopped in mid-pull of his other boot. McCloud was sure he was about to say something, but he stared off into space. "Well?"

"Well, what?" asked Rose as he finished putting on his boot.

"Why did you ask?"

Rose sighed, then started to shrug, stopping in mid-gesture. "Danes has a new ship. Or rather he's the new captain of an ancient ship. He's calling it the *Tracy K.*" McCloud chewed her lip at the new information. "I asked if the name meant anything, and he said no, but that was obviously a lie. I guess he's too polite to say bum off."

"If he named the ship after his dead wife ..."

"His wife is dead?" asked Rose in shock. "You didn't mention that."

"I was about to, but you interrupted."

"What happened?"

McCloud rolled her eyes and took a deep breath. "If you'll let me finish, I'll tell you what I know. Or should I say, I'll tell you what I've heard." Rose started to speak, but choked back his reply. He felt like he'd just taken a scolding, but baiting Rachel would only delay getting the information he wanted. She was trying not to look smug and nearly succeeded.

"So, she was hauling for one of the Guard units during the Clan War. As was typical during that phase of the war, her Lyrans were on the run. Whichever Clan they were fighting was overrunning the base and had the Guards backed up to their DropShips. A few of the DropShips made good their escape, but several others were captured while still on the ground. Two of the ships were destroyed. One belonged to Captain Danes."

Rose sat on the end of his bed and contemplated this new information. If McCloud's information was accurate, Danes might be looking to even the score with the Clans, or he might be looking to settle with the Federated Commonwealth, or he might just want to be getting on with his life. Rose had no way of knowing.

"How did he take the news?" he asked.

McCloud shrugged. "I don't know. As I said, I know him by reputation only." Rose tried not to be frustrated, but it wasn't easy. He was about to trust his life, and the lives of his company, to Sinclair Danes. If there were problems, he wanted to know about them now.

"Didn't Bell fight with one of the Lyran Guard units?" asked McCloud, almost as an afterthought.

Rose slapped his forehead. "The Twenty-sixth." He rolled over on the bed and reached for the comm unit on the nightstand. "Ria, could you ask Antioch to come see me for a moment? Thanks." He set the handset back down and stood up.

"Do you have any idea what happened to his last ship?" asked Rose. McCloud shook her head, but had no time to answer before a knock sounded at the door.

"In," said Rose.

Antioch Bell poked his head inside the door and smiled. "You wanted to see me, Captain?"

Rose waved him inside. "Come in and shut the door behind you, Antioch." Bell looked concerned for a moment, but the look quickly vanished as he closed the door. Rose looked preoccupied but not distressed. In Bell's mind that meant the problem couldn't be too serious.

"Hi, Rachel," Bell said cheerfully. "Ria had another place set tonight. You'll stay to chow with us, won't you?"

McCloud smiled. "Of course, Antioch. Your commander hasn't invited me yet, but I thought I'd hang around for a while."

Rose seemed to miss the implied message in the exchange. "We're looking for information, Antioch," he said to Bell, who nodded and leaned against the door. There wasn't much space in the small room, and the presence of the three full-sized bodies didn't offer the luxury of getting comfortable. Although Bell would never have been so casual in the presence of his former commanding officer, he knew Rose would take the relaxed posture for granted.

"Have you ever heard of a DropShip captain named Danes?" McCloud asked.

Bell frowned. "Like our new DropShip captain?" he asked.

"Like our new DropShip captain's late wife," said Rose. Bell's eyes went wide as he looked from Rose to McCloud and back again. "Her ship was probably either captured or destroyed during fighting with the Clans along the Steiner border. Rachel thinks that she might have been working with one of the Lyran Guard units." Rose paused to let Bell speak, but the fair-haired man remained silent. "Any ideas?" he finally prompted.

Bell slowly shook his head as he stared at the floor between his boots. "Sorry, sir. I don't know anybody like that with the Twenty-sixth. She might have been with one of the other units, but I just don't know." Bell looked up to McCloud. "Any other details?"

McCloud tried to dredge up other facts from her memory, but her mind was blank. "Sorry, but that's all I know." She shrugged. "There are too many DropShips out there to remember the names of every captain, especially one who's been dead for almost five years."

Bell pulled himself off the door and started to leave. "I'll check it out with some of the other Thorns. Maybe one of them knows something."

"Hold on, Antioch," said Rose. "Let's keep this quiet for the time being." Bell scowled. "Danes might be a great guy," continued Rose, "or he might be a loose cannon."

"Do you think we're going to have problems?" asked Bell, suddenly concerned.

Rose shook his head, but the look Rachel gave him told Bell the situation might be otherwise. "He seemed fine when I met him a couple of days ago," said Rose. "The problem is he's flying a new DropShip. A piece of junk, I might add. His first mate walked out on him . . ."

"You didn't tell me that," said McCloud.

". . . and I think he just named his new ship after his dead wife," finished Rose with a stare at McCloud.

"You think he's a pirate," concluded Bell, leaning back against the door. Rose shrugged, but McCloud nodded. The nod took Rose by surprise.

"Really?" he asked.

"Jeremiah, of course he's a pirate."

"But he's here at the request of the Combine government. They don't take acts of piracy lightly," Rose countered.

"Officially, no," she conceded. "But consider where we're standing. If there is any location in the Inner Sphere that is more unusual than this, we've never heard of it. We're in the middle of Smoke Jaguar territory, for God's sake. You've accepted a second contract. One that runs concurrently with your present contract, you'll remember. That is not, as I understand it, common practice. Even before the Clans invaded, independent DropShips worked both sides of the border between Successor States. Even if Dane has raided several F-C bases for parts, the Kuritas are likely to look the other way."

"As long as he's somewhere the Federated Commonwealth can't see him," continued Bell. "Teddy isn't supporting the piracy. He's just using all his available assets."

Rose nodded. It made good sense. With the tight control on Wolcott, it was unlikely that any of the other Inner Sphere leaders knew who, or what, was here. As long as Danes, or any other captain or MechWarrior, for that matter, stayed on the good side of the Kuritas, he could always find a job on Wolcott.

"You know," Rose said, "this assumes the worst about the man. There are other explanations for the evidence we've seen."

"You're right," said McCloud. "Nobody has ever accused him of anything. If the Kuritas were upset, they'd never have brought him to Wolcott."

"You said he was a pirate, Rachel. How do you know?" asked Bell.

"It's the only explanation," she said, but Rose and Bell still looked baffled. "Look, I'm not saying he spends all his time preying on passenger liners, but he's a pirate. He probably spends part of the time 'outside the law' and part of the time hauling high-risk cargo to questionable locations."

Her two companions didn't look convinced. "I can tell you ground-pounders are having trouble figuring the situation. But think about it for a minute," McCloud went on.

"Jeremiah, have you ever wondered why I hate the idea of combat? Well, it's not just because of the obvious danger, but because the financial burden would ground my ship faster than any lasers. Yes, it takes thousands of C-bills to repair a BattleMech, so imagine how much more expensive it is to repair a DropShip. Not only are parts harder to find, but they cost more.

"If you're an independent, like me or Danes, one good battle can cost you hundreds of thousands of C-bills, and that assumes you're not assessed for damages to the cargo. That's a burden most captains can never recover from. If they want to keep flying, they have to either join up with one of the Houses of the Inner Sphere or look for some easy money."

"Sounds like a risky line of business you're in," commented Bell with a sad shake of his head.

"For some of us, yes. Of course, not everybody is in the same situation. Some ships are owned by giant merchant companies; those captains work for the company. Maybe they call the ship their own, but it belongs to the company. Those captains don't set their own course; they go where the company orders. Military captains are in the same situation.

"The question is one of independence. I could eliminate all my worries by simply signing on with a House or mercenary unit. Then it would be their problem if the *Bristol* ever got damaged. The price is my freedom. If the stories about Danes are true, he decided to run from the Commonwealth bankers. It could have happened when his wife died or it could have happened following an attack."

"Or, it might never have happened at all," continued Rose.

"I admire your unflinching trust in your fellow man," said McCloud sarcastically. "But if he's an honest trader, how did he acquire an Inner Sphere DropShip? One riddled with weapons fire and so badly damaged it almost collapsed on landing."

"How did you know about that?" asked Rose.

McCloud snorted. "I've been living at the spaceport, remember? Danes' landing sent the crash crews scrambling. He didn't think the leg would support the weight of the landing. He was damn near right."

Rose nodded, letting the room fill with silence. McCloud might be right, but he hoped not. He had to be able to trust Danes, and the idea of working with a pirate unnerved him. The Clans were the biggest threat humanity had ever faced, and the thought of someone preying on the misfortunes of the Inner Sphere during the Clan invasion was infuriating. Still, Rose knew that such things happened every day. He didn't want to believe it, but he had to prepare the Thorns for the possibility.

"Thanks for stopping by, Antioch. Let's keep this between the three of us until I decide how we should handle it." Bell grinned slightly and threw a half-salute at Rose. "Rachel and I will be going down to dinner in just a minute. Better have Riannon round up the troops." Bell nodded and winked a goodbye to McCloud as he left the room and closed the door behind him. Rose sighed and pinched the bridge of his nose. He could feel a headache coming on.

"This never should have happened," said McCloud as she sat down on the bed. Rose released his nose and sat down next to her.

"Done is done, Rachel. I think we can survive working with Danes. In truth, he doesn't seem like such a bad guy. He's just got a shady past." Rose smiled and put an arm around McCloud's shoulders. "Some people would say the same thing about me, remember? After all, the Com Guards aren't one of your more reputable units, at least not to the rest of the Inner Sphere."

McCloud relaxed and Rose could feel her body lean against his for a moment before she pulled away. He knew that she was about to give him the bad news.

"I'm leaving," she said simply.

"I know. Will it be soon?"

McCloud looked at him, her eyes starting to fill. She stood suddenly and stepped away from the bed. With her back to Rose, she brushed the tears from her eyes and took a deep breath. She turned back to him, but kept her distance as she regained control of her emotions. She took another deep breath and looked at her chronometer.

"Thirty-eight hours and twelve minutes till lift-off."

Rose whistled and tried to lighten the mood with a smile. "That's pretty precise timing. Must be an important mission."

McCloud laughed and tears started to well again. "Hardly. We just have to follow a precise pattern to reach the JumpShip at the proper time. Too early or too late . . ." McCloud let the sentence drift off to silence. They both knew what would happen if the *Bristol* was too early or too late.

Rose sat on the bed in silence, knowing he should say something, but unsure what. "Rachel," he started slowly, "you know . . ."

"Wait, Jeremiah. I don't want a goodbye confession. I know how you feel, even if you don't. I just wanted to say goodbye. If all goes well, I'll be back in thirty days. Maybe we can talk then. Will you still be here?"

Rose nodded. "The launch date hasn't been assigned yet, but we should be here for that long and a little more. We're scheduled for training and a couple of practice runs before the real thing, so you should get back long before the Thorns leave."

McCloud accepted the news in silence. Rose wanted to talk to her, but this wasn't the time, she'd said so herself. He *would* talk to her, however. He promised himself he would get past his own emotional barrier and give McCloud the kind of love she deserved, but for now there were too many ghosts and doubts. Those would have to be banished before he could build the relationship he wanted with McCloud. The silence continued as Rose and McCloud each remained lost in thought. Finally McCloud slapped her thighs and looked at Rose.

"We'd better head over to the mess room. I'm on a sched-

ule and the Thorns will wait all night for you to show up."
She gave Rose a smile, then held out one hand to him. They
would go together to eat their goodbye dinner with the rest
of the Black Thorns.

=== 16 ===

A harsh buzzer had just begun to wail when the floor of the ship dropped away from Rose. As he slipped into free fall, his stomach lurched upward with the same familiar nausea. Next time he'd bypass breakfast, Rose promised himself, no matter how hungry he was. Within seconds, the nausea subsided and he was able to enjoy the euphoria of falling through space. This part of a drop felt like flying or floating, and it was the one time when Rose could understand why spacers acted the way they did and why aerojocks so loved their crafts.

There was a brief lurch in his ride and a stability warning light went off on his 'Mech's control panel. He was fifty kilometers above Wolcott and falling fast. As the last MechWarrior out the door of the *Tracy K*, Rose knew that the rest of the Thorns had been kicked loose on time and on target. Once his 'Mech left the ship, however, he lost the direct link to the bridge and was as blind as the rest of the Black Thorns.

Checking the altimeter and flight profile readings piped in from the drop cocoon, Rose could tell that his descent was going precisely to plan. Encased in his metal cocoon, or coffin, as the aerospace pilots liked to call the drop pods, he watched as the altimeter reading continued to fall. At forty kilometers above the plains, a drogue parachute deployed with a sudden jolt that ripped through the cocoon and pushed Rose down into his seat. The chute remained deployed for almost ten seconds before releasing, and Rose had to fight back another wave of nausea. All readings were still in the green.

At thirty kilometers, the main chute deployed. Rose could feel the drop pod swaying from the end of the giant chute as gravity tried to pull him down. The chute remained deployed for almost two minutes before Rose prepared to hit the release.

This was the most critical time in the drop. It was certainly possible for a BattleMech to drop from an aircraft to the ground using nothing but cocoons and jump jets, but Rose felt some of his men were too inexperienced for that method. Instead of a free-fall descent in a drop pod, they were using parachutes to slow their initial descent.

The first chute served only to stabilize the drop pod and correct any tumbling that might occur as the 'Mech exited the ship. It did very little to actually slow the descent. It was the second parachute that did all the work, serving as a safety measure that the dropping 'Mechs could keep deployed all the way to the ground. Rose paused with his hand above the parachute release and checked the gauges one last time.

In most cases a MechWarrior released the main chute at the designated drop altitude, which occurred somewhere between five and ten thousand meters, depending on the nature of the drop and the individual 'Mechs involved. Light 'Mechs with more reaction fuel could deploy quite low to the surface, giving them less time as an airborne target. Heavier 'Mechs required more of a safety cushion to descend safely. It was just one of many reasons why the light 'Mechs were always sent in first.

If the pilot deployed too late, even maximum thrust from the jump jets wouldn't be enough to slow the fall, and both 'Mech and pilot would end up at the bottom of a very large crater. Deploy too soon and the reaction fuel would burn out before the 'Mech was safely on the ground. The result of deploying too high was the same as deploying too low; the only difference was that pilot had more time to think about it.

Rose remained with his hand poised over the release button as he checked the gauges a fourth time. If any of the gauges or indicator lights showed a problem, Rose could stay with the parachute and ride it to the ground. The landing would certainly damage the 'Mech, perhaps even destroy it, but the pilot's chances of surviving were reliable.

Every pilot knew that combat drops were the quickest way to an early and permanent retirement, and so Rose couldn't chance this mission on pilots without drop experience. No matter how dangerous it was to even practice a drop, sending an untrained crew into an actual mission was worse.

He wasn't surprised at all to learn that of the thirteen members of the company only he, Bell, Jamshid, and Myoto were drop veterans. What did surprise him was that Myoto was among those who had earned their "drop boots," which was the reason he'd asked Myoto to sit out this particular exercise. The *Tracy K* could hold only twelve 'Mechs, and the other members of the company needed the experience more. He could have eliminated one of his own veterans instead, but he wanted the unit to work as a team as much as possible.

He knew the decision had hurt Myoto, but she kept a poker face and volunteered to work with the ground crew supervising the drop. That was typical. Every day she stood shoulder to shoulder with the Black Thorns, exposing herself to the same tests they faced. Although it earned her high marks among the unit, the Thorns sometimes wondered if she were simply a little crazy for doing so. Rose technically outranked her, but Myoto's status as liaison officer gave her privileges above her rank when dealing with the mercenaries. She could have declined to follow any order, and Rose would have had to accept it.

In the past eight weeks of training, Myoto had proved to be an excellent 'Mech pilot but a miserable marksman, completely missing easy targets that she ought to have been able to hit blindfolded. At first Rose thought it might be a problem with the targeting computer, but Hawg and Esmeralda went over the system three times and were unable to discover any problems. It was only when Riannon requested background information on Myoto that the Thorns learned that she was simply a poor shot. Bell volunteered to help her with her aim by teaching her small-arms shooting, an offer she eagerly accepted.

An alarm in his neurohelmet suddenly jerked Rose back to the present. Parachute release in ten seconds. He checked the controls one more time. Five seconds. Another check. When a green light appeared at the top of the console, Rose triggered the release. His stomach dropped again as the chute broke away cleanly. Rose counted the seconds silently to himself, and at six hit the trigger again.

A brief series of explosions all around his 'Mech and then he was free. The shards of the drop pod spilled away, revealing the blue sky around him and the brown-green of Wolcott below. Instantly the radio came alive, squawking in his ear as a host of connections were established. Rose checked his attitude adjusters, confirming that he wasn't in immediate danger of crashing, and then examined the short-range sensor.

As the last pilot out of the DropShip, he was able to see the rest of the company scattered below him. He confirmed eleven other blips as he thumbed the communications channel to life. Splitting his vision between the altimeter and the scanner, he watched as the IFF, Identify Friend or Foe, beacons were identified on each 'Mech. Call names began appearing above the blips, and the computer processed information and assigned names.

"This is Black Thorn One. Count 'em off, people, just like we planned it."

"Recon Four, green." Rose felt himself relax slightly. Kitten was the least experienced member of the company. Also the youngest, she was everybody's little sister, even Ria's. Although a veteran, her term of service had been brief and seemed to have consisted mostly of ceremonial duties. Kitten had listed several battles on her service jacket, but Rose doubted she'd seen much in the way of real fighting. This drop concerned him because there was so much that could go wrong. If something happened, Kitten would have only herself to rely upon. That wasn't necessarily bad, but it still worried Rose. He was glad she seemed to be handling the drop.

"Recon Three, green." Leeza was another question mark, but like Kitten, she seemed to be handling the drop all right.

"Recon Two, yellow." Rose started to question Yuri, but stopped with his finger over the comm channel. Yellow meant there was a problem, but not immediately life-threatening. Before the drop, Rose had made sure everybody understood that a status of red indicated a life-threatening emergency. Once the 'Mechs were free of their cocoons, any red status would have been announced immediately unless there was a problem with the radio, hence the countdown. Yuri would have to wait for the rest of the members to call in.

"Recon One, green."

"Battle Four, green."

"Battle Three, green."

"Battle Two, green."

"Battle One, yellow." That was Esmeralda. Rose noticed that her flight path on the scanner indicated that she had released from the DropShip poorly and was scattered away from the rest of the company. Her yellow status was likely caused by the poor flight path.

"Command Four, green."

Silence. Rose counted to three, then hit the comm. "Command Three, what is your status?" Rose glanced at his altimeter and cursed under his breath. "Command Three, pass."

"Command Two, green."

Rose eyed the altimeter again and began to slow his descent while trying to find Bell on the scanner. Normally a *Masakari* did not mount jump jets, but a special drop pack had been rigged to the back and legs of the OmniMech, just as it had with all the other non-jumping BattleMechs. The jump packs were light on fuel and not nearly as efficient as the internal jump jets of a jump-capable 'Mech, but the bulky pack allowed the Thorns to drop all their 'Mechs into battle.

"Lance commanders, handle yellow status and report if necessary." Rose worked the jump pack with one hand as the other flew over the scanner. He knew that dividing his concentration was dangerous, but he was responsible for every member of the team, and he wanted—no, he needed—to know what was happening with Antioch Bell. Rose triggered a series of short bursts followed by one long blast of the jump pack to slow the descent. Rotation was nominal, so he let that go and finally managed to pick up Bell on the scanner.

Zooming in on Bell's *Banshee* with his visual sensors, Rose could see that the entire right side of the 'Mech's head was blackened. Despite the damage, Rose could see the telltale exhaust of the jump pack strapped to the back of the *Banshee* as it fired. Evidently Bell was all right but unable to communicate. Rose checked the altimeter and fired his thrusters one more time. His fuel was already running low, and his velocity was down as well. A few more quick bursts and he'd be ready for touchdown.

Satisfied that Bell was not in danger, or at least not in a situation he could do anything about, Rose focused on the altimeter and the final stages of landing. He checked his speed and fired three quick bursts of the jump pack, killing some of his velocity and all of his spin. At one hundred meters Rose triggered the thrusters and held the button. He descended into his own smoke as the jump pack expended its remaining fuel in an attempt to fight gravity. Rose quickly lost sight of the terrain and kept his eyes glued to the altimeter as his height counted down. At ten meters he killed the thrusters, happy to see there was still a little fuel left in the tanks. Flexing at the knees, he dropped the last bit and let the OmniMech's powerful gyroscope and his own sense of balance, which was transmitted through the neurohelmet, land him safely.

Rose felt the clawed feet of the *Masakari* dig into the rocky soil and grip tightly. He started to lean to the right, but a quick step in that direction corrected his balance. He took one tentative step, then another, walking out of his own exhaust to greet the other Thorns.

"Status report. Recon?"

Ajax answered immediately. "Recon down and ready. No damage sustained in transit."

"And the yellow status?" asked Rose.

"Nothing affecting performance, sir." That was good news. Considering the number of new recruits in recon, the results were excellent.

"Battle?"

"Battle down and ready. Minor failure on Battle One, but nothing affecting performance."

"Command?" continued Rose.

"Command down and ready, sir." Riannon's voice was clear but slightly rushed. He suspected her first experience with a drop had been anything but routine. He'd have to get the details later. "Command Three is still silent, but he gives a thumbs-up."

"Good thing he's got a thumb."

Rose laughed in spite of himself. Although he couldn't identify the voice, it had to be Hawg. He was the only one capable of disguising his voice to any degree. He was also the only one likely to make such a comment.

"Cut the chatter, Thorns. We're still a long way from home. Recon lead us out of here, just like we planned. Riannon, confirm the drop with the ground crew and tell them we'll meet at the primary landing zone.

"Good work out there today, people," said Rose with obvious pride. "Just remember, the next time you get the chance to do this, there might be Clanners shooting back."

17

Mercenary Garrison District
Wolcott, Draconis Combine
15 July 3057

"Jeremiah, wake up."

Rose turned over in bed and came to full alert at the sound of another person in his room. It took a second to realize that the other person was Riannon. He reached out and hit the switch on the night stand lamp. Squinting against the lights, he checked his chronometer. Four twelve A.M.

"Trouble, sis?" he asked as he swung his legs out of bed and rubbed his hands through his hair. He didn't doubt the answer would be yes.

"This just came over the comm, in code," she said solemnly. As Rose took the slip of paper, he noticed that Ria was dressed in her shorts and tee shirt. At first he'd assumed that they were her sleep clothes, but then quickly realized it was the attire she wore in her 'Mech under her cooling vest. His sister was already prepared for combat.

Rose took the note and read it three times before turning back to his sister. "Anybody else know?"

Riannon shook her head. "Priority signals are duplicated on my terminal with an alarm. Esmeralda didn't flinch when the alarm went off. I read the note and pulled the hard copy from the communications center. I decided I'd better wake you, so I came here first—or second rather." She grinned. "I got some coffee started first."

Rose nodded. "Good thinking." He checked his watch again and reached for the communications unit on the night stand. Thumbing the system to public address, he lifted the handset to his mouth.

"Attention, Black Thorns. Rise and shine. Our departure date has just been moved up. Repeat, our departure date has just been moved up. This is not a drill. Report to your 'Mechs at oh-five-hundred prepared for immediate departure from the compound. We will leave the compound at oh-five-thirty. Repeat, we will depart the compounds at oh-five-thirty. This is not a drill." Rose dropped the handset and turned to his sister. She beamed anticipation. Rose lifted the handset.

"Coffee will be available in the mess room. Lance commanders, see to your command. Antioch Bell, to my quarters." Rose dropped the handset on the bed and stood. Despite the early hour, the call to action had him pumped with adrenaline and fully awake.

"Ria, ask Myoto to come in here after Antioch and I are done. Transfer command from the base to the 'Mechs, effective oh-five-hundred. How soon can you move out?"

"Ten, maybe fifteen minutes."

"Get on out to the warehouse as soon as you can. Set up the communications link with the *Tracy K* and monitor all inbound traffic."

"I'll check on the *Bristol*," said Riannon, as if reading his mind.

Rose smiled at his sister. "Thanks, sis." There was a knock on the open door as she turned to go.

"Antioch Bell, reporting as ordered, sir." Bell flashed the thumbs up sign to Riannon as she squeezed past him in the doorway. Rose couldn't see her face, but could easily imagine that the expression she gave in return was something between the rush of excitement and fear of the upcoming mission. Rose knew the excitement couldn't be helped, especially in the early stages of a mission. He also knew Ria was veteran enough to know the danger of the situation and to temper her excitement with respect as well as a little dread for that danger. Fear was an absolute necessity if a MechWarrior was going to survive long in the profession.

"Antioch, Ria is going to have her hands full, so I need you to handle a couple of things." Bell nodded. "Saddle up as quick as you can and leave the compound. I want you to handle the base defenses and arm everything the minute we clear the gates. I don't expect trouble, but since McCloud isn't back yet, we don't have anybody here to mind the store."

"I'll have to do some of the work from the ground."

Rose nodded. "I understand. That's why I want you on the other side of the gate. You can activate everything from the outside. Remind Ria to transfer the deactivation codes to the mercenary liaison office in case something happens." Bell nodded. The thought was not a pleasant one, but it had to be considered nonetheless.

"Anything else?" asked Bell.

"Yes, have Hawg put together some ration packs for everybody. We know the *Tracy K* will fly, but I have no idea how far they've gotten with the rest of the ship. The last time I was aboard, most of the so called extras were off-line. Until now I never considered food and fresh water an extra." Bell and Rose smiled.

"I guess you're just soft," said Bell.

"That must be it," agreed Rose as Bell turned to leave.

Rose reached for his flight suit and slipped it on while waiting for Myoto. Unlike the other Black Thorns, Rose did not wear standard MechWarrior garb when at the controls of his BattleMech. Instead of shorts and tee shirt, he wore a Star League-era MechWarrior combat suit.

The cockpits of all 'Mechs were shielded from the intense heat created by the armored giants, but the heat levels were still high enough that the only way a pilot could remain conscious at the controls was to wear special cooling gear. Current technology called for a MechWarrior to wear as little as possible to help keep the body cool. As a result, shorts and tee shirts were considered proper field attire. In the cockpit a MechWarrior also wore a cooling vest over his torso. The vest circulated a chemical coolant through mesh tubes to keep the upper body cool. Although the system worked, it was not as efficient as the one used in the old Star League.

While still a member of the Com Guards, Rose had had access to the advanced technology of the Star League. ComStar alone in the Inner Sphere was possessed of Star League-era technology. Equipment designed in that period of man's history could not be duplicated today, but examples of the tech still existed if one knew where to look. Rose's combat suit was one such item.

At first glance the suit looked no different than standard coveralls, but upon closer examination the fabric was much different, a synthetic that helped keep the body cool. When plugged into the cooling system of a BattleMech, the suit transferred standard coolant across the pilot's entire body, not just the torso. The suit was also padded at the elbows and knees for additional protection, and the entire surface was laced with ablative fibers to dissipate laser fire. In addition, the whole suit was more flexible and less confining because the coolant tubes built into it were much smaller than those of a modern coolant vest. Rose knew that he sacrificed some agility when wearing the suit, but the added protection was more than worth the trade-off. As he was adjusting the cuffs, Myoto reported in.

"*Chu-i,* has Danes finished the conversion?" Rose asked her.

"*Hai,* sir. It was finished yesterday morning."

"Good," said Rose. "It looks like you get to bring your *Grand Dragon* along with us after all." Myoto bowed. Rose suspected it was partially to hide the smile she couldn't quite contain.

The Black Thorns were a full company of twelve 'Mechs. As such, they took up the entire standard cargo compartment of a *Union* Class DropShip. When Rose told Myoto she'd have to leave her 'Mech behind, she'd come up with a counterproposal.

Since Yuri's *Dasher* and Leeza's *Mercury* were much smaller than normal, couldn't the two of them share a compartment? Rose knew the idea was possible in theory, but difficult in practice. After several conversations on the matter, he'd finally given his blessing, provided Myoto could sell the idea to Sinclair Danes. The next day she had announced to him that Captain Danes was making the appropriate alterations to the *Tracy K.* Rose wondered how she had managed to win approval for the work, but eventually decided it didn't matter. The extra BattleMech would come in handy on the raid, and Rose was confident Danes would not put his ship in danger, no matter what Myoto offered.

"Do you know anything about the accelerated launch date?" Rose continued. Myoto shook her head. "No, sir. I've placed several calls to liaison headquarters, but have learned nothing new. The first I heard about the change in plans was when you awakened us."

Rose considered her answer. Myoto might be telling the truth, but he found it hard to believe that she didn't know about the change in plans. Still, if she had known, she would probably have delivered the orders herself instead of receiving them over the communication lines.

"I've got a hard question to ask, and the only way I know how to do it is ask straight out. Before I do, though, I want you to know it's only because I feel it is vital that I know the answer. Is that clear?" Myoto paused and examined Rose with a harsh stare. Rose could almost see her mind going over the possibilities before she finally nodded. Rose sighed.

"In effect, I need to know what you're doing here. How did you get this assignment and what are you doing as a liaison? You're too young to merit this kind of assignment unless you've got some excellent credentials. But if that were the case, why aren't you pulling duty in some hotshot combat lance?"

Myoto didn't answer at once. Rose waited silently and let the silence add pressure to his questions. After a long minute, Myoto spoke. "You ask a difficult question, but it is one I am prepared to answer— on one condition."

"Which is?" prompted Rose.

"You will tell no one else what I am about to tell you. I believe I can trust you with the truth, but it is not information I would want spread throughout the company." Myoto looked down and remained silent while Rose considered the condition. It didn't take long for him to decide.

"Done," he said simply. Myoto looked up and held Rose's eyes with a calm, yet firm gaze.

"I am a blood relative of Theodore Kurita." It was only with great effort that Rose managed to keep his face expressionless. Although shocked, he knew any outward sign of surprise would be seen as disbelief and, therefore, an insult to Myoto. She waited several seconds for Rose to work through the implications of the statement before continuing.

"Be assured, the blood line is distant, but solid. As a result of this, I have had a special place in society since the moment of my birth. My gender and station in life made my dream of becoming a MechWarrior almost impossible. As a result, I have had to overcome numerous obstacles to reach even the rank of *chu-i*. My current assignment, that of liaison offer, was, in effect, the best choice from a poor list of alternatives. I was not given the opportunity to serve on a frontline unit." Myoto hung her head.

The situation now made perfect sense to Rose. As a member of the Kurita noble house, Myoto had a certain responsibility to the entire Combine. In most cases that meant she was expected to serve the government in some way. For royal women that meant a cultural position, not a military one. He could well imagine the problems she would have had overcoming her relatives' opinions about a "proper" career for a woman. Not that all Kurita society felt that way. It was acceptable for women to serve in the military—and many did—but Kurita nobility observed different customs and had different expectations placed upon them.

"How did you end up on Wolcott?" he asked.

"I volunteered, just like everybody else who remains here. As there was a need for more liaison officers, the request was reluctantly accepted."

"And the *Grand Dragon*?"

"A gift from a nameless benefactor. Undoubtedly one of my relatives, but I do not know which one."

"You didn't receive the 'Mech upon graduation?"

Myoto looked at her feet and shook her head. "My marks

weren't good enough to merit a BattleMech," she said to the floor. "I was somewhere at the middle of my class in nearly every subject except history."

Rose blew out a long breath and rubbed his chin. That certainly made sense. From what he'd seen of Myoto, she got by on determination and fear of failure more than anything else. She was somewhat clumsy and a poor shot, but Rose had to find a way to make her part of the team.

"All right, *Chu-i,* we'll keep this conversation between the two of us. Thank you for being honest with me. I'd like to respect your right to privacy, but there are some things a commander needs to know. I hope you understand."

Myoto finally looked up at Rose. "I understand, Captain Rose. I will strive to do my best on the assignment."

"That's all then. Oh, by the way," he added. "Since you'll be going with us, I plan to assign you to the battle lance. Any problems with that?"

Myoto did not hesitate in responding. "Captain Rose, although you have your doubts about me, you have never failed to treat me with respect. The other members of your unit have granted me the same respect. Were the situation different, I believe I could easily call several of them my friends. I wish my own commanders thought as much of my position and my abilities."

"You report to Zimmer, right?" asked Rose.

"Yes, sir."

Rose scratched the stubble on his chin and considered Myoto's frank admission. "Well, *Chu-i,* I haven't had time to examine all the motives and such, but I'd guess you're just caught between the old guard and us mercenaries. I suspect they don't like us much and I'm more than happy to return the sentiment. Throw in a little resentment for your social status, and most of the narrow-thinkers are more than happy to find reasons to dislike you." Myoto nodded. Rose obviously wasn't telling her anything she hadn't figured out for herself.

"So where does that leave us, *Chu-i?*" he asked as he reached for his weapon belt.

"I will continue to fulfill my duties to the best of my ability. However, I understand and accept the simple fact that I lack the tactical experience to aid or correct you once we are on the ground. Having worked with you for these many weeks, I know you will do everything in your power to fulfill the contract. You do not need me to watch over the Dragon's interests."

"You seem to have a pretty good idea of what this is all about, *Chu-i*," said Rose. "How come you haven't volunteered this information before?"

"There was no need. I fulfilled my duties, as did you and the rest of the Black Thorns. That was only training, however. We have entered the next phase of your contract with the Dragon, and additional information is required if you are to be successful. I have merely provided that information.

"I will always place my duty before personal motivations, but I have reasons to behave as I do."

"You trying to prove something, *Chu-i*?" asked Rose. He hoped the answer was no. Warriors following the call of glory or trying to prove something usually got themselves killed in the first moments of a battle. Bad enough the waste of a warrior and BattleMech, but the loss of the 'Mech usually meant other warriors had to pay the price for one person's foolishness.

"Yes," replied Myoto, "but only to myself." That was not the answer Rose expected, but it seemed like a good one. He supposed it was ultimately the reason most warriors went to battle.

"All right. See what you can find out from the liaison office. I'll let Esmeralda know you'll be with her lance." Myoto bowed and saluted, holding the salute until Rose returned it, then she left.

Rose grabbed his duffel from the wardrobe and threw his few possessions inside. He secured his portable computer containing the company's supplemental information files, then dropped it on top. At some point in the mission, all the files would be loaded into his 'Mech's computer system, but until then he'd work on the portable if necessary.

Rose threw the duffel over one shoulder and headed for the mess room and a cup of coffee. He was still wired with adrenaline, but decided something to drink was in order. Grabbing some coffee, he put down his duffel and made a quick inspection of the barracks.

He was not surprised to see Ajax and the rest of the recon lance already on the move toward the warehouse. The small lance commander had managed to instill recon's basic principle in all the recruits: Always keep moving. On the battlefield Rose could count on the recon lanced to provide quick and accurate information about the enemy. Ajax felt the best way to ensure that kind of readiness was to practice it all the time. He was hard on the members of his lance, but the foursome seemed to take a lot of pride in their unique position in the company. Rose decided not to interfere with Ajax's methods, especially when the other members of the lance didn't seem to want any interference.

Antioch and Riannon were already gone, leaving Jamshid to close down the command lance's section of the base. The task wasn't that difficult or time-consuming, so Rose knew Jamshid would have the work done by the allotted time. Esmeralda and O'Shea were working in the battle lance's meeting area, both moving with a swift but relaxed air of confidence. They had both been through this routine countless times and knew exactly how long was needed to accomplish their tasks.

Rose found Greta and Hawg in the mess room. Working together they were stuffing field bags with ration kits and supplemental food containers. Hawg grinned as he worked, his movements swift and sure. Greta managed to keep up with the big man, but just barely. Hawg paused when Rose entered the room, saluting as Rose reached for some coffee. While Rose sipped coffee and waited for Esmeralda and O'Shea to appear, Hawg and Greta finished their work.

Hawg grabbed three of the stuffed sacks and in one motion threw the entire bulk onto his back. While keeping the weight steady with one hand, he reached down for his own kit with the other, then stood up. The simple action was a feat of strength Rose knew he would never even have attempted, let alone matched. Greta grabbed the remaining sack of rations and her kit, then hustled to follow Hawg out the door. Getting the heavy load all the way up to the cockpit of a 'Mech was going to be a problem, but Rose knew Hawg would figure something out.

He glanced at his chronometer just as Esmeralda and Badicus came in. There was still a little time available, so Rose held out the coffee pot as the two approached. Producing twin cups, they watched as Rose poured in silence. Rose replaced the pot and flicked off the burner.

"Once more into the breach," said Badicus. Rose chuckled, but Esmeralda just nodded and sipped her coffee.

"I suspect you're right," she commanded. "This could be a nasty fight." Badicus scoffed and began to shuffle toward the door. Rose followed them out, locking the door behind him. Across the tarmac, the lights of the warehouse indicated that the Black Thorns were in full action. As they approached, Bell's *Banshee* took a step forward, then turned toward the gate. The mission was officially underway.

18

DropShip **Tracy K,** *Pirate Point 5N/Lu0013Zulu*
Wolcott System, Draconis Combine
25 July 3057

Rose sat staring at the communications unit in the DropShip quarters. He knew it wasn't likely the unit would activate by thought alone, but he sat there in the fervent hope of hearing from McCloud before he left Wolcott. He glanced over at the stack of hard copy reports on the bunk and considered breaking the final news to the rest of the Thorns, but for the seventh time in the last hour, he decided to wait a little longer.

Rose and the rest of the company had been trapped—Rose could think of no other word—in the *Tracy K* for three days. The trip had been mercifully uneventful, but the lack of information on McCloud and the *Bristol* was grating on his nerves.

The *Tracy K* had lifted off without a problem, despite the damaged appendage. Under a thick cover of aerospace fighters, the ship had successfully run the Clan blockade and was now preparing for the final approach to the JumpShip. Not that the ship was already in the Wolcott system, but Danes had to trust that it would be by the time the *Tracy K* arrived at their rendezvous point.

The mission required split-second timing on the part of the DropShip and JumpShip crews. Although no Clan ships had trailed the *Tracy K,* at least as far as the crew knew, the

JumpShip would not remain long in the Wolcott system. After undocking any DropShips it had carried into the system, the starship would meet up with the *Tracy K,* then jump immediately to the Black Thorns' destination. Because of the time-space relationship between the pirate point in the Wolcott system and the pirate point of their destination star system, any mistakes would doom the mission before it started. Of course, that assumed the ships survived the mistake in the first place.

Rose glanced over at the reports, then suddenly jumped to his feet, grabbing the reports and heading for the mess room. As usual, the Black Thorns had appropriated the largest mess room on the ship as their de facto headquarters. When Rose got there, the room was surprisingly empty, but a quick call over the public address system remedied that situation. While waiting for the room to fill up, he thought over the briefing report, but still wasn't really sure where to start even after all his people were present and looking up at him expectantly.

"Well, ladies and gentlemen, we're approaching the Wolcott jump point. I'm not really sure where that is, but Captain Danes assures me we're on course and on schedule. If all goes well, the JumpShip will arrive within the next couple of minutes. That means we'll be making the jump to the target within the hour." Rose stopped to take a sip from a fresh cup of coffee. He noticed that the Thorns were unnaturally quiet, as if they were awaiting news of great import. Despite the importance of the mission briefing, Rose suspected they were looking for something more.

Wrapped up in his own feelings about McCloud, he had not stopped to consider how much the rest of the Thorns held her and the *Bristol* in special regard. To them she was a part of the company. They worried about her and her ship just as they would any member of the team. McCloud had been gone for over a month and there was still no news of her status, despite repeated attempts to gather information from the liaison office. Even unofficial channels had proved fruitless. Rose wanted to give them the news they awaited, but he simply didn't have it. Instead he continued with the mission briefing.

"Upon arrival in the Courcheval system the *Tracy K* will debark immediately and head for the planet's surface. We'll be approaching the world through an asteroid field, which means two things. First, the course will have to be somewhat circular to avoid the densest areas of the field. In this case that doesn't really affect us, as we would have taken the same course even if the way had been clear. The course will keep the Clans from tracking the DropShip's path back to the JumpShip.

"The asteroid field also provides us with some cover for the inbound trip." Rose rubbed his head and laughed briefly. "Who'd have thought there would be cover in space? Sort of defies logic. In any event, the latest intelligence reports seem to indicate that the asteroid field is the back door to the planet. The Clans don't patrol it heavily because they consider the approach too dangerous to try, even from a pirate point. We're counting on that fact to get us to the surface with a minimum of fuss."

"That seems like a pretty wide gap in the Clan's defenses," said Esmeralda. "Do we really think they'd leave a opening like that?"

"No, we're sure they've got some defenses, but they're mostly passive in nature. Remote sensors, listening posts, things like that. It seems likely they'll eventually learn about our approach through one of these devices, but they'll still have to scramble a squadron of aerospace fighters to intercept us.

"Remember, the Clans don't look at aerospace assets the way we do. To them fighters are something to bargain away before a fight. Piloting is probably the one area of the combat where the Inner Sphere holds the edge. I'm not saying they'll let us land, but they're not as good at successfully making deep-space interceptions as we are."

"Won't the JumpShip be vulnerable?" asked Riannon.

Rose sighed and nodded. "It will be the most vulnerable when it first jumps into the system. If we happen to land near a listening post or within range of a recon patrol, the mission has about zero chance for success. The odds of that happening are very small, however, so I wouldn't worry about it. Once the *Tracy K* is away, the JumpShip will power down all non-essential systems and deploy the solar collector. Rigged for silent running, there is very little chance of the ship being detected. Even the Clans don't have the capability to spot a JumpShip in a million square kilometers of space.

"While we're on the mission, the JumpShip will recharge its lithium batteries for another two jumps. When we rendezvous again, we jump back to Wolcott. The JumpShip will make a second jump out almost immediately, carrying whatever cargo turns up on Wolcott."

"Who's piloting the JumpShip?" asked Esmeralda.

"The vessel belongs to the Combine," said Rose.

"They won't leave without us, will they?" she asked in return.

Rose shook his head. He didn't want his company to worry about the ride home. He knew they were going to need all their mental faculties focused on the mission if they were to be successful. "No chance," he said. "For two reasons. First, they're Kuritas. You can count on them to do their duty, even if it means they get themselves killed in the attempt."

Rose scanned the room. "Am I right, *Chu-i*?" All heads turned toward Myoto, who was sitting at the back. She nodded silently.

"Second, the return trip will be at least as difficult as the arrival. The JumpShip will have only a narrow window of opportunity for a jump back to the pirate point here in the Wolcott system. The ship can't leave until it has recharged the batteries and the window is open." Rose saw his people nod in understanding. Although they understood the fierce Kurita sense of duty, they were more heartened by the complex physics of the operation.

"Remember, Thorns," continued Rose, "just as you can count on the JumpShip waiting for us until the proper time, you can count on them leaving us behind if we're late. We have to get in, hit the Clans hard, then get away quick. Unless, of course, you want to walk back to Wolcott."

Rose paused to take another sip of coffee and let the warning sink in. He didn't want the Thorns worried about the ride home, but he did need them to understand just how critical timing was to this mission. Mistakes on the part of a single MechWarrior could doom the other members of his lance, and maybe even the entire company. Rose wanted to believe he would never abandon a fellow Black Thorn, but he prayed he'd never have to make that decision.

"Anyway," he continued, setting the empty cup down, "we arrive on Courcheval and deploy by combat drop. The altitude will be roughly the same as we practiced back on Wolcott, so there should be no problems there, right?" There were murmurs of agreement from the Thorns.

"Antioch, did you ever figure out what happened to your 'Mech last time?" asked Rose.

The tow-headed MechWarrior nodded. "Faulty cocoon. When the explosives split away from the cocoon, it ignited a secondary explosion near my head. The blast peppered the side of my 'Mech with cocoon bits and sheared away some of the communications gear. The Kuritas put it down as a freak accident."

"Let that be a warning to all of you," said Rose. "Triple-check the cocoons. Damage like that could take you right out of the fight, and even if it doesn't, it will make everyone's job that much harder.

"Back to the subject. The *Tracy K* heads for a part of the planet known as the Graveyard. It is an arid plain with naturally occurring rock formations in the shape of tombstones. Catchy name, eh?" Rose reached for his empty cup and motioned for more coffee. Hawg passed the pot forward as Rose continued. "The formations should provide some cover for the DropShip. Given that the Graveyard is a thousand klicks from any population center, it should be a reasonably secure location for pickup.

"We assemble after the drop and head for the primary target. Once there, we assess the situation. If it looks like the target is lightly defended, or accessible, we'll hit it. This is a simple raid, so we're not interested in what we hit. Do maximum damage in the shortest amount of time, then hit the trail.

"If all goes well, we'll continue toward the secondary objective and run the same drill as before. That done, we head back to the Graveyard and the *Tracy K*.

"Any general questions about the mission so far?" asked Rose.

"What are we hitting?" asked Hawg.

"Both the secondary and primary targets are manufacturing centers. Neither plant is currently operational, but the Nova Cats are hoping to bring both on line by the end of the year. The original owner was L'Outre Manufacturing. Now that the Nova Cats have taken control, they've diverted production from consumer electronics to military subsystems.

"The primary plant constructs heads-up display units for use in battle armor suits. The secondary plant constructs communications systems. From what I've read, these systems are primarily used in Elemental armor and infantry commo equipment. As I said, neither plant is operational yet, so I have no idea about any static defenses that may be present. I shouldn't have to tell you how critical these components are to the Nova Cat invasion effort, but I'll do it anyway. This is a chance to do some serious damage to their ability to wage war on the Inner Sphere. The Cats have spent considerable time and effort on these projects. It's up to us to make sure it's wasted effort.

"Now, I know you're wanting to know what we'll be up against, so I'll put your minds at ease. The defenders come from two units. The first is the Fourteenth Garrison Cluster of Omega Galaxy. Although we've got a name, about all we have to go on is that they use a non-standard organization. As most of you probably know, a Clan star usually consists of five 'Mechs. But the units we'll be facing on Courcheval have a point of Elementals attached to every star.

"We also know that a garrison cluster typically fields refitted Inner Sphere designs and second-class Clan 'Mechs. But don't forget that they'll also have heavy Elemental support. Count on refitted *Warhammer*s, *Battlemaster*s, and

*Shadow Hawk*s. Tactics for fighting these 'Mechs are the same as against our own Inner Sphere counterparts, but be careful. These 'Mechs all have Clan technology, so all ranges and heat output will be different. Think of them as tough cousins of the 'Mechs you know and love.

"Now for the really tough guys."

"Geez, commander, I thought those were the really tough guys," said Hawg.

Rose smiled but shook his head. "Hardly. The real danger on the planet comes from the Forty-sixth Nova Cat Cavaliers. We're hitting their home base." Rose anticipated groans and received them in abundance. "The Forty-sixth is a frontline BattleMech unit. That means we can expect about sixty OmniMechs with full fighter support.

"Now, it's unlikely the Forty-sixth will be assigned to garrison duty, but you can bet your final paycheck that they'll be called in to hunt us down after we've been spotted. If they catch us—well, let's not let them catch us, all right?" Rose paused and made sure the Black Thorns understood their situation. The Cavaliers were a crack unit with enough firepower to level the Black Thorns five times over. He held no illusions about his company's chances in a fight against such a potent opponent.

"Questions?" The mood of the room had become somber, and none of the MechWarriors seemed to want to speak. Rose knew there would be questions later, but for now each warrior was wrestling with the new information and coming to grips with his or her own fears. Rose glanced at his chronometer. If they were still on schedule, the JumpShip should have arrived several minutes ago.

"All right, then, prepare for jump. Once we're on the other side, I want all warriors in the cargo bays checking the drop pods. Report any problems to your commander. We'll handle situations as they occur." As Rose spoke, he noticed a DropShip crew member slip into the room. He didn't seem ready to speak, so Rose continued.

"You're not going to have much time to sleep or eat when we hit the dirt, so stock up now." Rose surveyed the room, trying to read the thoughts of each Black Thorn. If their faces were any indication, their feelings mirrored his own. Resolve mixed with expectation and fear. He knew they wouldn't have much time to worry before the drop.

"Then pack it up." Rose reached for his coffee cup and watched as a DropShip crewman came in and began to fight his way through the departing mercenaries. Eventually he stood before Rose and handed him a single sheet of paper. Rose glanced at the top and grabbed the crewman by the shoulder as he turned to go. The grip stopped the man in his tracks.

"When did this arrive?" asked Rose with too much force. The remaining Thorns stopped and looked at their commander. The crewman's eyes went wide with fear.

"I don't know, sir. Several minutes ago, I think," he stammered.

"Why wasn't I told of this?" Rose said as he scanned the note again. The man's eyes remained wide with fear and pain as Rose continued to hold him in place with a vise-like grip on his shoulder.

"I don't know, sir. The message was unauthorized. Captain McCloud should not have transmitted the message. It is very dangerous."

"A message from McCloud?" asked Ria. She crossed over to her brother and laid a hand on his shoulder, easing his grip on the frightened crewman. Rose seemed to have forgotten about him as he reread the message.

"Captain Danes would never allow you to reply, sir. It would be too dangerous," said the crewman. Rose didn't even look up from the sheet of paper, but Riannon motioned to the door with her head and the crewman took the hint. With amazing speed, he wove his way through the mercenaries and disappeared through the door.

"What is it, Jeremiah?" asked Ria. Rose slumped into a chair and handed his sister the message. He sat there stunned while she read it, first to herself, then aloud.

"To Captain Rose from Captain McCloud. All is well. The *Bristol* and crew are returning to base in good health and prosperity. We will be there when you return. God's speed. Signed Rachel McCloud. P.S. You're going to be a father."

$$=== 19 ===$$

The *Tracy K* slid away from the JumpShip seconds after the starship emerged from hyperspace. Their DockShip undocked without incident, then silently began to make its approach to the planet through the cover of the asteroid field.

"Welcome to the Courcheval system," said Danes over the DropShip's public address system. "We will be arriving planetside in another thirty-seven hours, fifteen minutes. Until then, please feel free to move about the cabin."

Rose listened to the light banter of the other Black Thorns, but did not take part. Even Danes' attempt at humor left no impression on him. All he could think about was the message from Rachel. He was happy that she was all right, but furious at not having had a chance to talk with her before they'd jumped to Courcheval. Even though the *Bristol* was long past communications range, Rose had tried to send her a message. The attempt failed miserably.

True to the crewman's word, Sinclair Danes refused the Black Thorns access to the communications room. Rose tried everything he could think of to get inside, but eventually had to admit defeat. Harsh words had been exchanged with Danes, but the DropShip captain took Rose's outburst calmly in stride.

Rose allowed himself only a few hours to sulk, then tried

as best he could to put the entire situation out of his mind. Becoming a father was something he'd never considered. He was a warrior, a fighter. He knew nothing about nurturing life, only about taking it. For now, he decided the best thing to do was to concentrate on the situation at hand instead. There were details enough to worry about without letting new feelings enter into the mix.

Rose worked nearly around the clock doing or overseeing everything he felt was necessary to get the Thorns ready for their drop. His biggest concerns were the drop pods, which he'd ordered triple-checked for safety. Finally satisfied that nothing remained to be done, he went back to his cabin and studied the maps and reports of their destination for several hours until he found himself dozing at his work table. He climbed into the rack for some sleep, but five hours later he was wide awake.

Rose went from cabin to cabin talking to the other mercenaries about trivial details of the upcoming mission. Everything was in readiness, but he knew the value of making himself available to the other members of the company, even when there was nothing special to discuss. The lance commanders did a good job, but every pilot wanted to be recognized and appreciated by the leader. Rose's visits helped foster that bond.

Six hours from planetfall, Rose assembled all the Black Thorns in the mess room and went over a final countdown. The recon lance would drop first, then the command lance, then the battle lance. If they encountered resistance, recon would identify the defenders and let the heavier 'Mechs of the command lance deal with the problem. The highest priority was to get to the ground in one piece and then reassemble the company. The drop was designed to place the lances within kilometers of one another, but the veterans knew the chances of that actually happening were pretty slim. Plan for the worst but hope for the best.

After the meeting the mercenaries went down to the cargo bays and began final preparations for the drop. Systems that had been checked six times were checked yet again. Lance commanders went over the 'Mechs of their command, while

Rose also checked everything over one last time. He finally climbed into the *Masakari* and had Danes' cargomaster seal the drop pod. Powering up the OmniMech, Rose went through the entire system checklist twice before switching on the communications system. He thumbed the selector switch to DropShip command.

"Black Thorn One, radio check."

"We read you, Black Thorn One," replied a dispassionate voice Rose did not recognize.

"Request a status report, Drop Command, and ETA to planet."

"Black Thorn One, we are green to go with clear skies to the atmosphere. Estimated time of arrival to upper atmosphere is ninety-three minutes. Commence final drop check and report when ready."

Rose nodded to himself and switched to the company channel. As suspected, the line was filled with chatter from the pilots as the lance commanders conducted final checks. Rose listened for several minutes, lost in thought of past battles. On the surface this sounded very much like every battle he'd ever been in, but beneath the banter there was something more.

Rose knew the Black Thorns were not the first Inner Sphere unit to strike back at the Clans, but it didn't seem to matter. Listening to the sounds of his company, he was overcome with intense pride for the unit and its actions. These men and women were following him on a mission of his choosing, not just for profit, but for the chance to help defend their homes. Rose knew most of the regular army units scoffed at mercenaries as simple wage soldiers, yet mercs weren't that different from house regulars. They might be a little wilder, but they fought for the same reasons: to build a better life for the future. Not only for themselves, but for their families. For their children.

Rose struggled past the thoughts of his unborn child. There were so many questions, and he didn't have a clue where to get the answers. Rose hated the Clans for what they had done to him on Tukayyid, and the fury swelled within him at times like these. They would pay for the damage they had done and the lives they had taken.

Rose rarely talked about his feeling toward the Clans, but it had been the overriding motivation for his all actions in recent years. To strike back at the Clans was the reason he had formed the Black Thorns in the first place and the reason he was at this moment sealed in a captured Clan Omnimech above a Clan-held world. He wanted them to pay like he had paid. Like he was still paying.

A red light went off on the communications panel, and Rose thumbed back to the drop command channel.

"Black Thorn One, this is Drop Command." Although Danes did not identify himself, Rose recognized his voice. "Don't be alarmed, but we're being approached by an aerospace squadron. It's nothing we hadn't expected, but it looks like they'll reach us before we hit the drop zone."

"Understood." Rose considered the new information. The BattleMechs would be especially vulnerable to aerospace fighters during the actual drop. Enclosed in their cocoons, the MechWarriors couldn't even eject. Rose chewed on the information and listened to the company channel. Eventually he announced his presence to the rest of the unit.

"This is Command One. Lance commanders, meet me on the command channel." Rose gave the appropriate people the chance to make the switch to the alternative frequency. The command channel was used only to convey specific orders and to hold conferences with the mercenary leadership. Besides Rose, that meant Esmeralda, Ajax, Antioch Bell, and Riannon were part of any command channel conferences.

"We might have some problems, so listen up," Rose began without preamble. "We've got a squadron of fighters on the way and interception is confirmed. That makes the drop hot. We're going to stick to the original drop sequence, but I'm going to request a lower drop run from Danes. It will mean a more dangerous drop, but less time in the air as a falling target.

"Questions?" Rose waited, but the line was silent.

"Very good. Remember, your first responsibility is to your

lance. When you hit the ground, assemble as fast as possible and then move toward the rest of the unit. Good luck and I'll see you on the ground."

Rose switched back to drop command and requested the lower drop run. Danes was initially against the idea, but finally let himself be persuaded. It wasn't that much more dangerous to his ship and it would give the Black Thorns an added measure of protection. When the conversation was over, Rose eased back into his chair and waited.

He tried to clear his mind and relax, but the meditation techniques he'd been taught while stationed on Luthien during his service to ComStar failed him for the first time. Eventually he succeeded to a small degree, but just as he started to achieve the desired mental state, the *Tracy K* began to rock. The sudden motion of the ship surprised him, but when no explosion followed immediately, Rose put it down to the turbulence of the upper atmosphere.

Then the ride got bumpier, and Rose abandoned his meditation. The DropShip rocked and wobbled as it descended into the gravity well of the planet. While cinching the safety straps of his command chair, he glanced at the chronometer inside his neurohelmet, surprised to find that they'd entered the atmosphere almost seventeen minutes ago. They were less than ten minutes away from the drop zone. The chop they were experiencing could be turbulence, but Rose suspected they were also nearing the engagement range of the Clan aerospace fighters. As if confirming his thoughts, the drop frequency went green. Rose thumbed the channel.

"This is Black Thorn One." The speaker near his right ear popped with static, and Rose flinched in spite of himself. He heard a voice on the other end, but despite desperately working the gain of the frequency, he could not bring the voice in. The DropShip shuddered violently as Rose worked. With another pop of static, the line suddenly went active.

". . . problems."

"Say again, Drop Command. I do not read you."

"We've got some problems on this end, Black Thorn One. The fighters are as thick as fleas around us." Rose recognized the once-dispassionate voice of the drop controller on the line, but all trace of the previous calm was gone. The man was far from hysterical, but his voice was starting to edge upward.

"Easy, Drop Command. I understand. Will we make the drop zone?" Rose asked. He slapped several keys on the communications unit and overrode the signal to Ria's BattleMech. She needed to hear this as well.

"At this point, we don't know. We're on our approach run, but we've still got five of the bastards swooping around us." As Rose listened, the man regained some of his composure, his professionalism and training beginning to take over. "Make that four of the little bugs," he continued. The ship lurched heavily to port side, but continued on its course.

"Any damage on our end?" asked Rose, more to keep the man talking than because the information would do him any good.

"Yeah, I guess you could say we've got some damage." Rose didn't like the sound of that. Severe structural damage could prevent the drop altogether, or at the very least prevent some of the 'Mechs from dropping as planned. "Most of the damage is limited to the engineering sections, but we've taken a couple of hits near the bridge."

"Is Danes available?"

"Yes, he's still on the job." The ship rocked with an explosion, followed almost immediately by a secondary blast. By the way the secondary blast echoed from deep within the ship, Rose knew that the engines had been damaged severely. The ship began to vibrate slightly as it continued on its course. The communications line faded out, then came back in.

"Rose, this is Captain Danes. Sorry to say, your time is up. I've got to kick you loose immediately." Rose glanced at the chronometer. They were several minutes from the drop zone and thousands of kilometers from their intended targets.

"I understand," Rose swallowed and discovered his mouth was suddenly dry. "We can always walk."

"Very good of you, old man," replied Danes. "I'll hold

out as long as possible, but be ready for the doors to open. I'm afraid this could get a little messy for you and the lads."

"We can handle it," said Rose, praying that the less experienced members of the Black Thorns could indeed handle all the additional variables that were being thrown into an already complicated process.

"There are still three of the blighters left, ah, make that two, so you may have company on the way down. Wish I could do more." The ship continued to shudder and the vibration got worse. Rose guessed the frame of the ship had been damaged, possibly irreparably. He tried to sound optimistic.

"We'll handle it from here, Captain. Good luck. We'll meet you at the Graveyard. Rose out."

Rose switched to the company frequency. "All Black Thorns, prepare for emergency drop. Repeat, prepare for emergency drop." The vibrations on the ship grew worse.

"Stick to the original plan," Rose continued, "and regroup on your lance commander when you hit the ground. Once the lances are formed, rally on the command lance. No stragglers, understand. We're going to have to drop a long way from our original zone, so look lively. There's no telling what we'll find when we hit the ground. Lance Commander, you . . ."

Rose never got to finish the sentence. Without warning, the ground beneath his 'Mech opened up and Rose fell from the DropShip. As he descended, the direct connect to the other members of the company was severed and the comm line went dead. He would have to wait until the cocoon fell away before he could use his 'Mech's standard communications gear.

Rose watched as the drop pod's altimeter set itself based on the external data and its preprogrammed instructions. The first reading was 44,350 meters above the ground. That number surprised him. It was high enough to allow reaction to the changing conditions, but low enough to keep him from being a prolonged target. Danes had obviously pushed the *Tracy K* well into the atmosphere in order to give the Thorns the best possible chance.

Rose felt the first parachute deploy, then the second. He rode the giant parachute for several minutes waiting for the explosions that would indicate he'd been targeted by a passing aerospace fighter. Time wore on, with Rose's hand hovering over the chute's release switch. He watched his instruments and waited. Agonizing seconds later, the light popped green and Rose hit the switch.

The drop pod fell away cleanly and Rose scanned the skies. It was still dark, which surprised him, but the heavens and the scanners remained clear. He double-checked the scanner and realized there were no other 'Mechs on the screen. With sudden dread, he increased the sweep area until he saw the computer identify Riannon, Bell, Jamshid, and Hawg. He watched the altimeter and prepared for his descent. The rest of the battle lance was probably scattered to his right. He hoped the recon lance was off the screen to the left.

"This is Command One, report Command Lance."

"Command Four, green."

"Command Three, green."

"Command Two, green." At least the command lance is all right, thought Rose with a heartfelt sigh.

"I've got Battle Three on my screen. Anybody have additional Black Thorns?"

"I've got all of Battle Lance, Command One," said Jamshid. "They should put down sixty to eighty klicks to the east." Although that was horrendous scatter, Rose was glad to know the entire lance had made it out of the DropShip alive. The ship itself was long since out of range, assuming it had survived.

"I've got Recon Lance, Command One. All present and accounted for," said Riannon. "They're going to end up about a hundred and fifty klicks to the northwest of us."

Rose hit the thrusters and sorted the information. The entire company had cleared the DropShip. That was good news, but they were going to be widely scattered when they hit the ground. Rose fired the thrusters again and toggled to a wide-range sweep of the landing area. The analysis didn't look good.

Rather than landing in a grassland plain, the command lance was going to drop into light forest, where a warrior being impaled on a tree was very real possibility. Rose adjusted the range, sacrificing area for added detail. One way or another he was going to have to land, so he needed to find a safe place. As he studied the screen and the altimeter, a red triangle popped into place, then another and another. When the triangles finally stopped appearing, Rose knew that five enemy BattleMechs were waiting on the ground directly below.

20

Courcheval
Nova Cat Occupation Zone
28 July 3057

Rose watched the altimeter countdown and fired his thrusters. His descent slowed as he continued to apply thrust. Finally, with a gasp, the thruster fuel ran dry, and Rose dropped the final fifteen meters to the ground below. The legs of his massive 'Mech coiled to absorb the shock, but Rose landed much harder than he'd intended. The *Masakari* threatened to topple over, but Rose kept his balance by stepping forward. Shouldering a young cedar out of the way, he stopped and stood up in his 'Mech.

He triggered the explosive bolts on the jump pack, then felt suddenly lighter as the heavy unit fell away. Two more toggles and the additional thrusters on the legs joined the jump pack on the forest floor. Rose hit the scanner, toggling from short-range to long-range. By pure luck, the rest of the command lance had landed to the west. Rose, as the far eastern 'Mech, was closest to the approaching Clan Battle-Mechs. Knowing that the rest of the unit would not play a part in the upcoming battle, Rose switched to the lance channel.

"Command Lance, get to the ridge line and form on me." He turned the *Masakari* toward the nearby ridge and increased the throttle. His 'Mech's giant feet tearing hunks of sod from the loosely packed soil, he began to race up the hill. Continually checking the scanners for enemy 'Mechs, Rose maintained the pace all the way to the top.

The opposite side of the slope was not as heavily wooded, and Rose could just see the shapes of several 'Mechs as they moved through the trees. He released the safeties from his weapon systems and focused on the leading 'Mech. He caught glimpses of it as it ran between the trees, but he couldn't acquire a lock because of the foliage. With eroding patience, he waited and watched his lance move to support him.

His patience was finally rewarded when a light gray 'Mech stepped between two trees at the base of the ridge. For an instant Rose took in the sight and identified the enemy 'Mech. It was a *Griffin*—or more accurately, a *Griffin IIC,* a deadlier version of its Inner Sphere counterpart.

Although the Clan version resembled the venerable Inner Sphere machine, the two 'Mechs were completely different beneath the skin. The Clan model was faster on the ground and in the air; it also carried more armor and its weapons had greater rage. It was easily a match for any Inner Sphere 'Mech of twenty tons heavier. Rose eyed it coolly, and let the *Masakari*'s Clan-constructed targeting computer center its targeting cross hairs on the *Griffin*'s chest. With a tight-lipped grin, Rose triggered the primary target interlock circuit and felt the sudden spike of heat he always associated with 'Mech combat.

The target interlock circuit, or TIC, was a reconfigurable weapons trigger that allowed the MechWarrior to fire a set of weapons with a single pull of the trigger. The *Masakari* had three separate circuits that could be fired simply by pressing a different trigger on the weapons control stick. In addition, Rose could fire each weapon individually by toggling through the weapons control panel on the left side of his cockpit. The primary TIC fired all four of the extended-range particle projection cannons. Firing from a stable position and guided by the targeting computer, there was little chance Rose could miss. The four azure beams intersected on the *Griffin*'s chest, the combined energy vaporizing the medium 'Mech's torso armor and blasting through the engine shielding. The fusion engine died instantly. The blue beams continued their path, cutting through the *Griffin*'s gyro and large laser. With unabated fury, two beams passed entirely through the *Griffin,* blowing out the rear armor in a hail of debris.

The death blow came so quickly the Clan pilot had no time to register the damage. The legs of the *Griffin* simply quit responding. The arms of his 'Mech flailing, the pilot fought to control the falling machine with no success. The *Griffin* ground to a halt at the foot of the ridge amid massive internal failures.

Rose backtracked partially down the ridge, using the hill as protection for the *Masakari*'s legs. The other 'Mechs of the Clan star sought cover amid the trees of the ridge and paused in an effort to regroup.

Rose had no doubt these were the 'Mechs of the Fourteenth Garrison Cluster. Although the *Griffin IIC* was an excellent 'Mech by Inner Sphere standards, it was strictly second class when compared to the OmniMechs of frontline Clan units. The cluster's pilots would also be second-line, warriors who had failed to win a place in a frontline unit, pilots a notch below their frontline counterparts. Rose's grin grew more feral. Had they been frontline pilots, they would have redoubled their charge up the hill. Even a momentary pause gave the advantage to the Black Thorns, and acquisition of the high ground only compounded that advantage.

Rose scanned the terrain and moved to his right. The rest of the command lance was making their way up the ridge behind him. He had no doubt the Nova Cats knew the other Thorns were on the way, but it didn't matter.

"Command Four, break left and sweep wide. Two and Three, hold the center. I'm moving to the right." Without waiting for confirmation, Rose began moving along the ridge line. The Clan 'Mechs had also begun to move, but they were not taking any chances with an OmniMech on the ridge. Even though Rose had not identified the other 'Mechs of the star, he guessed them to be mediums, heavies at best.

Rose kept his targeting cross hairs toward the enemy and shuffled toward the right. One of the Clan 'Mechs started to move, but never quite cleared the cover of the trees. Rose could feel the temperature drop in the cockpit as the *Masakari*'s heat sinks worked to cool the BattleMech. The ER PPCs had long since recharged and were ready for firing. He glanced at the scanner. Bell and Riannon were just below the ridge line, and Jamshid was roughly opposite his own position at the other end of the ridge.

"Prepare to engage," said Rose as he moved slightly forward. The Clan 'Mechs began moving toward him, hesitantly at first, but then with vigor. Although the trees still blocked them from view, Rose knew they were coming after him instead of the unidentified 'Mechs of the lance, probably in retaliation for the destruction of their comrade.

The external speakers picked up the sound of a large tree splitting, and Rose knew his next opponent would be much larger than the *Griffin*. He stopped his lateral movement and targeted the projected path of the nearest enemy 'Mech. Keeping the cross hairs steady, Rose stepped over the ridge line and began walking down the far slope. As he moved, the second Clan 'Mech stepped into view.

At first Rose tagged it as a *Rifleman,* but a glance at the scanner told him he was wrong. The 'Mech before him registered five tons heavier on the scanner, making it about seventy-five tons in weight. The 'Mech shared a common ancestry with the *Rifleman,* but instead of twin weapon barrels on each arm, this machine sported a single reinforced barrel. It came toward Rose like Frankenstein's monster, its arms held straight out as its lumbering walk smashed aside trees.

The 'Mech spotted Rose and hitched its stride slightly before pointing both arms at the *Masakari.* Rose adjusted his aim, but there was no time for the kind of shot he'd made on the *Griffin.* He simply aimed for the center of the 'Mech and hit the primary TIC. Heat rose through the floor of the *Mansakari*'s cockpit as the four ER PPCs stabbed toward the Clan 'Mech. One beam passed between the outstretched left arm and torso, but the other three found their mark.

The first beam traced a black line up the inside of the 'Mech's left arm. The ugly gash went deep, but Rose wasn't surprised to see that the shot had failed to penetrate the thick armor of the Clan heavy 'Mech. The other two shots savaged the left torso and burned their way inside. As the azure beams died, Rose waited for the secondary explosions that would indicate critical damage to the breached area, but there were none.

He gritted his teeth as the enemy 'Mech returned fire with its Gauss rifle. Both arms bellowed smoke as the weapons fired, but the damage from Rose's shot had affected the pilot's aim. The range was less than a hundred meters, but only one of the shells hit the *Masakari*. With a resounding clang that Rose felt all the way up inside the cockpit, the rifle shell slammed against the flat armored plates high on the *Masakari*'s right hip. The armor held, however, and Rose didn't even have to compensate for the damage. The *Masakari* remained rock steady.

He glanced at the weapon control panel. All four PPCs were still recharging, so he thumbed the long-range missile launcher and moved down the hill. Though he was well under the missiles' minimum range, Rose would use them in a pinch until the PPCs were ready again. The enemy 'Mech fought to keep its balance in the wake of Rose's assault, eventually managing to do so. Pivoting to the left, the 'Mech followed Rose down the hill.

The cannons came back on line as Rose hit the bottom of the hill, so he toggled off the missile system and readied the two secondary TICs. One was configured to fire the PPCs mounted in the *Masakari*'s right arm and the other to fire them from the left. The Clan 'Mech stepped down the hill, and Rose spotted its right leg for an instant. Without thinking, he fired the right-arm weapons and was rewarded with a strike on the Clan 'Mech's shin before the trees once again obscured the view.

He glanced at the scanner. Bell and Riannon were moving over the crest of the ridge. If Rose could hold the position, they would fall upon the Clan defenders from above and behind. Jamshid was moving in from the left, but he was still too far away to shoot. Rose began slowly backing up to give his lance more time to engage, but the Clan pilots out-guessed his ploy and came at him in a rush.

From his right came the sound of jump jets, and Rose knew that one of the Clan 'Mechs was taking flight. If it got behind him, he would be in serious trouble. Rose tried to get a shot on the jumping 'Mech, but was unable to acquire a lock because of the branches overhead. He turned to the right with his right arm upraised, and one of the enemy 'Mechs took the bait.

Breaking through the trees at a dead run came a 'Mech Rose had never seen before. The 'Mech was humanoid-shaped with heavy shoulder pads and thick lower legs; its two hands pumped the air as it ran. The construction lines of the 'Mech were graceful, with thousands of bends per metal plate. The entire effect gave the 'Mech a sleek, curved shape as close to human as anything Rose had ever seen. A single weapon port showed in the center of the 'Mech's torso.

The *Masakari*'s left arm barely moved as Rose fired the two PPCs in that arm. He'd used the trick before and doubt-less would use it again. Most pilots assumed their opponent was right-handed. When the Clan warrior saw Rose's right hand so far out of position, he got bold. Then he got killed. A natural lefty, Rose impaled the onrushing 'Mech with both shots. The charged particles actually stopped the 'Mech in its tracks. It tottered and started to fall, but Rose was no longer watching.

The look-alike *Rifleman* had cleared the trees and was fir-ing on Rose again. One Gauss shell ricocheted off his right torso, furrowing, but not breaching, the armor. The second shot passed over Rose's head by less than a meter, but a miss was all that mattered.

Rose dropped his right arm and locked onto his target. Without thinking, he held his breath and double-checked the lock, centering the cross hairs on the damaged left torso of the Clan 'Mech. Releasing half his breath, Rose fired the right-arm PPCs. True to his aim, the twin bolts passed through the breach in the damaged left torso and gutted the insides. The shot burned away the remaining internal struc-ture and set off a series of small fires. With a snap that was audible two hundred meters away, Rose saw the Clan 'Mech's left arm drop away.

Over-balanced by the loss of its arm, the 'Mech tottered to the right and slammed into a small cluster of trees. Shredding limbs and bark, the enemy 'Mech tried to stand but could not do so. The remaining arm was nothing more than a rifle mounted on the shoulder. With neither elbow nor hand, the 'Mech couldn't acquire the leverage to stand in the loose soil. As Rose approached, the pilot stopped struggling and tried to bring the remaining weapon in line. Rose circled wide and was soon out of range.

He glanced at the scanner and saw that the remaining two Clan 'Mechs were on the run. He pointed his right arm at the cockpit of the fallen Clan 'Mech and the struggling ceased. Rose stood immobile as the rest of the command lance centered around him.

"Report," he ordered, more coldly than he'd intended.

"Command Four. I traded shots with something. I don't know what it was. Neither of us got a hit, however, because of the intervening trees. It blasted off and landed on the far ridge." That would be the second fleeing 'Mech, thought Rose. It must have decided to get out when the other two went down.

"Command Three, no contact."

"Command Two. I got a passing shot at something, but I don't know if I hit. The 'Mech landed in the trees and kept moving away." That would be the first 'Mech, Rose said to himself. Fear is still the better part of valor, I guess. The pilot must have decided to make a break for it rather than damage me from the rear.

"I don't recognize either of these two designs," said Rose, pointing to the two 'Mechs at his feet. "Did you get recordings of the designs you spotted?" There were affirmatives all around, and Rose was heartened by the news. Tangling with new BattleMech designs was extremely dangerous, and the more information a warrior had about the opposition, the more likely he would survive the first few encounters. His battle with the *Rifleman* look-alike was also recorded.

"All right, people, let's move out." Rose switched to long-range scanning and checked for the other two lances. "Any contact with Battle or Recon?" he asked.

"Nothing since the landing," said Riannon. "Both of them should have an approximate idea of where we are, so it shouldn't take too long to link up."

Rose nodded but wasn't convinced. They were a long way from their intended landing zone and separated by heavy woods. If either of the other lances had dropped into a hot zone, well, Rose didn't want to think about that.

"Riannon, give us a fix on the last known position of Battle Lance. Command Four, lead the way. We'll link up with the closest unit first, then try to hook up with Recon."

"We could wait here," said Riannon. "Let them find us instead of blindly trying to run into each other."

"No chance, Command Two. That first 'Mech might have been on the move back to base before I finished off the other two. If that's the case, you can be sure there will be company heading our way immediately, if not sooner. We stay here and we're going to find ourselves surrounded."

"What about this guy?" asked Bell, indicating the fallen but not destroyed BattleMech at Rose's feet. Rose considered the options, then turned on the *Masakari*'s public address system.

"Ten, nine, eight, seven," he began. He moved the *Masakari* next to the fallen BattleMech's head and dropped the right arm to the cockpit.

"Six, five, four, three," he continued. A hatch suddenly opened in the BattleMech's head and out popped the pilot. Diving into the dirt, he just managed to roll clear of the 'Mech as Rose reached count zero. Rose stabbed the PPC trigger once and destroyed the cockpit. Without a second thought for the Clan pilot, he turned and followed Jamshid through the woods.

21

Star Colonel Denard Devereaux sat motionless at his desk and stared toward the far wall. Two pilots from the Fourteenth Garrison Cluster stood before him. Like their commander, they had remained immobile for the last thirty-seven minutes. Unlike their commander, they were standing at full attention.

The first pilot was a male whose close-cropped red hair was already beginning to recede, despite his youth. Though the other members of his star tolerated him, none would have called him friend. By Clan standards he was a capable gunner and an above-average pilot, but that was all. He lacked the drive and the ability to achieve his proper place in Clan society, and that failure placed a stigma on him. He was a MechWarrior, but he would remain a second-class pilot and a suspect ally.

The second pilot was female. Her blonde hair was also short, but the cut seemed to add character to her face, giving it a vitality the other pilot's would never have. Like her counterpart, she was a capable gunner and an above-average pilot who had occasionally shown flashes of brilliance. She had the right to dream of more than simple garrison duty. If she survived, this warrior could one day pilot one of the OmniMechs of Clan Nova Cat.

Denard still did not move. The strain had long since become apparent on the face of the male warrior. Denard was certain that the female was equally tired, but she did not show it in any of the ways most people would have perceived. That is good, thought Denard.

The two pilots before him were the only survivors of the morning's brief combat. What had started as a simple training exercise had become a deadly engagement when the training star had stumbled upon an Inner Sphere raiding party. Denard had known the raiders were in the system, but it hardly seemed worth the effort chasing down a single enemy DropShip. After all, how many 'Mechs could it hold? Barely two stars' worth. Better to let it land and hone the skills of his warriors. It was a good plan, but poor execution had cost him three BattleMechs.

From the corner of his eye, Denard saw the male flinch. Though the movement was barely perceptible beneath the man's combat suit, Denard caught it easily enough. That young warrior's fate was decided.

Denard raised his hands from his lap and placed them palm-down on the desk before him.

"You may relax." Neither MechWarrior moved. "I have several questions about this morning's events that I would like to have clarified." With deliberate slowness, Denard spread his fingers wide. He looked at the male.

"You broke off the engagement." Denard's voice was silky-smooth and very, very low. "By whose command?" he asked.

The man licked his lips and kept his eyes forward. "No command was given," he replied in a shaky voice. Denard remained silent for several moments, and the man's nerve broke. He gulped audibly before adding, "Star Commander Ortin was dead."

Denard turned to the woman. "You did not engage the enemy. By whose command?"

"Star Commander Ortin," she replied simply. Denard remained silent, but she refused to elaborate on the point. She was obviously very confident.

"Describe to me, in your own words, what happened this

morning, and please do not merely repeat what was in your report." Denard paused before continuing, his voice dripping menace. "I have already memorized that trash."

"We were deployed in a standard crescent," she began. "I was on the north point. We detected the drop pods and moved to intercept the last cluster. Star Commander Ortin believed that it had to be their command unit.

"As we approached, the Star Commander discovered that the raiders possessed two OmniMechs, a *Masakari* and a *Mad Cat*. He ordered me to return to base with that information."

Denard nodded and stood up. Moving with deliberate slowness, he came around the desk and stood before the woman. She was nearly six feet tall, but being an Elemental, Denard towered over her. She stared at his sternum until he hunched over to eye level.

"Tell me why you believe Star Commander Ortin ordered you to flee combat." The warrior's eyes flared briefly, but she quickly regained control. Excellent, thought Ortin. She is furious at the thought of being called a coward, but she still does her duty.

"We were over-matched in weight and firepower," she said. "Knowing we would lose. Star Commander Ortin sought to buy time so our intelligence could be returned to base. OmniMechs in the hands of Inner Sphere raiders is a serious matter."

Denard stood and began pacing the room. Soon he was behind the two pilots. They could not see him, but his heavy boots and deliberate stride made it patently obvious where he was at every moment. After three tours of the office, Denard walked to the door and flung it open.

"Star Captain Thrace," he bellowed. "My office." Without closing the door, he returned to his desk and sat down. A second Elemental rushed into the room. The female equivalent of her commander, Thrace was a mass of well-proportioned muscle backed by agility and the skill to put that mass to good advantage. Despite the somber air in the room, Thrace was smiling.

"Yes, Star Colonel?" she asked. Denard found it hard not

to smile back at his assistant, but succeeded in maintaining his calm. He started to speak and looked at the female MechWarrior.

"What is your name, MechWarrior?" he asked.

"Ailbrenn, Star Colonel."

"Star Captain Thrace, former MechWarrior Ailbrenn is now acting Star Commander of Pursuit Claw, Trinary Growler. She will need replacements to fill several spots recently vacated by combat losses."

"Very good, Star Colonel," responded Thrace.

"Take our new Star Commander over to the tactical center for a briefing on the massacre this morning, then get back here. We have things to discuss."

"Aff, Star Colonel." Without another word, the two women left the room, Thrace pulling the door shut behind her. When his assistant returned ten minutes later, Denard was still where she'd left him, but the other pilot was nowhere to be seen.

"Did you eat him?" she asked, only partially in jest. Denard snorted and rose from the desk.

"It wasn't necessary," he replied with a slow shake of his head. "The fool practically choked himself to death in front of me."

"Batchall, *quiaff*?"

"Aff. He expects to die in combat, and I will not disappoint him." Denard indicated an empty chair, the only piece of furniture in the room beside the Star Colonel's own chair and desk, then reached into a desk drawer. Thrace sat down, stress-testing the chair as Denard pulled out a chip and slipped it into the computer. After pressing several keys in silence, he pushed the monitor toward his assistant and leaned back. She read the text swiftly, then glanced at Denard.

"Could this be more than it seems?" she asked slowly. Denard frowned. It was not a question he expected from her. Indeed, he had not expected her to question him at all.

"It is not likely," he said. "Whoever these raiders are, I cannot believe they are anything more than what they seem on the surface. Mere Inner Sphere scum."

"With at least two OmniMechs," she reminded him.

Denard paused, then nodded once in silent acceptance of the facts. "What is the current tactical situation?" There was no doubt in Denard's mind that his assistant would have been given a full briefing on the current status of the raiders while she was had been at the cluster's tactical center.

"All their 'Mechs have reached the ground. Only one unit was engaged upon landing, but another was pursued for several kilometers before making an escape." Denard reached for the computer as she spoke. "Composition estimates?" he asked without looking up.

"A heavy company. The engaged unit was probably their command lance . . ."

"How do you know that?" he interrupted.

"The engaged units were the last four 'Mechs to release from the damaged DropShip. Intelligence reports indicate that Inner Sphere units always drop the command lance last in order to coordinate the drop. The exact opposite of the way it should be done, of course. The *Timber Wolf* was the last pod ejected. If the hypothesis is true, it is piloted by their company commander.

"Perhaps a worthy opponent, *quiaff*?" smiled Denard. Thrace looked at her commander. The reflected light of the computer monitor bathed his face with harsh shadows, casting a deathly pale green over his features.

"Perhaps," she agreed warily. She continued to study her commander, who was lost in thought before the computer. Star Colonel Denard was something of a legend among the giant Elementals.

Like many before him, he had won a bloodname and the right to fight in the front lines of the Clan advance into the Inner Sphere. First as a Star Commander, then as a Star Captain, he had always been at the head of forces participating in the thickest part of the fighting. Losses were heavy, but new warriors were eager to fight under the leadership of this legend-in-the-making. Thrace had been assigned to Denard's point while he was still a Star Captain, then become his assistant following the battle of Luthien. Through setback and victory the two had fought side by side. Then came

Tukayyid and the success that ruined the warrior she once knew.

Without proper logistic support, the Nova Cats had been routed off the planet by Com Guards in less than a week. First at Joje and Tost, then at Losije. Although the Nova Cats had enjoyed some initial successes, the Com Guard counterattacks had completely destroyed the Cats' positions. It was the Nova Cat Clan's worst defeat and their lowest moment. Only the failure of the Jade Falcons two days later and the exploits of Denard had made the shame bearable.

Harassing the enemy in a series of bold maneuvers, Denard's star of Elementals had kept up the pressure on the Com Guard forces throughout the engagement. Popular accounts said Denard had lived in his armor for that whole week, and Thrace knew it wasn't far from the truth, for she had rarely left his side. In the end, however, it did not matter. The Clan was defeated, and Denard was lifted off the planet with the final star of defenders.

Desperate for a hero, the Nova Cat Khans had decided Denard was their man. Tales of his exploits and his prowess grew and multiplied until even Thrace was hard-pressed to say where truth left off and the fiction began. Ultimately it did not matter. Clan Nova Cat had a new hero, and their faith in themselves was repaired, at least in part, by the exploits of that hero. Then came the promotion.

It was delivered without ceremony. Star Captain Denard was now Star Colonel Denard, newly appointed commander of an entire cluster. But when Thrace heard that the command was of a second-line garrison cluster instead of a full blown combat cluster, she thought the news would kill him. Star Colonel was as high as Denard had ever wanted to rise. To him it was the ultimate command position, yet now that he had it, he would be forced to watch the fighting from the back lines.

Thrace looked for any signs of aging in Denard's profile. Certainly there were lines and scars. Every commander revealed the weight of command in the depth of his wrinkles. Denard was no exception; but as with most males, the lines added character to his face and empowered it. His dark eyes were still as clear as the day she'd first met him, and if either his numerous injuries or his age had taken any of his speed and agility, he more than made up for it in wisdom and experience. None of the Elementals in the cluster could defeat him, and Thrace doubted there were any in the entire galaxy who could last in a Circle of Equals with him. With the new command, however, all that ability was wasted. For more than a year Thrace had been watching Denard die a bit each day as he pined for the chance to get back into the fight. She was tempted to pity him, but fought against it. He deserved more than her pity.

Denard looked up from the monitor, silently prodding her to continue. If there was a prolonged silence, he did not seem to notice it.

"Estimated ground strength is one company," she continued. "That is twelve of their 'Mechs. Given current information and estimates, we project four assault, four heavy, and four medium or light. Of those twelve, two are known OmniMechs—the *Timber Wolf* and *Warhawk* of the command group. The rest are unknown."

Thrace looked over the computer and saw that Denard had linked into the main tactical system of the cluster. As she spoke, he had been making notes with the light pen on the raiders' known locations. He continued to stare at the computer while speaking to her.

"They should link up about here." Denard drew a circle on the map and increased the magnification. The map grew in clarity until a ten-by-ten-kilometer section was displayed on the screen. Thrace knew that the computers in the tactical center would have given them better resolution, as well as three-dimensional holovision, but she didn't suggest that to Denard. He was working on an agenda of his own; she could tell it by the fire in his eyes. When he was ready, he would brief the rest of the cluster, but for now it was their secret.

"Send Trinary Fang to this area. Use Trinary Growler and Binary Pouncer to herd them into the area." Denard turned from the screen. "Then crush them. We have no need for prisoners. If we can salvage the OmniMechs, so much the better, but it is not necessary, *quiaff*?"

"Aff. What of the DropShip?"

Denard slammed his knuckles down on the desk with enough force to bounce the computer. "Those fools of the Forty-sixth. Cavaliers? Ha!" He rapped the desk a second time, and Thrace began to fear for the computer's components. The screen flickered slightly but remained active.

"Luckily, they only damaged the DropShip." Denard grabbed the light pen and moved it across the map, indicating a point in the center of the continent's northern plains. "The captain managed to set the ship down in good shape right about here."

"And the kill belongs to the Cavaliers, *quiaff*?"

"Neg," Denard bellowed. "None of the aerospace fighters survived the attack. I have claimed the ship, as it landed of its own will."

Thrace scowled but held her tongue. If the DropShip had been forced down by the fighters of the Forty-sixth Nova Cat Cavaliers, then the ship was rightly the isorla, or property, of that cluster. By declaring that the ship landed by will rather than damage, Denard claimed the prize by right of being commander of the garrison cluster responsible for defense of the planet. The Cavaliers were only using Courcheval as a staging area. Although there was friendly rivalry between the two clusters, until now matters had always been cordial. Thrace doubted Star Colonel Bondan would accept the loss of an entire star of aerospace fighters without some claim on the downed ship.

"The Cavaliers—," she began.

"—are of no concern," Denard told her. "They may be angry, but there is little they can do." Denard pierced Thrace with a deadly stare. "The DropShip is mine."

"But we have the BattleMechs, including two, maybe more, OmniMechs. That is enough, *quiaff*?"

"Neg," said Denard with a slowly spreading smile. "The DropShip is the prize, not the 'Mechs."

"But surely, Star Colonel, we have better DropShips than these raiders can possibly possess, *quiaff*?"

"Aff, Star Captain. Aff. But it is an Inner Sphere DropShip, and that makes all the difference."

22

Courcheval,
Nova Cat Occupation Zone
28 July 3057

Rose moved slowly through the forest and tried to split his vision between the *Masakari*'s long-range scanner and the main view screen. Although such activity was common when in combat, he'd rarely had to perform such actions when not engaged with the enemy.

For the last four hours the Thorns had been pursued by several groups of enemy 'Mechs. Just as the enemy would reach the edge of scanner range, they'd fade away again. Rose had tried to lose them, but the pursuers remained doggedly on his tail.

The command lance had linked with the battle lance within an hour of landing on Courcheval. Unlike the command lance, the battle lance 'Mechs had landed unopposed. Once they'd regrouped, the five had headed toward the command lance and kept up a continuous pace until finally reaching the command lance. For the last three hours they had been trying unsuccessfully to find the recon lance. Rose was tempted to wait and let the recon lance find him, but every time he wanted to stop, the unidentified pursuers would show up to the south. Unless he wanted to engage them, he was forced to continue north. Rose was starting to suspect he was being herded.

The Thorns were moving through a wide valley formed by

a series of low running hills. The woods had thinned slightly, but there was still plenty of cover, especially for Clan Elementals. Rose had deployed the unit in a line sweeping north. Despite the tactical limitations of such a formation, he believed that the wide scanner area provided by the formation was worth the risk.

"Contact," came the call over the company frequency. Rose double-checked the scanner, but nothing appeared. It looked as though the gamble had paid off. As he was positioned in the center of the Black Thorn line, that meant the contact was either to the east or the west, probably just outside his scanner range.

"Identify," he responded.

"Four 'Mechs moving in single file to the west." By now Rose had identified the speaker as Greta. Stationed at the extreme left flank, it made sense that she would spot the approaching 'Mechs first. "It looks like they're moving at a pretty good clip, Captain," she continued.

"Keep an eye out for additional targets, Thorns. Command Two, try to raise Recon One. Command Lance, swing left. We're going to meet them halfway."

Rose turned to the left and allowed Riannon and Jamshid to pass him up a few seconds later. He knew that Bell would be positioned behind him once he started to move, so he fell behind Ria in the march to the west. It didn't take long for the recon lance to appear on the scanner, but there was no contact. Rose tried to raise Ajax several times, but was unable to establish a connection. With each attempt he grew more frustrated and worried.

As a product of Clan technology, his *Masakari* BattleMech was the ultimate achievement in military construction. Like every military vehicle, however, it was designed for a specific purpose. In the case of the *Masakari*, the primary emphasis was on long-range stopping power. As a result, the 'Mech mounted four of the single most powerful weapon available to modern man: the extended-range particle projection cannon. The 'Mech also mounted an advanced targeting computer to increase the accuracy of the four primary weapons. It was well armored, but that was only one item on the list of outstanding features.

As a command vehicle, however, the *Masakari* was strictly run-of-the-mill. Of course it still outclassed most of what was available in the Inner Sphere, but it lacked many of the features common in first-rate command 'Mechs. Ajax's *Raven*, constructed in the Capellan Confederation, had a much more advanced electronics suite that gave it a wider scanning range and sophisticated electronic counter-measures. Riannon's *Phoenix Hawk*, built on New Avalon in the Federated Commonwealth, had been upgraded following their stint on Borghese. Instead of the standard communications gear, the *Phoenix Hawk* had been outfitted with an advanced company communications suite. The new equipment gave the *Phoenix Hawk* increased range and a host of abilities not even the OmniMechs could match.

Rose hoped his sister was having better luck reaching the recon lance than he was. He continued to move forward, keeping his eyes focused on the scanner, but several more minutes passed with still no word from Ria. On a hunch Rose toggled the scanner display from tactical to topographic to check whether some unseen terrain might be blocking the signal. What he saw shocked him.

The Thorns had entered the far western edge of the valley. Although the terrain could not be called mountainous, the surrounding slopes were much steeper on this edge of the valley than toward the center. Given time, he knew that all the Black Thorn 'Mechs could scramble up the hillsides, but that could be slow going in most cases. Only the jump-capable 'Mechs would be able to make any kind of time up the slope. The recon lance was moving into the valley along a washout between two hills on the other side. If the terrain was as wooded on that side of the hills as it was in the valley, the washout would make a perfect road for moving into the valley and linking with the rest of the Black Thorns. Given the speed of the recon lance, Rose guessed they were being pursued much the same as he was.

Rose paused and slowly brought the *Masakari* to a halt. He could almost sense Bell stop behind him. Scanning the valley, Rose suddenly saw the trap. This wasn't the classical box canyon seen in the trideos, but it was close enough for modern combat. The steep hills would slow any 'Mechs trying to ascend them long enough for emplaced BattleMechs to pound them to dust. The feeling of being shepherded returned with a vengeance, and Rose felt his stomach roll. By swinging to the west, he had let the trap shut all the tighter.

"Battle Lance, this is Command One," he said as he flicked the scanner back to tactical. "Deploy in standard defensive box formation. Watch the hills, Thorns. I've got a bad feeling about this one."

"Command Two, any luck with Recon?" he continued. He toggled through all the *Masakari*'s active scanning capabilities; thermal, visual, electromagnetic, and seismic. He stopped on the last setting when the scanner picked up the flicker of a disturbance behind the northern hill.

"Negative, Command One," reported Riannon. "Something is interfering with the signal."

Rose adjusted the scanner as she spoke, trying to bring the seismic contact into better focus.

"Multiple contacts, bearing four-seven degrees," came the voice of Antioch Bell. "They don't look like friendlies."

Rose thumbed back to electromagnetic scanning, the standard mode for detecting enemy BattleMechs. Bell was right. Five 'Mechs were racing down from the north toward the mouth of the valley. By their speed, Rose guessed them to be medium or light 'Mechs. Rather than engaging, these 'Mechs were positioned to keep the Black Thorns from fleeing the valley. He knew what would come next.

"Multiple contacts along the north," reported Esmeralda. "Looks like another two stars." Rose confirmed the report. Ten enemy 'Mechs were moving down the slope toward the Thorns. The slope that was keeping the mercenaries trapped in the valley proved no hindrance to the Clan 'Mechs as they half-slid, half-walked down the side of the hills.

"Battle Lance, deploy to the north. Keep them off Recon Lance as they enter the valley. Command Lance, provide support. Once the rest of the unit gets here, we'll continue to the northeast."

Rose swung the *Masakari* to the north and began moving forward. The enemy 'Mechs were just out of range, but that would change before long. He locked the targeting computer onto the nearest descending 'Mech and continued advancing into firing range. He wasn't surprised that his target acquisition system failed to identify the enemy. Rose had been trying to repair the OmniMech's onboard computer following the unit's landing on Courcheval. The system's failure to identify the first group of 'Mechs worried him, but he could not find any malfunction in the system. The computer didn't know these designs either because it had been damaged in the fighting on Borghese or, more likely, because the information had not been loaded into it in the first place. Whatever the case, the end result was the same.

Rose readied the long-range missiles and triggered them the moment the target lock went green. Ten missiles sped from their launchers over the *Masakari*'s head, but Rose didn't wait to see the results of the launch. He continued his pace and fired the right-arm PPCs the moment those weapons were in range.

Rose was rewarded with a series of hits along the center and right torso of the smaller 'Mech, but he couldn't tell the extent of the damage. Another five steps and he triggered the left-arm PPCs. Another hit, this time on the right leg of the enemy 'Mech, staggered the Clan machine, but it did not fall. Rose picked up his pace and continued toward the Nova Cat line as Bell fired at the same 'Mech. The *Banshee*'s two Defiance PPCs flailed away at the damaged Clan 'Mech, the onslaught snapping the right leg and bringing the enemy 'Mech to a permanent halt. Rose switched targets as the Clan forces drew closer.

Several Clan 'Mechs tried long-range shots at the approaching Thorns. The afterimage of lasers burned into Rose's retina as he continued the advance, but he wasn't hit by any of the bolts. The reload complete, he fired the long-range missiles, ten of them directed this time at an enemy *Rifleman*. Rose recognized the familiar yet subtly different shape and aimed his right arm at the 'Mech. Blossoms of flame wreathed the *Rifleman*'s shoulder and right arm as the enemy 'Mech returned Rose's fire. Despite the explosions all around him, the Clan pilot's arm was perfect.

Four lasers burned away at the *Masakari*, two striking the assault 'Mech's right arm, boiling away more than a ton of armor from the shoulder and upper arm. Another struck the opposite arm, and the final bolt pushed into the *Masakari*'s damaged leg. Rose fought against the sudden loss of weight caused by the destroyed armor. At a full run, the *Masakari*'s center of balance was dangerously extended, and it took Rose several bone-jarring strides to return that precise balance to true.

Rose centered the cross hairs on the *Rifleman* and held the aim for just a moment. He tasted blood, and realized suddenly that he had bitten his lip during the struggle to remain upright. Rose snarled and stabbed the primary TIC. All four PPCs speared the *Rifleman,* followed closely by the staggering impact of Bell's Gauss rifle. Azure beams rent the armor over the *Rifleman*'s damaged torso before burrowing their way inside. The Gauss round punched through the armor and shredded delicate control circuits hidden beneath.

The *Rifleman* took a halting step and stumbled. The right leg refused to follow the left, and the entire 'Mech fell facedown into the dirt. The outstretched laser barrels of the arms bent and snapped under the driving weight of the 'Mech. Rose was tempted to laugh at the ease with which the Clan 'Mech was destroyed, but he refrained. Selecting another target, he continued the attack.

"Status report, Battle Lance," he said as he closed on an enemy *Marauder*. A small part of his mind told him to be careful, but with Bell providing backup, he chose to ignore the warning. The Clan 'Mechs would have to be destroyed, or at least damaged, if the unit was to get away.

"Recon just entered the valley. Ajax will swing to the south and head for the mouth on the eastern edge." Esmeralda paused, and Rose could hear the massive roar of the *Mad Cat*'s long-range missile launcher over the microphone. Forty missiles flew toward the Clan lines as Esmeralda was saying, "We're moving around as fast as we can, but we're taking a pounding."

"Anybody down?" Rose asked immediately.

"Not yet, but it's just a matter of time." Rose picked up the sound of an explosion and knew Esmeralda had no time to continue the conversation. He triggered the right-arm PPCs at the *Marauder* and toggled the recon channel.

"Recon, continue movement east. Punch past the star in the center of the valley. We'll meet you on the other side of the hills." Rose unconsciously braced himself as the *Marauder* fired all three PPCs. Two more hits on the *Masakari* staggered Rose, but he refused to fall. Bell returned fire on the *Marauder* before switching to another target, then Rose hit him again and the *Marauder* finally stumbled and fell. As the 'Mech struggled to rise, Rose scanned around for another target, but didn't like what he saw.

Lumbering from the north was the biggest 'Mech Rose had ever seen. At first glance it looked somewhat like a *Marauder,* but this design was much larger. Giant cloven feet sank nearly two meters into the soil with each step, and each arm ended in a huge gun barrel. Rose wondered what could be housed under such protection, but hoped he'd never have to find out. Over the back of the crab-shaped 'Mech were two more gun barrels reaching out over the front. Rose shuddered to think of the damage the four weapons could do. Bell fired on the fearsome 'Mech as Rose watched and waited for his weapons to recycle.

Despite a pair of solid hits from Bell's Gauss rifle and one from his PPC, the giant Clan 'Mech continued its lumbering pace toward Rose. As his own weapons blinked on-line, Rose began to walk backward. He was just about to hit the target interlock when the Clan 'Mech's four barrels roared at him.

Explosions shook the *Masakari* as Gauss rounds slammed into the 'Mech. Then twin lasers stabbed at the *Masakari*'s chest, and Rose had to fight for balance, knowing it was a lost cause. With his 'Mech already moving backward, the added impact and loss of nearly three tons of armor threw him to the ground. He slammed onto his back as the *Masakari* fell. Looking at the clear sky above him, Rose could see the trails of long-range missiles overhead. The view was quickly obstructed, however, as Bell moved the *Banshee* over the fallen *Masakari*.

Rose rolled to the right side and tried to stand. The task was difficult because the *Masakari*'s arms weren't much help, but with Bell providing protection, he finally managed to right the assault 'Mech. Then he swung all four PPCs at the first 'Mech he saw, the enemy *Marauder*. It was not his first choice for a target, but Rose hit the trigger and watched the Clan 'Mech fall a second time. He doubted it would stand again.

"Damn, that thing is big," Rose muttered as he watched the approaching 'Mech. Its armor had been scored by nearly a dozen hits, but nothing had breached the monster's thick hide. Rose glanced at the *Masakari*'s control panel and grimaced. Although his armor had not yet been breached, a single hit from a pop gun could damage the internals.

"Battle Lance, where are you?" he asked as he and Bell backed away from the lumbering Clan 'Mech.

"We're at the mouth of the valley. Haul your butt over here, and we can get out of this place." Rose gulped in surprise and looked around him. The remaining Black Thorns were all to the east of him, moving slowly to the northeast. Though several of the Thorns were waiting for him and Bell, the main body was moving away. Rose hastily counted the friendly blips on the scanner and sighed in relief when he hit twelve. Around him were the damaged and destroyed remains of Clan 'Mechs. Although the behemoth coming at him wasn't the only operational Clan 'Mech left, the other enemy pilots had apparently left the trap and any remaining kills to the lumbering giant.

"Bell, get ready to break on my command. Three. Two. One. Now." Rose triggered every weapon he had and turned to flee. Bell did the same and followed closely on his commander's heels. Despite the targeting computer, Rose hit with only one weapon, and Bell scored with only two. The Clan 'Mech lumbered on, but the faster 'Mechs of Bell and Rose began to widen the gap.

The Clan 'Mech continued to fire at Rose as they fled, burning a scar into the back of the *Masakari*'s left leg before it finally stopped shooting. Rose charged past the fallen forms of three Clan 'Mechs, presumably the ones that had been charged with keeping the Black Thorns penned in the valley. Ahead of him Esmeralda and O'Shea backed slowly away, their large guns covering their commander's retreat.

"Follow Recon Lance," Rose ordered. "Ajax, get us out of here and keep moving north. We might have won the battle, but it's a Pyrrhic victory, at best. Another victory like this will reduce us to scrap."

=== 23 ===

Rose kept the 'Mechs in a single file, his attention on the back of Jamshid's 'Mech. Almost two hours had passed since the battle in the valley, and Rose could tell that the unit was still feeling the aftershock. It was not uncommon. Warriors often experienced a letdown following the rush of combat. He scanned the line of 'Mechs proceeding up the hill, and suddenly realized what was keeping the unit in such a dark mood. Battle Four was missing. When he'd counted the 'Mechs of the company, he'd forgotten to add on for *Chu-i* Myoto.

Rose toggled a personal channel to Battle One. "Esmeralda," he said softly, "what happened?"

Rose expected a professional report from a combat veteran. Instead Esmeralda sighed into the microphone. "There were just too many of them, Captain," she said finally. "Battle Four went down with a blow to the engine. I think Greta managed to get the engine off line, but there wasn't time to pick her up. Several of the Clan 'Mechs swarmed past her fallen *Charger,* and we had to fall back." Esmeralda paused again, breathing deeply and audibly. "I'm sorry," she said finally.

Rose knew that if Esmeralda had felt forced to leave Greta and the *Charger,* it meant there was nothing she could have done. He had absolute faith in her loyalty to the unit and her charges. He was tempted to tell Esmeralda that she wasn't to blame for the incident, but he knew that would not be enough. She wanted absolution, not sympathy.

"I understand, Ese," Rose told her gently. "It's never easy to lose a member of your command. Believe me, I know. I have no doubt you did the best you could, but sometimes that just isn't enough. There isn't any blame. We're at war, and wars inflict causalities."

"Understood, sir. Thank you."

Rose changed his tone, reverting to his command voice. "Check battle damage and compile a status report. Command One out." He switched to the recon and command channels and gave the same orders. Within minutes the grim news was displayed on his computer screen.

Each of the 'Mechs of the command and battle lances had sustained damage. Although none of the surviving 'Mechs had lost limbs, Jamshid's right arm hung limply at his side. Several 'Mechs had suffered internal damage, but only O'Shea's *Warhammer* had taken a serious internal hit. A short-range missile had damaged the heavy 'Mech's engine shielding, spilling waste heat into the cockpit and engine compartment. In any future battles the *Warhammer* would run very hot, limiting its effectiveness.

The recon lance had not suffered heavily in the exchange. They had rushed around the battle and command lances and headed straight for the light and medium 'Mechs at the valley's east end. In a single passing attack, Ajax and Yuri had destroyed two of the Clan second-line 'Mechs while Kitten and Leeza accounted for a third. Return damage had been light, but a destroyed foot actuator had Kitten's otherwise speedy *Panther* hobbling somewhat. In all, Rose should have been satisfied with the outcome. He triggered a private channel to Ajax at the head of the column.

"Any ideas?" he asked abruptly.

"None." Ajax sounded glum. "These hills seem to break up to the north of here, but we'd never make it on the plains. Clan fighters would have a field day picking us apart."

"Agreed," said Rose. "We've got to stay here and find a place to regroup. Any hot prospects?"

"Negative. The entire terrain is pockmarked with hills, stands of trees, and loose gravel. The woods are too thin to provide protection from air cover, and the hills are too widespread to provide a suitable defense."

Rose nodded silent agreement. "Do the best you can then. See if you can find a large body of water. At least that way we can cover one side from attack."

Rose fell back into silence and concentrated on piloting his 'Mech. He and his people were in desperate straits and he knew it. So did the other Black Thorns. They were completely out of contact with the DropShip and thousands of kilometers from the pickup area. To make matters worse, the DropShip was on the other side of a very dangerous stretch of flat ground.

"Contacts, dead ahead," came the call. Rose thought he recognized Yuri's voice, but the tight warning was muffled by the sound of an explosion.

"Enemy star dead ahead, sir," reported Hawg. Rose broke to the right, followed closely by Bell. Riannon and Jamshid moved to the left. "They're sniping at the recon lance from the cover of boulders on the path ahead."

"Battle Lance move right and cut them off. Recon Lance disengage." Rose started moving forward. The recon lance was built for speed, not a toe-to-toe fight with snipers in protected positions. Although the recon 'Mechs were very capable when in the open, the hills hampered their movement.

Rose moved up behind Hawg, who was scrambling toward the Clan 'Mechs on the hillside. Also moving up the hill, Rose realized that the Clanners had chosen an ideal position for an attack. Although the position of the snipers prevented them from retreating without being dangerously exposed, they were dangerous opponents while they were in the cover of the rocks. As he watched, Rose realized something else about the ambush.

The Clan star was in a suicide position. Judging from the 'Mechs Rose could see, the snipers were all light and medium 'Mechs. Once the heavy Black Thorn 'Mechs made it to the front of the line, the ambushers would be overrun. Sure, the enemy 'Mechs might inflict damage, maybe even take out a Black Thorn 'Mech or two, but they would also die in the attempt.

"Command Two, sweep the rear!" bellowed Rose. "Anything coming up from behind?" Rose was aware that a strong follow-up attack from the rear could save the Clan ambushers, but if enemy pursuit was out there, they were still beyond the distance of a long-range scanner. And if such pursuit arrived, it would be too late to do the ambushers any good.

"Affirmative," Riannon reported. "I've got another star moving on our six. They'll be within range in the next five minutes." Rose frowned. Five minutes was enough to kill the ambushers three times over. Could the Clans have made such a critical mistake, he wondered? It didn't seem likely even though they were second-line units.

Rose focused on the fighting in front of him and watched as Hawg and an ambushing *Shadow Hawk* traded volleys. Hawg staggered back a step, but the *Shadow Hawk* crumpled into the boulders. Coolant dripped like blood over the boulder that failed to provide cover for the fallen 'Mech. A flight of long-range missiles streaked past Rose, and he involuntarily flinched as they exploded behind him. He scanned for the attacker, but the firer had already ducked behind the protection of the boulders.

Hawg moved toward the ambushers' position, his right-arm PPC leveled at the rocks. Rose followed and Bell brought up the rear of the small column. Across the narrow trail, Esmeralda, O'Shea, Myoto, and the rest of the command lance mirrored the movement.

An enemy 'Mech popped up from cover and fired at Esmeralda. As the Clanner's shot slammed into the *Mad Cat,* the same 'Mech was skewered by return fire from five different Black Thorn 'Mechs. Rose smiled in spite of the situation. Even Myoto had managed to hit with her snap shot. The enemy 'Mech fell backward behind the boulders, but Rose knew the shots had been fatal.

"One Cat," said Hawg, "D.R.T." None of the Black Thorns responded to the cryptic announcement. After a moment of silence, Hawg came back on the channel. "Dead Right There."

Rose laughed at the grim epitaph delivered so calmly by Hawg. He continued to work his way forward, but silently wondered at Hawg.

"I've got—," began O'Shea before a metallic thump cut the sentence short. The command line picked up the hollow ringing of metal across the company frequency, and Rose knew instantly what it was. He'd heard the same sound during the battle of Borghese right before an Elemental had tried to kill him.

"Battle Two, you've got two Elementals on your shoulders and another on your head," warned Esmeralda. Rose fell back and turned toward the other side of the trail. He knew that the rest of the unit could take care of the remaining ambushers, but O'Shea was in serious trouble.

As he focused on O'Shea, Rose realized that the situation was worse than he'd initially thought. The Clan warriors had chosen their target well. The *Warhammer* lacked true arms, mounting PPCs in place of the lower arms and hands of a standard humanoid BattleMech. The added flexibility of arm-mounted weapons gave the design a greater firing arc, but the loss of the hands hampered fine movement. That loss was about to be critical.

The Elemental on the 'Mech's right shoulder ripped off a handful of armor over the joint and thrust his clawed hand inside. Bracing himself, the Elemental turned slightly and fired his arm-mounted small laser and both shoulder-mounted short-rage missiles at the *Grand Dragon,* the closest 'Mech to O'Shea. Myoto had no choice but to accept the stinging, as any shot that hit the Elemental would doubtless injure the *Warhammer.*

The Elemental on the left shoulder tried the same trick, but lost his grip as O'Shea stepped laterally into a tree. The trunk snapped and the Elemental dropped off, but began to get up almost from the moment he hit the ground. If the ten-meter fall had even knocked the wind out of him, the Clan infantryman didn't show it.

Rose locked onto the small target and fired both of his right-arm PPCs. Although such giant weapons were certainly overkill versus a target like the Elemental, the warrior's small size effectively countered the advantages of the targeting computer. The first blue beam scorched the ground to the right of the Elemental, but Rose's second beam caught him before he could jump onto the back of the *Warhammer*. Vaporized under the electrical attack, the Elemental and his armor simply ceased to exist.

Rose switched back to the *Warhammer* and watched as O'Shea flailed at the two remaining Elementals. Bringing the 'Mech's right arm across, he tried to swat the Elemental off his head, but to no avail; the Clanner was inside the arc of the long arm. Standard tactics called for a pilot to try to scrape an Elemental off or, if possible, to jump. The shock of jumping and landing was often enough to dislodge the powered infantry, but the *Warhammer* was earthbound, so that was not an option.

"Battle Five," yelled Rose, "get that Elemental on O'Shea's shoulder." Then Rose began to concentrate on the other Elemental burning his way through the armor of O'Shea's cockpit. Because of the angle of the attack, only Rose had a shot on the Elemental. Any other assistance would have caused too much damage to the *Warhammer*'s head. Rose lined up his shot and fired a single left-arm PPC. The shot was true, but a sudden movement by O'Shea spoiled his aim, and the azure beam passed harmlessly in front of the *Warhammer*.

"Damn it, O'Shea. Hold still!" Rose bellowed. Rose had one last PPC on line. This would be the final shot. Taking careful aim, he sighted on the Elemental and released half this breath, but didn't pull the trigger.

The Elemental on the *Warhammer*'s shoulder finally succeeded in fully breaching the armor over the joint. Slashing, tearing, firing the small laser, he wormed his way into the joint as Myoto fired. Her aim was perfect, but the Elemental had caused too much damage. The PPC bolt killed the Elemental, but finished off the damaged shoulder joint. With a rending tear, the *Warhammer*'s left arm dropped away. The sudden loss of the arm tilted the *Warhammer* to the right. O'Shea tried to keep the 'Mech steady, but the giant machine began a slow-motion fall to the ground.

Rose offered a quick prayer and fired the final PPC. The shot caught the Elemental in the rear, blasting away the back half of his armor and destroying the flesh underneath. The warrior died instantly. As the 'Mech fell to the ground, the Elemental fell away from it. Rose moved down the hill and across the trail. As he approached, Myoto stepped into view from the cover of a cluster of trees. The remaining two Elementals of the point were crawling up the torso of her *Grand Dragon*.

As Rose approached, the higher Elemental thrust his laser into the long-range missile ports of the *Grand Dragon*'s nose. Rose saw the flash of the Elemental's small laser as the warrior fired into the unprotected launcher. There was the flash of an explosion that threatened to dislodge the Elemental, but a quick grab with the power claw kept the warrior lodged on the 'Mech. Rose moved closer, but realized there was little he could do. To his left he heard the sounds of the continuing gunfight with the ambushing 'Mechs, but he knew that fight would be decided without him.

He centered the cross hairs on the nose-mounted Elemental, but again he was forced to hold his fire. The shot was too risky, and the *Grand Dragon* had advantages the *Warhammer* did not share.

Reaching up with her 'Mech's left hand, Myoto grabbed the Elemental who had ruined her 'Mech's missile system with a huge battle hand. Ripping the Clanner away from her machine, she continued to apply pressure. The Elemental's struggles grew more frantic as the warrior tried to free himself from the hand's grasp. With a sudden jerk, however, the Elemental armor failed. Myoto crushed the warrior and dropped the limp body to the ground.

The final Elemental, wary of the *Dragon*'s arm, moved onto the 'Mech's back and began pulling away the armor there. Rose aligned a shot, but the Elemental scampered over the *Grand Dragon*'s shoulder, keeping the body of the 'Mech between him and the *Masakari*. Rose tried for several shots, but the Elemental managed to stay one step ahead of him. Although Rose was preventing the infantryman from doing further damage to the *Grand Dragon,* he could not remove him from his perch.

Rose had chased the Elemental to the *Grand Dragon*'s shoulder when two lasers suddenly picked off the Clan warrior. Rose pivoted to see two small hovercraft approaching at flank speed. In these hills, with their tightly clustered stands of trees, Rose knew such actions were nothing short of insane, but the two pilots continued their headlong charge. Approaching from the rear, they had been shielded from the scanners of most of the Black Thorns, and Rose had been too busy trying to dislodge the Elemental to register the new players in the battle.

The Elemental struggled to rise, finally succeeding as the lead hovercraft closed the distance. The Elemental fired first, but the shot sailed past the hurling hovercraft. The hover's return shot knocked the wounded Elemental off his feet. Rose covered the Clan warrior with one arm while the other tracked the twin hovercraft.

He scanned the battlefield as the two hovercraft slowed to a stop at the feet of the *Warhammer*. The ambushers had all been eliminated from their cover on the hills. Hawg reported four dead BattleMechs in the cover of the boulders. The five Elementals seemed to have made up the rest of the star, an unusual formation for the Clans but one that had been predicted by the briefing the Thorns had received prior to the mission.

As Rose watched, the cowling of the lead hovercraft cracked open, and the pilot jumped out of the craft. It took a moment for Rose to realize that it was a woman, but when she removed her helmet in trying to enter the 'Mech's cockpit, Rose saw a mane of long red hair. Then he caught a glimpse of her face as she slipped into the cockpit. Several seconds later she emerged from the fallen *Warhammer* and scrambled to her craft. Rose thumbed the public address system of the *Masakari*.

"How is O'Shea?" he asked in a booming voice.

She looked up at him with sad eyes and shook her head. "Is that the pilot's name?" she asked. Rose adjusted the gain of the address system and answered.

"Yes."

"He's dead," the woman replied, climbing back into the cockpit of the hovercraft. Rose was stunned. "D.R.T.," he whispered softly to himself.

The remaining Black Thorns clustered around the fallen 'Mech. Although the *Warhammer* belonged to Esmeralda, Rose knew she'd miss the pilot more than the machine. It was an uncommon sentiment in these times. Another battle, another victory, and once again the cost was too high. Rose bit his lip and looked at the hovercraft pilot.

"Who are you?"

"We're with the resistance, such as it is," she said, stuffing her hair back into her helmet. "You fighting for Kurita?"

"Yeah," Rose answered simply.

"Did you arrive on a *Union* Class DropShip?" she asked.

Rose scowled. How could she know that, he wondered? "The *Tracy K*?" he asked.

"I don't know the name of it, but if you came to Courcheval on a *Union* Class ship, you'd better follow me." While speaking, she'd been buckling herself in on the hovercraft. Without waiting for a response, she started to close its cowling.

"Why?" asked Rose, suddenly concerned.

She stopped pulling on the cowling and stared up at Rose. "Because your DropShip has become the property of the Nova Cats," she replied levelly, "and that means you're not likely to get back to Kurita space anytime soon." She paused and seemed to consider the next sentence. "That also means you're not part of the regular army anymore. You just enlisted in the Courcheval resistance."

24

Star Colonel Denard stood in the middle of the cluster's tactical center and fumed. Not even the bravest of his aides dared look him in the eye or call unwanted attention to himself. Denard studied the replay of the battle in the valley and the ambush in the hills for the third time. As before, the obvious errors of the Clan warriors stabbed at him like a dagger through the heart.

"An entire Trinary lost," he said aloud. "One third of my command destroyed by a pack of illiterate mercenaries from the Inner Sphere." He stopped the playback as an Elemental killed the enemy *Warhammer*. It was his only moment of pride in the two battles. Shortly after the attack, the Clan 'Mech recording the battle had been destroyed. If the mercenaries hadn't been in such a hurry, the battle ROMs of the Clan 'Mechs would have fallen into their hands, not his.

"Are you listening to me?" he roared at the assembled aides. To a man, the members of the tactical unit stopped in mid-stride. "A pack of unwashed barbarians defeated us." He looked around at his warriors, taking pains to meet the eye of every individual in the room. "Is no one but me shamed by that fact? Does no one but me blush red at the dishonor of such a defeat?" Denard paused and looked around the room. "Answer me!"

"Aff," resounded the warriors in chorus. Denard's right hand clenched into a fist, and Thrace thought he was going to destroy the holograph projector with his bare hands. Despite the thing's combat casing, she had little doubt that the Star Colonel could do it. She made a mental note to requisition another unit as Denard raised a fist, then paused, then brought the fist crashing down on the projector. The holographic 'Mechs disappeared as the projector failed. An unidentified component flew past Thrace's right eye, but she did not move. Denard smashed the projector with a powerful left jab, then stood back. He wasn't even breathing heavily.

"We will endeavor to prevent anything like this happening again," he said to the room at large. "Is that clear?"

"Aff, Star Colonel," came the hearty replies.

Denard stabbed a finger toward one of the Star Captains in the room. "Take Trinary Growler and run the mercenaries to the ground. They have been damaged by their previous fights and should represent no challenge." He paused and walked around the room. "Put Star Commander Ailbrenn in the lead. I suspect she has a personal score to settle with these Inner Sphere mercenaries."

"Aff, Star Colonel," the man responded. He dropped the electronic clipboard he was holding onto a table and dashed from the room. Denard ran a hand through his short hair, rubbing his scalp vigorously.

"What is our current situation?" Across the room, a MechWarrior consulted her clipboard in response to the vague question.

"Five Elementals dead, Star Colonel. Twelve BattleMechs damaged. Of that total, four will have to be scrapped. The remainder are being repaired as we speak." She glanced at the clipboard a second time. "Five 'Mechs damaged but operational."

"When will we be back to full strength?" asked Denard quietly.

The answer hung in the officer's throat for a moment before she managed to speak. "We can field a fully repaired star in just over six hours. A second star will be available seven hours after that." The officer stopped.

"Did that answer my question?" Denard asked the officer.

"Neg, Star Colonel. In truth, we will have to await reinforcements before returning to full readiness. Until that time we will be short one star and one point of Elementals" Denard raised a finger to his lips and tapped them slowly.

"I see. So you are telling me I lost an entire star, had two more damaged, and in return I have destroyed two enemy 'Mechs, *quiaff*?"

"Aff," the officer responded.

Denard turned to an Elemental. "Have we heard from Star Colonel Bondan?"

"Aff, Star Colonel. She asked if we required assistance to track down the raiders. I declined the offer."

Denard hitched his head at the response, but smiled slightly. "You overstep your authority, Paie." The man bowed his head, but Denard's smile grew wider. "Still, it is good to have a warrior one can trust." Paie nodded but kept his head low, shielding his smile from his commander.

Denard clapped his hands together and walked around the room.

"I do not think we have much time, but we have got some rebuilding to do." He pointed at Paie.

"Get over to the command center of the Fourteenth and ask Bondan to dine with me tomorrow. I need to keep on her good side, and a personal visit might help. Besides, I have an offer she might like to hear." Paie hustled from the room as Denard moved on to another warrior.

"See to the arrangements," he said simply, hitching a thumb over his right shoulder. The man left on the heels of Paie.

Denard turned to the remaining man in the room. "What is the status of the raiders' DropShip?" he asked.

"The surviving crewmembers have been transported here. We are currently investigating the crash site . . ."

"Stop," Denard interrupted.

"Stop, Star Colonel?" the man asked in shock. The order went against all his training. "Certainly the DropShip contains valuable information," he offered.

Denard rolled his eyes and looked at Thrace, who stood

alone in the corner of the room. She shrugged and Denard turned back to face the man.

"Of course it contains information. I want you to stop investigating the crash and start repairing the DropShip."

The man's face drained of all its color. "But, Star Colonel, damage to the ship was extensive."

Denard jabbed a finger toward the man, but choked back a hasty reply. Clenching his outstretched hand into a fist, he returned it to his side. "Of course. But the DropShip is a vital part in my plans. It must be ready to fly again and soon. I am understood, *quiaff*?" Denard glared at the man, daring him to reply.

"Aff, Star Colonel," he said in resignation.

Denard smiled. "Now was that so hard?" He looked over at Thrace, who remained impassive. "How many days until she is back in the sky?"

The warrior consulted the clipboard. "As I have stated, damage was extensive." He paused for several minutes, studying the clipboard intently. "Three weeks, Star Colonel. The ship could be ready in just over twenty days." He looked up and smiled, but his face fell when Denard sadly shook his head.

"You have five days."

The man's jaw dropped. "But . . . ," he stammered. Denard held up a single finger, and the man fell silent.

"Five days. If necessary, pull technicians off the BattleMech repairs." The man's eyes grew wide at the authorization, as did Thrace's, but Denard did not miss a beat. "Furthermore, treat the crew with respect. See to their comfort. They will be needed to provide access to the security files of the ship."

"Even the MechWarrior?" asked Thrace. Denard turned in surprise.

"A MechWarrior?" he asked. "Did I miss something?"

Thrace shrugged. "We captured a female MechWarrior following the first battle. We have been holding her with the other raiders until we determined what to do with her." Thrace shrugged again.

"Move her in with the others for the time being," Denard

said. "I will decide what to do about her later. Did she fight well?" he asked as if by afterthought.

Thrace nodded. "Well enough. She was overwhelmed by sheer numbers. Her comrades tried to fight their way back to her, but they could not. She is in the hospital with a concussion."

Denard looked over at the other man in the room. "You are still here?" he asked in mock amazement. "I would have thought you had too much to do to stand idly by while your commander discusses that which does not concern you. Perhaps you need further instruction?"

"Neg, Star Colonel." With eyes firmly on the floor, the man hustled out the door, leaving only Denard and Thrace in the room. The woman crossed the floor at a leisurely pace and stood before Denard.

"So, Star Colonel, what is your game?" she asked.

Denard feigned surprise. "Me? Surely you do not mean your cluster commander. Hero of his Clan." Thrace smiled with him, but the bitterness of his last words killed the smile. As she suspected, he hated his command. She watched him for a moment, but he remained silent. Finally, he laughed, a hollow, bitter sound.

"Have you ever had a dream, Thrace?" He ran a hand through his hair and began pacing. Thrace knew the question was rhetorical, so she made no reply. "A dream that kept you awake at night? A dream that filled you with passion and gave you the strength to go on when all hope seemed lost?"

"Aff," she mouthed silently, but her commander missed the reply. He stood and stared at a computer screen.

"I have had such a dream," he said, looking at her across the room.

"What was it?" she asked. Denard looked down at his hands. Already they were starting to bruise from the pounding they had given the protective case of the holographic projector.

"I dreamed I would be the best warrior ever to live."

She almost laughed, but caught herself just in time. Such a dream was shared by every Elemental in the sibko. Only the ones who held on to that dream survived the training and went on to see actual combat. It had to be an Elemental's one burning desire. Looking at her commander, Thrace saw that dream burning more fiercely than in any other warrior she had ever known.

"What happened?" she asked quietly.

Denard sighed and his massive shoulders slumped. Again he laughed, this time with a hint of mirth. He turned and looked her in the eye.

"I achieved it, Thrace," he whispered.

"On Tukayyid?"

"On Tukayyid," he said. "For one week I was the best the Clans had. I was one man against the storm. I fought and killed and I destroyed and I reveled in the power." His hand curled into a fist for the fourth time, but as Thrace watched, the hand slowly opened again. She knew he was slowly mastering his emotions. He slapped his thighs and looked around the room. "And this is what I get. Cluster commander of a second-rate garrison unit that cannot even defeat a gang of Inner Sphere raiders in an uneven fight."

Thrace remained quiet as her commander's words echoed through the empty room. What he had said was true. He was the finest fighter she had ever seen. Perhaps he was the greatest warrior the Nova Cats had ever produced. And surely that was the Clan's great aim. Carefully controlled breeding programs assured that the best warriors would live again in their offspring. If an individual warrior achieved greatness, he or she could be assured of living forever in future generations. The *giftake,* where the gene sample of the warrior was taken for use in future offspring, was one of the Clan's most sacred rituals.

Thrace looked Denard in the eye, trying to see a spark within. Anything to indicate that the man she had fought alongside on Tukayyid was still alive in the bitter shell before her. As she watched, Denard smiled. She found herself smiling too, but without finding the spark she sought.

"You have a plan," she said. It was not a question. There was no doubt Denard had a plan to reacquire some of what he had lost.

"I have a plan," he agreed, "but it all depends on that savashri DropShip." He almost snarled the words, but managed to hold his emotions in check.

"You plan to leave Courcheval," she stated. Denard looked at her as though he had been run through. To her the plan was so obvious she wanted to laugh, but bitterness ate at her and she remained solemn.

"Not just leave," he finally stammered. "Leave with a flair."

"Aboard a stolen Inner Sphere DropShip," she said. "That should really impress the Khans." Denard looked at his aide, eyes wide. In the several years he had known her, she had never spoken to him in this manner. Nor would she have ever allowed anyone to speak to him in such a way. He knew he should be furious, but the only emotion he felt was confusion.

"Listen to the plan, Thrace, before you pass judgment."

"I have passed no judgment, Star Colonel. I merely state what is obvious to me."

"Then just listen. We use the Inner Sphere DropShip to return to their waiting JumpShip. We both know it has to be hiding out there somewhere. Inner Sphere pilots are not fond of either glorious death or suicide missions, so they must have a JumpShip in waiting. Once we have docked, we seize the JumpShip and return to Wolcott." Denard held up a hand to stall protests. "I know what you are thinking, but hear me out.

"We release the DropShip at Wolcott and await the next incoming vessel. We already know that the Kuritas pick up and deliver during the same run. The Elementals remain on the JumpShip and take over the approaching DropShip. The JumpShip course is already laid to either Pesht or to Luthien. We arrive at our final destination and attack the Kuritas in their own homes."

Thrace examined the plan dispassionately. She assumed Denard was no fool, which answered several questions, but more remained. "Who is on the first DropShip?" she asked.

"Two BattleMech stars from the Forty-sixth Nova Cat

Cavaliers. We are forbidden to assault Wolcott, but raiding is certainly acceptable."

"Any Cavaliers selected would die," she responded.

"Of course, but they would not die immediately. Certainly there are ten warriors among the Cavaliers willing to face the challenge of such a raid. Given the information on the JumpShip, we might even be able to arrange a pickup."

Thrace doubted that, but she also knew there would be no lack of volunteers among the MechWarriors of the Forty-sixth for such a raid.

"After we get to Luthien, how do we return to Clan space?" she asked. Denard's eyes went wide and he laughed, the first genuine laughter she had heard from him since he had assumed command of the garrison cluster.

"We will arrive in Luthien like hunting cats among the flock. If we jump to Luthien, we destroy their space station and flee. If it is Pesht, we take what fortune provides." His smile was firmly in place, but Thrace doubted the joy reached below the surface.

"Surely," he continued, "capturing a JumpShip would represent no significant challenge to the Elementals selected to accompany us." Thrace nodded. He naturally assumed she would accompany him on the mission, and Thrace knew he was right.

"Then why?" she asked finally. Denard's smile fell away. Back was the shell of the man she had come to know over the last year.

"To prove I can still do it? Maybe," he mused. "Actually, it is because I want my offspring to be part of the retaking of Terra. I want them to succeed where we have failed."

Thrace scowled. "You have your bloodname. You are a Star Colonel. You have already participated in the *giftake*," she countered passionately.

"Aff, Star Captain, but when? Unless I prove my ability one more time, my offspring will not be born for one hundred years, if that soon." He thumped his chest. "My son or daughter will surpass me in ways I cannot even begin to imagine."

Thrace nodded. In addressing her by rank, Denard had put

an end to the conversation. They were no longer talking as one soldier to another. The discussion had moved to commander and aide. She looked at him one last time, piercing his soul with a stare as direct as she could muster. Still there was no spark in the man's eyes.

She turned to leave the room, knowing full well that Denard did not plan to return to Courcheval. His gene sample was securely stored away on a nameless shelf in a nameless lab on their homeworld. All that remained for Denard was to find a way to die as gloriously as possible. Not me, Thrace silently vowed. If there is some way for me to survive this raid, I will find it.

25

Courcheval
Nova Cat Occupation Zone
29 July 3057

Rose followed immediately after the two hovercraft, which he now recognized as Savannah Masters, down an unseen side trail. Moving in silence behind him was the rest of the Black Thorn line, each warrior mourning the loss of Badicus O'Shea in his own way. Rose went through the standard piloting functions by reflex, giving them no more thought than he gave his feet when walking down the street. The other members of the Black Thorns would spot trouble long before the *Masakari*'s scanners picked it up.

Night was falling and the hovercraft finally began using aviator lights to see the way. The standard headlights of each vehicle had been darkened to mere slits, allowing the pilot to see the terrain before him without giving away his position to reconnaissance aircraft. The 'Mechs simply switched to low-light scanners, which made the ground jump out in vivid green detail. The system worked well when moving slowly over nearly any terrain, but it failed miserably when used at any type of speed. As many of the Black Thorns already knew, low-light destroyed depth perception.

It was fully dark when the two hovercraft stopped before an undercut in the hillside. To Rose it looked as if a giant machine had gouged out a portion of the hill and carried it away. He was to learn later that that was exactly what had happened. As he watched, a man stepped out from the underbrush and moved toward the vehicles. Rose could see him exchange signs with the hovercraft pilot, then step back.

As the hovercraft moved forward, Rose followed. Nearing the undercut, he saw that it was actually a large entranceway cut into the side of the hill. The hill itself would completely obscure the doorway from the air, and even on the ground, someone° could easily miss the entrance because of the concealment provided by the surrounding foliage.

First one, then the other hovercraft disappeared from view. Rose went in next, crouching low as he walked the *Masakari* through the entryway and down a sloped tunnel. One hundred 'Mech steps later the tunnel leveled out and elbowed to the right, opening into a large cavern. The lights of the cavern cast a faint glow, making low-light unnecessary so Rose switched back to standard vision. He rounded the corner and stopped in awe of what he saw.

The cavern was twice as tall as the *Masakari* and nearly as large as the Black Thorns' compound warehouse back on Wolcott. Halogen lights had been placed near the rooftop, fully illuminating the entire chamber, which contained several vehicles and a host of people scurrying around them. There were no 'Mechs in the cavern, but Rose saw a Harasser missile platform, a brace of Scorpion light tanks, and a single Hetzer assault gun. There were other vehicles here as well, but Rose couldn't determine their parentage, let alone their purpose, because they seemed to have been patched together from so many different parts. Except for one or two civilian vehicles, the rest were all obviously war machines.

As the Savannah Masters slid into adjacent stalls, a flagman motioned Rose to follow him. Rose moved down the cavern, creating a sensation as the technicians and pilots all stopped their work to gape and gasp at the huge OmniMech. The succeeding Black Thorns were similarly guided, and soon the entire company was berthed in work stalls. Rose began the shutdown process on the *Masakari,* locking all systems down for exit. Then he set his neurohelmet on the shelf above the command couch and stood up to unlock the exit hatch at the top of the *Masakari*'s head. By the time he climbed down the retractable ladder to the ground below, a small crowd had gathered at the 'Mech's feet. Rose descended silently into their midst.

The braver of the technicians held their ground as Rose stared at them. Others shrank away and returned to their duties until the crowd became less than half the original size. Rose greeted each tech brave or curious enough to remain, but most only mumbled a greeting and continued to inspect the *Masakari*. Several of the Black Thorns joined him, all obviously bursting with questions that they were holding until their guide rejoined them.

As Rose watched her approach, he could tell that she was a ranking member of the Courcheval resistance movement, if not the leader. Not only did the others defer to her, but she carried herself with a confidence few of the others could match. Her wingman walked alongside her. The two could not have made an odder pair. She was short and walked with almost too much intensity. Her arms swung in wide arcs as she moved and her hips swayed in counterpoint. Rose knew most men would find her attractive, maybe even beautiful, but he didn't share that opinion. His tastes ran toward taller, leaner women.

Her wingman ambled alongside her, easily keeping pace with her short stride by moving with a deceptive shuffle that ate up the distance. He was rail thin, with stooped shoulders and an unruly crop of thick black hair. If she was fire, he was water. His hands were shoved into the pockets of a long coat, a posture that initially made Rose nervous. He hated not being able to see another person's hands. Several other Black Thorns must have had the same reaction, for Rose noticed some members of the company subtly adjusting their stance and dropping their hands toward their weapon belts.

The woman walked up to Rose and extended a hand. "Welcome to the underground," she said with a smile. "My name is *Sho-sa* Elaina Cantrell." Rose took the offered hand and swallowed the small appendage in his own. Despite the difference in the sizes of their hands, her grip was as firm as his.

"Captain Jeremiah Rose, commander of the mercenary company the Black Thorns." Rose surveyed the cavern, obviously impressed. "Quite a place you have here, *Sho-sa*."

She responded with a lopsided smile. "Not mine actually. I just look after some of the military assets. The actual resistance is headed by one of . . ." She stopped and brought the other side of her face up in a smile. "Well, I should probably let them introduce themselves." She turned to one of the technicians at the foot of the *Masakari*. "Can you fix it?"

The man shrugged. *"Shirimasen."*

"Round up the others and give me an estimate," she said to the man's back as he examined the damage to the *Masakari*'s shin. The man nodded silently and continued his inspection. Cantrell tapped Rose on the sleeve and motioned to a side tunnel.

"Leave them to their job," she said. "They're some of the best technicians I've ever seen, despite the primitive equipment. They'll give us an estimate when they've looked the 'Mechs over." Rose nodded and followed Cantrell as she cut across the busy cavern floor. The rest of the Black Thorns followed them in a clump, looking more like a sight-seeing group on a tour than a group of warriors. Rose would have laughed, but the situation was too unusual.

"Excuse me, *Sho-sa* Cantrell," he said as they entered the side tunnel, "but you seem to be accepting us pretty much on faith at this point. If you really are resistance fighters, which means you're against the Clans, shouldn't security be a little tighter?"

Cantrell continued to smile. "Well," she began, "you're not exactly new to us. We've been requesting assistance for quite some time now and . . ." Once more she paused. "Sorry, but I'd better not tell you that.

"In any event," she said while walking, "we spotted your ship the moment it entered the atmosphere. We figured you were heading to the industrial centers north of here, but when the ship was attacked, you all sorta got chuckled out." She smiled at a private joke but didn't interrupt her train of thought. "We lost you in the drop, but Dusty and I have been scouring the hills for you ever since.

"Right, Dustin?" she asked of her sidekick. The man simply looked at Rose and nodded.

"Dustin doesn't talk much," Cantrell offered as an explanation.

"Why were you looking for us?" Bell asked from his position behind Rose.

Cantrell cocked her head at the question. "Well, you're the third company-sized raiding force to hit this planet in the last two years. That's not too remarkable. The remarkable part is that you're the first ones to land near our base and you're the first ones to lose their DropShip."

Rose stopped and reached for the woman's arm. Cantrell winced with sudden understanding. "Sorry. You didn't know about the ship, did you?" His shocked look told her the truth, but Rose shook his head anyway.

"Tough break," she said. "Sorry you had to get the news so abruptly, but your ship went down a couple of hundred kilometers from here. Since then it's been crawling with Clan technicians."

Rose didn't like the sound of that, but his brain was still stumbling over the loss of the DropShip. Were they really trapped on the planet, as Cantrell suggested? The ramifications of their current situation hit him like a physical blow. Things were even worse than he thought.

Cantrell led the Black Thorns into a side room off the passage they had been following. Inside the room were several tables and a series of bunks bolted into the cavern wall. As the ceiling was lower in the tunnels and side chambers, the high-intensity halogen lights had been replaced with standard florescent bulbs. Cantrell looked around the room.

"You can stay here for the time being. The previous users of this room don't need it anymore." She paused for a moment, and Rose knew exactly what she meant. "We don't have running water, but there are several underground wells nearby. I'll have one of the techs bring you some buckets and show you to the well. I suspect you'd like to get cleaned up.

"A couple of things before I leave, though. First, always carry a flashlight when you travel. The power is fairly dependable, but even a short-term blackout can leave you with a case of the screaming meemies if you're caught all alone. Second, always carry your sidearm. I see most of you already take that to heart, but in case you think it's even remotely safe here, think again."

Cantrell turned to go, but Rose stopped her with a gentle hand on her arm. "*Sho-sa,* a moment please. This is all happening rather quickly, and there are a few questions I'd like answered, if you please."

Cantrell looked at her chronometer and glanced at Dustin, who shook his head. "All right," she said, "but make it quick."

"First of all, we never heard a thing about an organized resistance to the Clans here on Courcheval. Do the Kuritas know you're here?"

Cantrell snorted and gave Rose a strange look. "I hope so. We communicate with them three or four times per year. Mostly it's through pirates running the border, but occasionally we'll get word from a military vessel." Cantrell shook her head, stopping Rose's next question. "The particulars of any contact like that are on a need-to-know basis, and, well, I'm sure you understand."

Rose nodded. "This place seems like a fairly large operation. How have you managed to keep the base a secret?"

Cantrell scratched her head and pondered the question for a moment. "Well, I guess you'd have to put some of it down to luck. In truth, we're really not that big. There are only a few hundred of us at the base at any one time. Mostly we're infantry, which means we rarely get involved in direct shooting matches with the Clans. We pop up, hit a base, and drift away."

"What about all the vehicles? Don't they see action?" asked Hawg.

Cantrell shook her head. "Not very much. We use the two hovers quite a bit, but that's about all. They're fast and maneuverable, which gives them an edge. The rest of the gear is too old and slow to be of much use. We keep it around, but I suspect it's more for reassurance than because anybody thinks it will do any real damage."

"So you're guerrillas," observed Bell.

Cantrell turned toward Bell and nodded. "Close, but we're very selective. We were a little less so about our targets in the early days, and the Cats took it out on the populace. Now we only hit military targets. It's more like commando tactics than guerrilla tactics. In truth we're not even commandos. We're more like a recon force. We provide intelligence reports about the Clans and strike an occasional target, but we're not equipped to do much else, if that makes any sense."

Not really, thought Rose, but he held his tongue. The resistance movement obviously knew what was going on, which was all that mattered. "How did you know we were coming?" he asked.

Cantrell checked her chronometer again. "We didn't. We requested a strike on the factories to the north over six months ago. The Cats have them almost ready for production, and we thought a surgical strike could set them back maybe a year or even more. Seemed like a good idea, but the factory was too heavily guarded for us to take on ourselves.

"Unfortunately, the factory garrison was beefed up with a trinary from the Nova Cat Cavaliers, a frontline OmniMech unit. If you'd landed anywhere near the factories, the Cavaliers would have pounded you into snail snot." She laughed lightly. "No offense," she added.

"None taken," responded Rose automatically.

"Well, I've got to report in. Somebody will be back to show you around. Your 'Mechs will be repaired as best we can manage." Cantrell smiled at Rose, a gesture of sincere friendship. "After all, we're in this together, right?" Rose nodded, but his mind was engaged in trying to figure out the next move.

"One more thing," said Ria. "Where are we?"

"This is the Silverton and Sons mines. We're currently standing in one of the old crew quarters. Right outside is primary tunnel number forty-seven, which leads to the active mines several levels below. The entire complex is a maze of tunnels and shafts."

"I'd have thought this would be one of the first places the Cats would look for any resistance operation," remarked Esmeralda.

"It was," smiled Cantrell, "but the Tabbies were too efficient. Back then we were too unorganized to have an operation like this. We only moved into the mines fourteen months ago."

"And they haven't been back to check the place out?" asked Bell.

Cantrell shook her head. "S and S closed down five years ago when the entire complex was declared unstable. I guess the facility sits on some type of geological fault. The planetary government declared the mines unsafe and forced the closure of all operations. When the Tabbies checked it out, the place was still abandoned."

"So this whole place could collapse at any moment?" asked Bell somewhat nervously.

Dustin laughed, the first sound he'd made since meeting the Black Thorns. "How long you want to live anyway?" he asked through crooked teeth. Bell grinned back, but clearly was not comforted by the response. Cantrell punched Bell in the shoulder and flashed a thumbs-up. Bell returned the salute half-heartedly as the pair left the quarters.

"I think I'm really going to hate this place," said Bell as he looked around the room. Several of the Black Thorns nodded agreement.

Rose ignored the comment. "We've got to start making some plans. Let's get settled in; we might be here a while. Take *Sho-sa* Cantrell's words to heart. In addition, pair up. Nobody leaves this room alone, got it?" He looked at the assembled company to make sure everyone understood the importance of the order.

"We've got another problem," offered Myoto from the back of the pack.

"You're telling me," mumbled Bell with a quick look at the ceiling.

"I mean the DropShip," she continued. "If what *Sho-sa* Cantrell says is true, the Nova Cats have access to the computers of the *Tracy K.*"

"And?" asked Riannon with a puzzled look.

"That means they have access to the control codes and mission files," said Rose.

Myoto nodded gravely. "It is not impossible that the Nova Cats could link with the JumpShip and return to Wolcott aboard the *Tracy K*."

"A Trojan horse," said Esmeralda.

Myoto frowned for a moment, then nodded. "If they managed to take over the JumpShip, they could travel not only to Wolcott, but to the JumpShip's next destination."

"Luthien," said Riannon. Myoto closed her eyes and nodded.

"This suddenly becomes bigger than us getting stuck on Courcheval," observed Esmeralda. "It sounds like we've just given the Nova cats the keys to Luthien's front door."

"As I said, it is not impossible," replied Myoto.

"They could also cut off Wolcott from its supply lines," said Yuri. The other Black Thorns looked at the young man. He shrugged. "Just an observation," he added self-consciously.

"You're all right," said Rose. "We've got a problem that requires immediate attention, but we're not in any condition to do anything about that now. Fall out and get some rest; that's an order. Ria, you and I will make the announcement to the resistance leaders. Everybody stick close to this room. When we know more, I'll want everybody involved in the planning."

"One more thing, Captain," said Kitten. "I'd like to have a brief service for Badicus and Greta." She looked down and swirled the dirt on the floor with the point of her boot. "Nothing fancy. Just a few words to remember them." She wiped a tear from the corner of her eye.

"Of course," said Rose. He checked his chronometer. "Service will be one hour after Ria and I return." Rose could almost see the blanket of misery fall over the company at the thought of their losses. It had been the same way when Angus died on Borghese. A small unit like the Black Thorns always felt the loss of a member more acutely than did a bigger, more impersonal unit. It would take time to heal the emotional wounds.

"Now fall out," he said, knowing it was all that was left to say. "You all look like you could use some rest."

26

Courcheval
Nova Cat Occupation Zone
30 July 3057

Star Colonel Denard walked down the guard-lined hall at a brisk pace, Thrace following in his wake. As expected, the Elementals at the end of the hall snapped to attention as Denard reached for the double doors that stood between them. Throwing the doors wide, he walked into the room with scarcely a halt in stride. Following behind him, Thrace turned and closed the doors, shutting out the others.

Denard walked down the short hall to the suite's main room, pausing in the entrance archway to survey the scene before him. Scattered about the room were several overstuffed chairs and couches, most of them within easy reach of a table holding a computer terminal. To the left and right Denard could see the closed doors that led to the suite's adjoining bedrooms. Directly across from the doorway was a huge picture window offering a view of the plains beyond the compound. From the room's location four stories above the ground, the view was spectacular.

Inside were only three people. Two were staring silently at computer terminals while the third looked out the large window. Denard did not doubt that the men had heard him enter, but none of the room's occupants bothered to look up. Denard smiled. The three captives were trying to show that they had retained at least a shred of their dignity, but by allowing themselves to be captured, the trio had forever lost their claim to it in the eyes of Denard and the rest of the Nova Cats.

"Captain Danes," Denard said, "at last we meet. I am Star Colonel Denard Devereaux." The Star Colonel crossed the room in several huge strides, barely giving Danes time to turn from the window before extending his hand. The custom of hand-shaking had no place in Clan society, but Denard's advisors had assured him that offering his right hand in greeting would put Danes at ease. They had forgotten to tell Denard that the DropShip captain's right hand was encased in a cast and supported by a sling. Denard withdrew his hand and looked out the window. Heads were going to roll after this meeting, but right now he had to recapture the initiative.

"A beautiful view, *quiaff*?" he finally offered.

"Yes," agreed Danes, "it certainly is a beautiful view."

Denard towered over the DropShip captain, but if the smaller man noticed, he didn't show it. "I trust you find your accommodations suitable," he said. Danes nodded but did not speak. Behind him Denard heard the other two crew members stand up and leave the room. Thrace remained on the other side of the room but well within earshot of their conversation.

"I must say," said Danes, "that I find our treatment something of a mystery. Tell me, are all prisoners treated so grandly?" Danes indicated the suite with a wave of his good hand.

Denard grinned and rubbed his chin. "Honestly? No, you and your remaining crew have been singled out for this rather special honor because of your unique status." Danes had assumed as much. He had something the Nova Cats wanted, and he was being treated with respect while they determined the best way to get it. He had no doubt about what would happen to him and the surviving crew once the Cats got what they wanted. Slavery, or worse.

"Tell me, is MechWarrior Podell recovering?" Denard's question caught Danes off guard, as he imagined it was supposed to.

The DropShip captain nodded and smiled slightly. "Your skill in medicine has helped her speedy recovery. She was up for awhile earlier this morning. I suspect she will make a full recovery."

"That is indeed excellent news. A warrior is an asset that should never be taken lightly."

"Tell me, Star Colonel," said Danes, "to what do I owe the honor of your visit? Your doctors have informed me that you are an important man on this planet. Surely you have more important things to do than talk with a lowly DropShip captain."

Nothing is more important than our conversation, thought Denard. He clasped his hands behind his back and turned toward the room. "Perhaps we could make ourselves more comfortable, *quiaff*?" He indicated a pair of chairs, and Danes chose the one nearest the window. Although that put Denard's back to the hallway and door beyond, he did not think there was anything to worry about with Thrace standing guard. He walked to the remaining chair and sat down opposite Danes.

Denard casually studied the DropShip captain as Danes struggled to find a comfortable position. From reading the reports of the DropShip's crash, Denard knew Danes was in considerable physical and emotional pain. He planned to use that pain to his own advantage, inflicting more if necessary.

The crash of the DropShip had killed most of the crew. The only survivors were Danes, the navigator, and the cargomaster. The bridge had been almost completely destroyed, causing the greatest number of casualties. Danes had apparently been thrown from his command chair into the navigation console. The fall must have broken his arm, but that was not listed in the report Denard had seen. Doubtless there were other injuries as well.

As it turned out, the navigation console was the only station that survived the crash. The rest of the bridge was reduced to debris when one of the support beams broke loose and collapsed. The pilot was killed by the falling beam, and the rest of the crew was killed by the collapse of the ceiling. It was a miracle a fire didn't break out from the extensive damage to the electronic systems, but the DropShip had been spared the subsequent fires so common in "high-risk landings." The cargomaster must have survived on dumb luck.

Danes finally stopped struggling in the chair. He had either found the position he was looking for or else had abandoned the effort. As Denard continued to watch him, he noticed the lack of color in the captain's face. He wondered if that was natural or an indication of his current physical condition.

"You did well to land your ship in one piece," Denard offered. Danes scoffed and looked around the room. He was obviously uncomfortable with the praise.

"I mean it," continued Denard. "I know of no other captain who could have done better. Considering the damage your ship suffered at the hands of the Nova Cat Cavaliers, I am amazed the ship survived."

Danes stared at Denard, content to let the giant man lead the conversation. He was sure he knew where the talk was going, but there wasn't much he could do about it. After regaining consciousness aboard the battered bridge of the *Tracy K*, he had tried to set the self-destruct mechanism, but the extensive damage had prevented the system from operating. With enough time, he could have destroyed the computer core, but he'd been barely able to move immediately following the crash. Danes had been captured by Clan Elementals less than five meters from where he'd awakened.

"You understand why I am here, *quiaff*?" Denard said at last.

"I understand," said Danes.

"The correct response is aff or neg, as appropriate. Do you understand?" Danes glared at Denard, but eventually nodded his head. "Good. Proper grammar is one of the cornerstones of good communication." Denard's eyes narrowed to slits, giving him a menacing appearance despite his body's relaxed posture. "I would hate to have a misunderstanding destroy a carefully constructed situation."

Suddenly the glare was gone and Denard almost smiled, a gesture Danes did not return. "You were not able to destroy your ship. Neither were you able to wipe clean the computer's memory. These are simple facts." Denard stopped and steepled his fingers in front of his face, index fingers lightly touching his lips. "Had you been able, you would have done both of those things, *quiaff*?"

"Aff," Danes responded in a whisper.

Denard nodded approval. "Good. I would expect no less from a committed warrior, especially a captain. However, you were unable to do so, and now I am presented with a rare opportunity." He smiled like the cat of his Clan's name.

"You know I have the precise coordinates of your waiting JumpShip, *quiaff*?"

"Aff," Danes responded. "At least, I know you will soon have those coordinates. It would be difficult to make use of that information, however."

Denard glanced over at the impassive Thrace and raised an eyebrow. I told you so, he seemed to say, but Thrace and Danes both ignored the look.

"Neg, Captain. I can make very good use of that information. That is where you come in." Danes shifted uncomfortably in his chair. Denard's feral smile spread.

"Many of your critical files are coded, *quiaff*?"

"Aff," Danes responded with a smile.

"And if my technicians are correct, those files are rigged to wipe themselves clean if not provided the proper passcode upon access, *quiaff*?"

"Aff."

Denard pursed his lips and nodded. He had suspected no less from a military vessel. The DropShip's computer contained too much information to be left to possible capture. His technicians had already removed enough explosives to destroy the hardware six times over. Now all that remained were the locks on the software.

"I will have your DropShip, and I will use it to seize the waiting JumpShip. There is nothing you can do about that. All that remains is the exact path to success." Denard leaned forward in his chair, elbows on his knees.

"You can either give me the information I need to access your coded files, or I will rip it from your mind. And do not deceive yourself. Our scientist caste has developed drugs that can dredge up information from your brain that you didn't even know existed." Denard leaned back in the chair. "Of course, the mind is all but destroyed by the process. You would live out your remaining days as a gibbering idiot."

"But you could not be sure of your information," countered Danes.

"The drug has a seventy-six percent success rate historically. Three out of four is good enough for me," Denard replied.

"I could agree, then give you the wrong code," taunted Danes. "The information would be lost—and nothing you could do about it."

Denard nodded and leaned forward. "Nothing except exact my revenge. First upon the MechWarrior, then your crew members, then the civilians of Courcheval. Rest assured, you would continue to be treated as a respected guest, but they would suffer tremendously because of you."

Danes wanted to deny the truth of Denard's words, but the man's cold look left no room for doubt. Danes knew that the Clansman was completely capable of committing the atrocities he alluded to without the least remorse. He might even enjoy it, Danes realized with a shiver.

"And if I agree to provide the access codes, what happens then?"

Denard looked at Thrace. No matter what Danes said now, both Elementals knew the DropShip captain would cooperate fully. Neither one had doubted that Denard would eventually be able to sway the DropShip captain, but the man had caved in much quicker than anticipated. Thrace was halfway convinced that she was along merely to rough up the crew members for Danes' benefit. Although she would have done so without a second thought, the warrior in her blanched at the prospect of assaulting anyone who could not fight back.

"We take you and the surviving crew members along with us," said Denard. "That way we have you as well as the codes. You might even be able to help us out once we're underway.

"Once we get to our destination, we drop you and your crew in the middle of nowhere and let you go." Denard spread his hands. "You go your way and I'll go mine."

"So in return for the freedom of me and my crew, I hand you my DropShip and the Combine JumpShip?"

Denard pondered the question. "Aff. That is essentially our arrangement," he allowed.

Danes shifted in the chair and considered his rather limited options. He had already resigned himself to life as a bondsman. When the Elementals had first captured him, he'd had no doubts about his fate. The thought of a life of slavery had been frightening, but he would gladly accept that over the label of traitor.

The Elemental's determination to capture the JumpShip cast a whole new light on the situation, however. The Clansman seemed fully willing to do whatever was necessary to achieve it. Danes knew he was just a tool to be used and tossed aside. If he accepted the offer, there was a chance he could make something happen, but he honestly had no idea what that could be. If he refused, other people were going to suffer.

"Can I think it over?" he asked finally.

Denard nodded solemnly. "Of course, Captain. I will return here tomorrow and we can discuss the situation. I'm sure the technicians working on your ship can find plenty to do until then." Denard stood and Danes tried to follow, but the Elemental stopped him with a firm hand.

"No need to exert yourself, Captain. I can see myself out." Denard turned without a second look at the DropShip captain, flashing a sly smile at Thrace as he walked past. Thrace remained impassive as Denard walked out. With a nod to Captain Danes, she turned and followed her commander out of the room. Denard's plan seemed to be going perfectly, she thought to herself. If his evening meeting with Star Colonel Bondan of the Cavaliers went as well, how could his plan fail?

27

Courcheval
Nova Cat Occupation Zone
30 July 3057

The meeting with the leaders of the resistance movement was every bit as discouraging as Rose feared it would be. As he suspected, they were more concerned with keeping their location hidden and their forces safe than they were in stopping the Nova Cats from using the captured DropShip. Only *Sho-sa* Cantrell was willing to argue for Rose's cause, and she was overruled by the political leaders who made up the council. They all agreed that the capture of the *Tracy K* represented a serious threat to the Combine, but because it did not directly affect Courcheval, they were unwilling to stick their necks out too far. It was the typical kind of short-sighted thinking that Rose had encountered among politicians all his life.

He managed to keep his temper with help from his sister, who offered a few carefully chosen words on the side. In the end all Rose was able to win was the guerrillas' agreement to repair the Black Thorn 'Mechs to the extent possible and then let the Thorns go on their way. Even that was a major concession from the resistance leadership, Riannon pointed out, considering that the Black Thorns now knew the location of their headquarters. If one of the Black Thorn pilots were ever captured by the Nova Cats, the entire resistance would be in jeopardy. Rose was not inclined to agree with his sister's optimistic attitude, but he did allow that the repair of the Battle Mechs was a significant concession. Although few of the surviving 'Mechs had suffered internals, nearly every Black Thorn 'Mech had some armor damage.

Back in their temporary quarters, Rose led the company in a short service to honor the memory of O'Shea and Podell. Although he had known O'Shea well, Rose stumbled when it came to talking about Greta Podell, whose acquaintance had been so brief. Kitten jumped in, however, and told the other Thorns what she knew about her. Rose was initially surprised at the depth of emotion Kitten expressed, but by the end of her short eulogy, Rose realized that the two had shared a deep kinship.

The next two days passed quietly for the Thorns. Rose reflected on the company's options while Esmeralda and Hawg led work teams in repairing the BattleMechs. *Sho-sa* Cantrell spent a lot of time with the Black Thorns providing them with additional information on the situation on Courcheval and on the Nova Cats in general.

The Black Thorns learned the local names for the unknown BattleMechs they had fought earlier. Many of the second-line Clan 'Mechs were simply refitted versions of standard Inner Sphere models and, therefore, bore the same name. The *Rifleman* look-alike was called the *Galahad*. The giant 'Mech Rose and Bell had fought was a *Behemoth*. To Rose's dismay he discovered that the garrison cluster had no less than three of the giants, maybe more. Even though the 'Mechs were considered only second-class, Rose had learned a healthy respect for the monsters.

By the end of the second day Rose had come to the inescapable conclusion that the Black Thorns would have to either capture or destroy the *Tracy K*. All that remained was to discover a method for accomplishing this feat. Myoto had assumed that fact from the start, but it was only after lengthy consideration that Rose and rest of the Black Thorns became convinced. Resistance scouts had managed to sneak close to the campsite that had sprung up around the downed DropShip, and they returned with additional information for Rose to consider. Cantrell offered some insight as well. On the evening of the Black Thorns' second day in the caverns, she arrived with unexpected news.

"Take a look at these," she said, dropping a stack of holopics on the table in front of Rose and Riannon.

"That's Danes!" exclaimed Ria, glancing quickly at the top picture. Rose confirmed it. The image clearly showed Danes being led into a DropShip. It didn't take much imagination to figure out where he had been taken.

"Is he still there?" asked Rose as he picked up the stack. Cantrell shook her head. "No," she said. "He stayed around for about an hour and then was escorted off the ship." Rose nodded absently as he scanned the holos. He'd seen enough of the type over his career to recognize several things about the photos.

They had obviously been taken with a high-powered zoom lens. That made sense, given the security around the DropShip site and the surrounding terrain. The photos had been taken with a military-grade lens designed for just such a purpose. The quality was very good, but the depth of field was typically bad. The pictures showed Danes in a series of poses, the result of a high-speed film advance.

"Your scouts do good work," said Rose as he passed the photos to Riannon. Cantrell beamed.

"Trained them myself." She smiled wider. "Of course, they've got a thing or two to learn, but they manage."

"How did Danes get to the crash site?" Rose asked.

"VTOL. The Cats have set up a small landing pad to the north of the crash site. You probably know that the Clans don't use vehicles in combat roles, but they do have several different support vehicles at their base."

"He doesn't appear to be in such good shape," observed Ria.

"Neither is his ship, but both are getting fixed, thanks to Clan Nova Cat," replied Cantrell. She paused and waited for Rose to finish staring at the pictures. "Is there a chance he'd work for the Cats?"

Rose nodded. "I doubt he'd do so for personal gain, but if they had something over him, he'd probably do whatever they asked—especially if they were holding his crew." Rose and Cantrell shared a knowing look. As commanders, both of them placed the safety of their men before their own personal interests. It was one of the attributes of a good commander. It was also a problem, especially now.

"That doesn't sound good," Cantrell finally offered. Rose agreed. Myoto's notion that the Clans might use the *Tracy K* against the Draconis Combine was scary enough, but to have Danes actually working for the Nova Cats would really complicate matters.

"Any idea where he's being held?" asked Ria as she continued to scan the pictures.

"I can't say for sure, but I'd imagine he's at the garrison base. There are quite a few buildings there, however, so I don't think that info will do you much good."

"Who's that?" asked Ria pointing to a woman who was in every picture of Danes. Cantrell frowned at the top picture, then thumbed through the stack looking for one that gave her a better view. She finally found what she was looking for.

"Star Captain Thrace. She's the garrison commander's right-hand man. Pardon the gender reference."

"Big woman," commented Rose.

"Epic is more like it," corrected his sister. "She's huge and I'm not talking just height. I mean, she makes Hawg look like a pipsqueak."

"Somebody mention me?" asked Hawg as he entered the room. Ria blushed.

"Just by reference," said Rose. Hawg walked up to the table and looked at the pictures over Ria's shoulders. Ria pointed to Thrace, and Hawg whistled.

"Now that is a whole lot of woman," his said with a slowly spreading smile.

"She probably outweighs you by forty pounds and she looks every bit as strong," commented Rose. Hawg just laughed.

"More to appreciate, Captain." Hawg turned to Cantrell. "What's she like?"

"Well, I don't have to tell you she's an Elemental. She sees to most of the detail work involving the garrison cluster here on Courcheval. Her boss, Star Colonel Denard Devereaux, is the planet big shot. He's an Elemental, too. They're both war heroes of some repute, but I'm not sure exactly why. By all reports, she's capable, smart, and somebody you'd rather not cross."

"Believe me," said Hawg. "I only want to get on her good side." Riannon blushed anew, and Hawg laughed.

"Her presence in all these pictures does mean something," said Cantrell. "She's Denard's top aide. If he assigned her to babysit Danes, you can bet it's because he thinks Danes is important, at least in the short run."

"That gives us more to consider, all right," agreed Rose. "Have your scouts got any idea how close they are to finishing with the DropShip?"

"Well, that's the weird part," said Cantrell. "In most cases I'd expect the Cats to strip the ship of all the important computer information, then set the whole ship on fire, figuratively speaking."

"They are pretty contemptuous of Inner Sphere technology," agreed Riannon.

"Believe me," continued Cantrell, "if what I've seen is true, the words Inner Sphere and technology are mutually exclusive as far as the Nova Cats are concerned. Still, they seem to be spending the time and resources to actually repair the ship."

Ria looked gravely at her brother. "Which pretty well confirms *Chu-i* Myoto's fears."

"The exterior work is almost done," said Cantrell. "I don't have an exact time, but the last reports tag completion for later today. Who knows what's going on inside that ship?"

"All right," Rose said. "I'm willing to assume the Nova Cats are planning to use the *Tracy K* to return to Wolcott and cause some major damage. That means we've got to stop them before they lift off from Courcheval. Once they're in the air, the Kuritas won't know they're around until the Nova Cats open fire."

"Plus they're taking our ride home," added Hawg. Rose exchanged looks with his sister. Hawg's point was equally important. "Time is not critical until they actually start loading the ship. Once they begin the loading process, we've got a couple of hours until they're out of reach.

"Hawg, round up the team and have them in this room in sixty minutes." Rose collected the pictures and handed them back to Cantrell. "*Sho-sa,* I need to talk to your superiors as soon as possible. Right now, as a matter of fact. I know they don't think stopping that DropShip is any of their concern, but the fact of the matter is, it is. You've got to make them understand and accept that fact."

Cantrell left the room with Rose close on her heels. Hawg smiled at Ria and slapped her on the shoulder before he turned away and headed back to where most of the Black Thorns were currently working in the main cavern.

Knowing what Rose would need when he returned, Ria began to construct a diagram of the crash site based on the photos and verbal reports collected from Cantrell's scouts. On the surface, the job didn't seem very demanding, but the lack of information and the compressed time schedule made the process nerve-wracking.

She started with the physical layout. A *Union* Class DropShip was designed to land on four stout legs. The spheroid craft usually took a severe beating in a forced landing because it couldn't be sure to land vertically. From what Riannon could tell, it looked like the *Tracy K* had come in for the final landing with a high degree of drift. That meant she was moving horizontally rather than coming down for a perfect vertical landing. The DropShip must have hit, bounced, hit, and bounced again before coming to a stop.

When the ship first hit, the legs would have absorbed the impact not countered by the thrust of the engines, but the northernmost leg had failed completely. That was probably the one damaged and supposedly repaired on Wolcott. The second bounce tore the foot off the moorings of the easternmost leg. The giant landing pad had not been sheared away, however, which was probably what had saved the ship from tumbling over when it hit the ground for the third time.

The *Tracy K* had finally come to rest after digging a thirty-meter furrow from the southwest to the northeast. The final set-down finished the job on the eastern leg, ripping the foot completely away, but not before the leg absorbed enough of the landing to keep the ship upright. The northern leg collapsed, but a broken spar became wedged in the primary joint, effectively locking it in place. The ship would have suffered severe metal fatigue over the entire surface and superstructure, but—depending on the internal damage—it should be able to fly again.

The Clans had built a small encampment around the ship, erecting several temporary buildings to the northeast, closest to the major damage. Reports indicated that the buildings contained power tools and the machinery needed to repair the landing legs of the DropShip as well as maintain the portable equipment. To the west, the workers had erected a small tent city. The structures were basic, but they provided the workers protection from the elements and had been put up in less than one morning. A small mess tent had been placed to the south and a large supply tent was located on the north. Next to the supply tent was a temporary building probably used by the technicians as an administrative center. The Nova Cats must have had this entire encampment packed away for just such an emergency, thought Riannon. The small encampment had gone up too fast—even for people with the Clan's military efficiency—for it to have been simply pieced together.

The crash site was protected by an ad hoc star of four BattleMechs and five Elementals. Not a standard Clan formation, but the Fourteenth Garrison didn't seem to fit the standard Clan mold. The Elementals normally stayed close to the base and assisted with heavy lifting as necessary, while the four BattleMechs swept the perimeter with military precision each day. Though the 'Mechs never followed the same route twice, their search area was almost always identical. As the crash site was on a broad plain, there wasn't much need for additional security. The defenders had little fear of any hostile force arriving before they had a chance to react to the situation. Although the Black Thorns could overwhelm the Nova Cat Star, the Courcheval resistance fighters hadn't the capability to even damage them. Ria doubted that the encampment had been set up to protect against the Black Thorns, but that was exactly what it was going to have to do.

She set the map in the center of the table and collected markers for the defenders. Small stones became the Elementals and larger stones the Clan BattleMechs. Crossing to the bunk, she pulled out her duffel and extracted a small bag of coins.

Then she spread the coins on the table and marked them with the first name of each MechWarrior in the unit. She'd just finished marking "Kitten" when Hawg arrived with the first group of warriors. Within moments her brother had joined them. He looked at the map with obvious approval, then gave his sister an appreciative smile.

"All right, Black Thorns, let's get to it. We've got a DropShip to capture."

28

Cantrell burst into the Black Thorns' quarters and slapped on the light. "Up and at them, guys. We've got some serious trouble." She looked around the room at the mixture of postures and smiled. Although she was sure most of the MechWarriors had been asleep for only a few hours, her noisy entrance had jarred them all awake. Several were actually on their feet, hands near their weapons. The smile disappeared when she heard the flick of a safety behind her.

Turning slowly, she saw the recon commander, Ajax, ease his pistol back into his holster. Till now she hadn't even seen him. "Not bad," she said when her heart left her throat and returned to its proper place. "You sure you're not in the infantry?" Ajax smiled but shook his head.

"What's the problem?" asked Rose as he combed a hand through his hair, the gesture that was becoming an all-too-frequent substitute for sleep and a shower. He rubbed his face and tried to wake up.

"The Cavaliers are on the move. They've got a trinary of BattleMechs heading toward the crash site."

"I thought this operation was being run by the garrison cluster," said Yuri. "Why would the Cavaliers be involved?"

"You got me," said Cantrell, "but they're on the way just

the same. I've got scouts at several points along the way, but once they hit the plains, we'll lose them."

"How long ago did they leave?" asked Esmeralda.

Cantrell looked at her chronometer. "They've been on the road for about an hour. They should pass my last scout in about thirty minutes. From there it's a four- or five-hour trip to the crash site."

"That gives us a two- or three-hour lead," observed Rose. "What's going on at Denard's place?"

"Nothing out of the ordinary," Cantrell said. "Except a small caravan of BattleMechs and infantry carriers packed to the gills with Elementals and support equipment."

"It's showtime, kiddies," smiled Hawg.

"What about the VTOLs?" asked Rose.

Cantrell frowned. "They're ready to roll twenty-four hours a day. Both carriers are at the garrison headquarters, but we've got no way of telling whether they'll be used in the immediate future."

"E.T.A. on the convoy?" asked Rose as he headed into the hall. Bell was right behind him and Cantrell was on his right side.

"Less than an hour if they move at full speed," said Cantrell, hurrying to keep up with Rose's long strides "The Clan vehicles don't pack weapons, but they've got some of the fastest hovercraft you've ever seen."

"No way we'll be able to intercept them," observed Bell as he shrugged on his cooling vest. Rose nodded. They reached the doors of the main cavern and stopped. The other Black Thorns surged around them and headed for their respective BattleMechs. The Courcheval resistance crews had replaced all the damaged armor, but the few internal components damaged in the initial fights were still off-line. The Black Thorns had worked virtually non-stop to repair the damage, but the underground simply don't have the tools or supplies to fix things even when the mercenaries could figure out what needed to be done. The loss of the *Grand Dragon*'s long-range missile launcher was the biggest problem.

"Everything ready?" he asked Ajax, who had just come

into the cavern. The smaller man shook his head and gazed up at his commander. Although Ajax was older than Rose and doubtless had more experience as a MechWarrior, he always deferred to him. Rose sometimes wondered if Ajax didn't allow him to make mistakes just so he could learn from them.

"You know this whole thing falls down around our heads if your team can't pull off their mission," continued Rose.

Ajax nodded in a motion that was more like a bow than an acknowledgment. Rose patted him on the back and smiled. "Good luck."

Ajax smiled back. "All we need is straight shooting, Captain. You're the one in need of good luck." With a parting laugh, Ajax headed toward his *Raven,* breaking into a trot as he cleared the first cluster of technicians. Rose was forced to agree with his recon commander's assessment of the situation. He was going to need some luck to pull off this mission.

Cantrell punched him in the arm and headed for her Savannah Master. Rose saluted her in farewell as he watched her pulling on her helmet and raising the hovercraft's cowling. Dustin already had the fans engaged as Cantrell pulled her craft in line and headed out the doors. Rose waited until the last of the Black Thorns had entered the main cavern, then headed toward the *Masakari.*

It was almost twenty minutes before the 'Mech was ready to move. Although the situation was urgent, Rose decided not to stress the machine's components by initiating a cold start of the fusion engine. The quicker process would have started the 'Mech in under five minutes, but the damage to engine components would have cost him in the long run. Assuming there is a long run, Rose told himself.

His thoughts drifted to McCloud and his unborn child. Although his recent days had been filled with tactical sessions and meetings, his thoughts were never far from her. For the nth time he wondered what the future would hold. Would he even have a future?

Thoughts of home evaporated when the communications channel crackled to life. "This is Rover One. How do you read me, guys?"

Rose switched to the private channel and triggered the radio. "This is Command One. We read you fine."

"I'm on the way to the site. Hope to see you soon. Rover One out."

Rose killed the connection and double-checked the *Masakari's* instruments. He was down several missile flights, but beyond that, the OmniMech was completely operational and fully functional. As he checked the panel, Ajax and the rest of the recon lance headed for the door. They were quickly joined by Riannon, who raised the right arm of her *Phoenix Hawk* in salute. Rose punched a private line to his sister.

"No problems, right, sis?" he asked when he established the connection.

"No problems, Jeremiah. You seem a little nervous about this. Is everything all right?"

Of course not, Rose thought, but I can't really admit that. He decided to change the subject. "Just remember, zip-squeal the message. The operational window is pretty tight, but it shouldn't be a problem."

"You're absolutely right, big brother. It won't be a problem. Just take care of yourself till I get back." Ria killed the connection before Rose could reply. It was probably just as well, he thought. I might have said something sentimental that would have embarrassed us both.

He checked the main viewer and examined the six remaining 'Mechs in the cavern. His sensors indicated they were all ready to go, so he opened the command frequency, which now included the whole battle lance. "This is Command One. Let's move them out, people." Hawg's *Battlemaster* broke loose at the first sound of Rose's voice and took the lead. Myoto followed just behind. The matching *Mad Cats* went next, followed by Rose and Bell.

Rose had decided to break the lances into two separate groups for their mission. All the lighter 'Mechs went into the first group, while the heavy and assault 'Mechs were in the second. If their timing was right, the two groups would reach their objective at nearly the same time. Rose also organized the 'Mechs under his immediate command in three squads of two. The tactic had worked well on Borghese when the understrength Black Thorns had been forced into combat against a numerically superior foe.

Rose followed Esmeralda up the tunnel and into the last glimmer of twilight. Courcheval's sun had all but disappeared behind the hills to the north, casting red shadows over the hills. The heavy 'Mechs turned to the north after moving well away from the cavern opening. Rose didn't hold much hope for the continued success of the resistance, no matter what the outcome of his mission, but he didn't want to insult the leaders by seeming indifferent to their situation. He was sure the only reason the Nova Cats had let them survive this long was because they hadn't become enough of a nuisance to bother eliminating. That would likely change very soon.

Rose watched the *Mad Cat*'s broad back as it led him through the hills into the plains beyond. By now the sun was completely gone, leaving the Black Thorn line in complete darkness. Even the stars had been obscured by the overcast sky.

On the plains the 'Mechs spread out, each covering the other with overlapping fields of fire. Rose was in the center of the formation, not because he was the most important, but because his 'Mech packed the most firepower. He could quickly adjust to any attack. They moved toward the DropShip site at almost sixty kilometers per hour and had been traveling for almost sixty minutes when Hawg announced, "Contact."

Rose picked up his pace and moved to right, cutting in front of Hawg. Jamshid and Esmeralda were soon by his side. The three OmniMechs moved toward Hawg's reported contacts, chewing up the soil as they sprinted toward their objective. By now Rose had a lock on the four enemy 'Mechs, the unit from the crash site on its nightly terrain sweep.

Rose and the twin *Mad Cat*s rushed the 'Mechs, but didn't fire. Although he was in range to use his PPCs, Rose did not trigger the weapons. Slowing slightly, he dropped the targeting cross hairs on the lead BattleMech, a Clan

Battlemaster. In the low-light scope of the main viewer, he could discern no real difference between the 'Mech in his sights and the one piloted by Hawg. Rose slowed to a walk as Esmeralda and Jamshid each opened a comm channel with the *Masakari*. There was no need to respond; the open channel was all Rose needed.

As he raised his 'Mech's left arm slightly, Rose centered the cross hairs on the *Battlemaster's* neck, just below the bulbous head. Releasing half his breath, he fired all four PPCs. Half a heartbeat later, the *Mad Cat*s struck the same target. Then all hell broke loose.

Until the moment he fired his weapons, Rose was sure the Clan pilots believed him to be a member of the Nova Cavaliers. Cantrell had gone to great lengths to make sure that the painted patterns matched those of the Cavaliers as much as possible. What Rose wasn't able to duplicate was the Cavaliers' radio frequency, so he was counting on closing the distance as quickly as possible. The less time the Clan pilots had to think, the better were his chances of a surprise attack. To their credit, the Clan 'Mechs returned fire almost immediately.

Rose hit the *Battlemaster* with all four shots, clustering the azure beams in a diamond pattern that burned through the other 'Mech's chest and into its heart. Guaranteeing the kill were the two *Mad Cat*s' large lasers, which burned away the engine shielding and destroyed the massive gyro. As the *Battlemaster* started to fall, the pilot ejected into the night.

A *Galahad* similar to the one Rose had fought before triggered twin Gauss rifles. The depleted uranium slugs hammered into the *Masakari*'s chest, staggering the 'Mech for a moment. Even as Rose fought for control of his BattleMech, he sent a volley of missiles at his attacker.

The ten missiles sped toward the *Galahad,* joined by concentrated flights from the two *Mad Cat*s. In all, ninety long-range missiles zeroed in on the Clan machine, which disappeared in a cloud of light and smoke as the missiles slammed home. Every part of the 'Mech was hit as it staggered backward and fell. Still the missiles landed around it, tearing up the soil and sending geysers of dirt into the air.

Rose switched to a new target, selecting the nearest 'Mech. The *Hellhound* was in the process of reloading, having fired its entire complement of weapons at Jamshid. Rose centered the cross hairs and silently cursed as the PPCs recycled. When the indicator finally turned green, he stabbed the trigger, sending two lightning bolts at the *Hellhound*. One bolt missed, but the other struck the 'Mech's triangular head, blasting through the cockpit and lancing into the sky. The 'Mech's actuators locked in place, and the *Hellhound* tumbled forward.

"That was for Angus," Rose spat into the commline.

Looking over the battlefield, he saw no other opponents. The remaining Clan 'Mech had bolted for the DropShip the moment the fighting started. Rose did not blame the pilot. The Clan *Peregrine* weighed in at only thirty-five tons and was no match for a single *Mad Cat*, let alone the three 'Mechs it would have had to face on its own. Neither the *Masakari* nor the *Mad Cat*s had a chance of catching the speedy 'Mech, so Rose triggered the commline.

"One light heading your way."

"Already have it in the bag," came Bell's immediate response. "*Chu-i* Myoto's *Grand Dragon* ran it to ground."

Rose was impressed. He knew the Kuritas were experimenting with extra-light engine technology, but he had no idea they could pack so much power into the frame of a 'Mech. That the *Grand Dragon* was as fast as the light Clan 'Mech was shocking.

Rose glanced over the battlefield one more time and prepared to move out. As the smoke cleared around the *Galahad,* he was surprised to see that the Clan 'Mech was actually struggling to rise. Ninety long-range missiles had come at it, Rose thought in amazement, and it still isn't dead. He swung the *Masakari*'s left arm toward the *Galahad,* but when Esmeralda suddenly appeared next to the fallen 'Mech, Rose took his hand off the trigger. The *Mad Cat* was well inside the firing arc of the Clan 'Mech and in no danger.

Esmeralda lifted the *Mad Cat*'s massive right foot and aimed it at the cockpit of the struggling *Galahad*. Then she slammed the foot against the *Galahad*'s head. The giant metal foot came up again and slammed back down into the torn and twisted metal. Esmeralda ground her 'Mech's heel in the debris and stepped away, moving north without a single word to Rose.

Apparently more than one Black Thorn pilot was to be avenged tonight.

29

Riannon moved into line with the recon lance and followed Ajax northwest. Moving at top speed, the reinforced lance was nearly twice as fast as the main Black Thorn column coming behind it. They needed every bit of speed they could muster to get into position in time and Ria knew it. Concentrating solely on piloting, she managed to keep up with the other 'Mechs of the lance.

Once they reached the plains she slowed to a halt to consult her map. Kitten in her *Panther* also slowed down, but the rest of the recon lance continued to move northwest.

"Good hunting," she called to Ajax as he led his team into the night.

"And good luck to you," he replied. "Recon Four, keep her safe. She's an honorary member of the recon lance now and we look after our own. Got it?"

"I got it, Recon One," laughed Kitten. "I'll guard her like she was my own sister."

As the two MechWarriors watched, the rest of the recon lance disappeared from view, then from the scanner. Ria sighed and began to power down the *Phoenix Hawk* as Kitten did the same. It took only moments to shut down the engines and switch to backup power. She switched off everything but the communication system and waited.

"This is Recon Four," came the loud call in the suddenly quiet cockpit. "I'm ready to roll."

Ria adjusted the volume and whispered into the microphone. "Command Two, confirm." Ria checked the chronometer on the *Phoenix Hawk*'s instrument panel and marked the time. All that was left to do now was wait silently in the dark. Wait and go over her part of the plan one more time.

Jeremiah had insisted, and she had agreed, that the Black Thorns had to get word to the waiting JumpShip in the event anything went wrong. She didn't like even contemplating that possibility, but her brother had taught her that preparing for unpleasant things sometimes prevented them from happening. The Courcheval resistance fighters didn't have the equipment necessary to get a message all the way out to the JumpShip, which left the *Phoenix Hawk* and its upgraded communications center to do the job. It could get word to the JumpShip, but it would be risky.

A tight-beam message was out of the question because the message would never arrive if the angle of the beam was off by even a fraction. And since the JumpShip was certainly not going to communicate with the planet, there was no way to be sure the broadcast was successful. That left a broad-beam message.

Which virtually eliminated the margin of error. The BattleMech computers could handle the calculation of milliseconds, but even though the message was coded and less than a half-second in length, Ria may as well have been playing the Nova Cats a symphony.

To keep the Clans from spotting them, Ria and Kitten had moved onto the plains and shut their BattleMechs down. Once their 'Mechs had cooled to the surrounding temperature, Ria would send the message. Then they would wait some more.

If they were lucky, the Clans would try to backtrack the message and pick up any unusual readings in the area. Normally a moving BattleMech or a hot spot on the terrain counted as unusual. One hour after after the message was sent, the Clans would probably stop looking for the sender.

It didn't really matter if they put the message down to a strange atmospheric bounce or a transmission from the resistance movement. All that mattered is that they didn't spend too long looking for the sender.

At the time it had seemed like a perfectly reasonable plan, and Ria had fought hard for its approval. Now that she was sitting alone in the dark listening to the metallic ping of her BattleMech as it cooled, she wasn't so sure. In the end she consoled herself with the fact that the others would still have a chance to complete their mission even if she was discovered. This was the Thorns' best chance for success, and she was happy to do the job that had to be done.

Ria hadn't wanted Kitten to accompany her, but Jeremiah had insisted. For all the good it did Riannon, Kitten might as well have been a world away instead of fifty meters. The two had to maintain utter silence, so she was just as alone.

As the chronometer ticked the minutes down, Ria watched the count time, then hit the send stud on the communications panel. Even before her finger had released the button, the message was gone.

She continued to wait as the time counted past ever more slowly, then began to nod off, some part of her brain reasoning that it was the middle of the night and she was sitting in a very quiet space. The sound of a buzzer jolted her awake and suddenly upright. Checking her chronometer as she keyed the communications channel, Ria discovered she'd been asleep for almost thirty minutes.

"We've got a fighter overhead, Command Two," came Kitten's whispered voice. That could be trouble or it could be merely a standard flight, Ria thought as she checked her 'Mech. There was nothing to give her away. In fact, with the power cycled down, there was nothing to tell her there were even fighters in the area.

"They're on the way back, Command Two. Suggest we prepare a proper greeting."

Ria keyed the microphone. "How do you know that, Recon Four? I can't see anything."

"I can hear them. I popped the hatch for some fresh air

and I picked up their engines. They're circling right now. It's just a matter of time," said Kitten resolutely.

Riannon cursed and slapped the toggles of the *Phoenix Hawk*, taking the fusion plant off of standby. From deep within the heart of the 'Mech a rumbling told her the 'Mech was coming to life as the fusion reactor fed power to the components. She toggled the scanner to extreme range and offered a quick prayer when nothing appeared on the screen. The long-range scanner wouldn't offer much warning, but she couldn't do much about that. Even set at extreme range, the scanner would give her less then five seconds' warning if the fighters arrived with any kind of speed.

She looked across at the *Panther*, barely able to make out the first signs of life as the 'Mech began the cold-start sequence. Ria didn't like doing this, but she agreed with Kitten. If there were fighters in the area, the two 'Mechs would have to be able to defend themselves as quickly as possible.

Riannon caught a flicker of movement from the *Panther* as the 'Mech began the final stages of start-up. She was still firmly locked in place, however, when the scanner flashed with two incoming targets. "Heading-three-four-four," Ria screamed into the microphone as the two fighters roared down from the sky.

She was still unable to move when the first fighter started the strafing attack. Six red beams of light appeared out of the sky and stabbed at the ground, chewing up the dirt on a path to her *Phoenix Hawk*. She tried to move, but the 'Mech didn't budge as she slammed the throttle forward.

Laser light washed over her like a wave, burning armor and rending the *Phoenix Hawk* across the back and shoulders and burning into the interior. Sparks exploded out of the instrument panel as the lasers cut into the *Phoenix Hawk*'s head. Ria screamed as the sparks burned her arms and legs. Then came a secondary rumbling, followed by an explosion as the antimissile ammunition ignited in the storage bay, the chain reaction setting off the ammunition in the adjacent bay. Ria passed out as a second wave of feedback blasted through her neurohelmet.

The explosions inside the *Phoenix Hawk* continued, driving shards of metal into the extra-light engine components in the side torso. The magnetic bottle around the fusion reactor began to fail as the engine absorbed more damage. The automatic safeguards kicked in, preventing a complete meltdown, but there was no salvation for the BattleMech. The ejection system blasted the cockpit skyward as the life support system failed. The BattleMech remained locked in place, refusing to fall even in death.

Kitten barely had time to register Ria's warning when her scanner indicated the approaching fighters. Without conscious thought she turned north and raised the *Panther*'s right arm. Kitten saw the first fighter begin the stafing attack on Ria, but she held her fire until the wingman began his attack on her. Guessing the angle, she fired her SRM launcher the moment the fighter's lasers stabbed the ground on their deadly path toward her 'Mech. Just as the lights washed over her, she fired the PPC.

Armor boiled and melted away as the *Panther* was bathed in laser fire. Warning lights indicated armor breaches in the left arm and right torso, but Kitten double-checked the instruments in amazement that none of the shots and damaged her 'Mech's internal components. To her right she caught the flash of fire and turned just as the ejection system of the *Phoenix Hawk* flew skyward. In the distance she saw a second explosion as one of the fighters crashed to earth.

Unknown to Kitten, her PPC has sheared nearly all the way through the right wing of the fighter. When the short-range missiles caught up with the fighter moments later, they collapsed the forward edge of the wing. The control surface was instantly destroyed, and the fighter flipped over onto its back. The pilot barely had time to register the surprise of being hit before the lighter aerospace fighter augured into the ground.

Kitten took a halting step forward and scanned for the ejection beacon. After frantic seconds of nothing, the system finally registered to the west of her. She had begun to head in that direction when she remembered the other fighter. Moving in a slow circle, she scanned the sky. When the fighter appeared, this time from the south, Kitten was ready for him.

The missiles leapt from their racks a moment before the enemy lasers sped toward the ground. Kitten aimed toward the origin of the lasers and thumbed the trigger, leaping her 'Mech to the side at the same time. The pilot tried to correct his aim, but was only partially successful. The lasers ripped across the legs of the *Panther,* but failed to reach the components inside. Kitten was jarred to the soles of her feet by the leap and subsequent landing, but she managed to survive the second attack.

In return her cannon slammed into the bottom of the fighter's fuselage. The ship bucked severely, but the pilot managed to keep it under control as the missiles swarmed past him and into the sky. He, too, had survived the attack, and that was enough for him. The burning rage at the loss of his wingman was quickly quenched by the desire to live just a while longer. He pulled the nose of the fighter up and headed back to base, all the while fighting the increasing vibration in the frame. Kitten listened to him roar away, then went to find Ria's ejection system once she was sure he was out of attack range. Only when she was about to exit the cockpit did she discover that she'd left the cockpit's back hatch wide open.

Less than a hundred kilometers away, Ajax and the rest of the recon lance sat in quiet ambush, the three 'Mechs scattered in a wide line between the Nova Cat base and the DropShip crash site. It had taken every bit of speed by the three fastest 'Mechs in the company to arrive in time to set the ambush.

Ajax sat between Yuri and Leeza as the three waited for their target to appear on the scanner. It took only moments to happen. Moving directly toward the DropShip site was a single VTOL. If Rose was right, the passenger compartment would contain the DropShip crew of the *Tracy K.*

Although the plan would have worked no matter which of the three ambushers actually pulled the trigger, Ajax was glad the task fell to him. In theory it was simple. He would fire toward the VTOL, but not directly at it. The idea was to damage the rotors without destroying them. Unfortunately, these vehicles were notoriously fragile. Ajax didn't doubt that he could bring down the aircraft with a single volley, but he was concerned that he might destroy it outright.

That was why he targeted the VTOL with all his weapons but only fired the short-range missiles. Flying toward the target, the six stubby missiles intersected the VTOL and continued their flight, which was exactly what Ajax had intended. Before launching, he had disabled the missile warheads. Although he considered it an almost criminal waste of firepower, the warheads were not required for the job. Backed by velocity alone, the missiles ripped past the VTOL without exploding. One missile did hit the undercarriage of the craft, but even it did not ignite.

Ajax listened carefully to the audio from the Beagle Active Probe. If the assault were successful, the rotor of the VTOL would have been damaged and the pitch of the blades would have taken on a decidedly different sound. At first he thought he'd missed and so prepared to initiate the backup plan, his two medium lasers. But then, with a deepening roar, the VTOL began to slide to the earth.

Ajax broke from cover and ran after the descending aircraft, calling for Yuri and Leeza to do the same. When the VTOL finally touched down, he and his two lance mates were waiting for it. He keyed the public address system as he watched the damaged rotors slowly spin to a stop.

"Please exit the aircraft immediately," Ajax called in a resounding voice. "You are now the prisoners of the Black Thorn mercenary company. Exit the aircraft with your hands in plain view." Ajax hit the spotlight mounted on the left wing of the *Raven* and called for the other Thorns to do the same. The area around the VTOL was instantly lit like broad daylight.

Ajax was preparing to repeat his message when the VTOL's side door opened. First one, then two Nova Cat crew members stepped into the open. They moved to the side, quickly followed by Danes and his two surviving crewmen. Despite the distance, Ajax could see the DropShip captain smiling from ear to ear. He waved at Ajax and even threw the giant BattleMech a kiss before glancing back into the VTOL. Apparently prodded by Danes, a sixth figure emerged. It was Star Captain Thrace.

Ajax whistled softly to himself. Here was a prize he had not counted upon. Although his mission indicated he was to take no prisoners, he knew he must bring Thrace to Captain Rose. He toggled the address system.

"Star Captain Thrace, do you recognize that you are a prisoner of war and stand defenseless before us?" The words sounded forced and somewhat phony to Ajax as he announced them over the address system, but everything he knew about the Clans indicated that they held their personal honor in high regard. The Elemental seemed to shake for a moment, and Ajax aligned the *Raven*'s laser over her torso. At this range he had no doubt that he could kill Thrace and miss Danes, the nearest friendly in the group. But such action proved unnecessary. Thrace nodded and bowed her head.

"Please move away from the aircraft." As the passengers and crew stepped away from the VTOL, the three 'Mechs inundated it with laser fire. In seconds the aircraft was a burning hulk.

"Captain Danes, please see to the prisoners," Ajax called. "I'm coming down."

30

Courcheval
Nova Cat Occupation Zone
4 August 3057

Captain Jeremiah Rose parted the plains grass with an outstretched hand and lifted the light-intensifying binoculars with the other. From across the distance, the crash site of the *Tracy K* leapt into view. Structurally, there was little difference between the view before him and the ones he had already seen in the holographs taken by Cantrell's scouts. He panned left to right and tried to spot any new features, but gave up after the third pass. He let the grass spring back into place and dropped the lenses. The only difference, as far as Rose could see, was the addition of a star of BattleMechs around the crash site.

These were not the second-line BattleMechs he and the rest of the Black Thorns had been fighting. These were front-line OmniMechs painted boldly with the insignia of the Forty-sixth Nova Cat Cavaliers. Cantrell had insisted there was more to the camp than the addition of some first-rate BattleMechs, but Rose couldn't see it. He shook his head.

"No difference," he whispered to Cantrell as he slipped into the shelter of a shallow depression. She grinned and began a crouched walk further away from the site. Rose followed her without a word, waiting until they were back at the Black Thorns' small base camp before speaking. It was still dark, but Rose was taking no chances of setting off alarms at the DropShip site.

A small copse of trees sheltered the small camp from view. Although sparsely placed, the slender trees provided the only cover for miles around. By keeping the trees between the *Tracy K* and the Black Thorns, Rose was able to remain near the site without being detected. And even though he was more than five miles away, he did not think that would be a significant problem when the actual attack began.

The Black Thorns had placed their 'Mechs in a tight circle facing outward, with Kitten's battered *Panther* in the middle of the protective ring. All the 'Mechs were fully powered and operational, but right now Rose and Esmeralda were on the ground with Cantrell, Leeza, Danes, and Star Captain Thrace. Ajax was responsible for providing protection from attack, so Rose wasn't worried about not getting ample warning. Once Ajax gave the word, Rose could be in the *Masakari's* cockpit before the enemy was in range.

Rose glanced up at the *Panther's* cockpit. No matter how many times they reassured him that his sister would recover, he was still worried about her. The neurohelmet feedback from the ammunition explosion had overloaded her senses and she had blacked out. When Kitten found her after the fighter attack, Ria's life signs were still strong. Rather than fill Ria up with chemicals she might not need, Kitten had simply extracted her from the cockpit and carried her up to the *Panther*.

Ria had drifted in and out of consciousness throughout the trip to the crash site, but Kitten couldn't spend time watching her without abandoning the controls of her 'Mech. Just retrieving Ria's body had placed both warriors in extreme danger when Kitten left her 'Mech. Rose tore his gaze away from the *Panther* and looked across the circle. Leeza was lounging next to the foot of Hawg's *Battlemaster* cradling a stub-barreled submachine gun in both arms. The barrel was pointed directly at Thrace, and Leeza's finger was tight on the trigger. Rose had given her permission to shoot if Thrace so much as looked like she might be considering causing trouble. By now the other members of the Black Thorns knew that Greta was still alive. Rose expected a heartfelt reunion once this was over, but at the moment they still had too much to do to give her a proper reception.

Cantrell hopped onto the foot of the *Masakari* and began pulling stickers off the cuffs of her pants. Rose did the same while Danes and Esmeralda stood watching. "The difference is in what you don't see," said Cantrell without prompting. "The Cavaliers left with a full trinary of BattleMechs. Ten of those 'Mechs are not in sight. The garrison left with a full star of Elementals in full kit. You didn't see any of them just standing around, did you?" Rose considered the question and shook his head.

"They're on the ship," said Danes.

Cantrell smiled wider and slipped down off the *Masakari's* foot. "Captain Danes, there are six plumes of steam coming from the *Tracy K* about two-thirds of the way up the body. Does that mean anything?"

"They're bleeding the altitude adjusters." Seeing Rose and Esmeralda exchange confused looks, Danes explained, "It's part of the pre-flight test. They'll go over every system on the ship before lift-off. It's the start-up sequence.

"Assuming they start with the largest systems first, they're probably two hours into the test, maybe a hair more. That means they've got about another hour to go."

"Which gives us time to work," put in Esmeralda with a wolfish grin and a look in her eyes that Rose didn't like. Ever since the death of Badicus, Esmeralda had been behaving with less and less regard for herself and those in her lance. She hadn't slipped to the point where Rose thought it necessary to speak with her—especially in the presence of people outside the unit—but he found the trend unsettling.

"Know what to do?" asked Rose, and Cantrell nodded her head.

"Just clear the way, 'Mechjock. I'll deliver the cargo," she said. Cantrell slapped him on the shoulder for emphasis, and Rose extended his hand, which she pumped once, smiling lopsidedly. Then she and Danes began to walk toward the Savannah Masters parked beyond the cluster of 'Mechs.

Rose went over to Leeza as Esmeralda headed toward her *Mad Cat*.

"Sorry you won't be coming with us on this one, Leeza," said Rose as he approached. The woman smiled at the words, but never took her eyes off Thrace.

"Maybe next time. Right now it's just good to be back in the fold, you know what I mean?" Rose did indeed know what it meant and it showed. He turned to Thrace, careful not to come between Leeza and her captive.

"Star Captain, I appreciate your assistance and cooperation in these matters." Thrace didn't even look at Rose as he spoke. Although they were roughly the same height, Thrace seemed to tower over Rose by virtue of her increased bulk. Her eyes remained firmly ahead. "Well," continued Rose, "I guess it doesn't really matter. Leeza has orders to let you go as soon as the shooting starts."

Thrace's head snapped around. "What do you mean?" she demanded with a glare. Leeza straightened up and shifted the SMG slightly, but Thrace didn't move. It was only her voice that made her seem threatening.

Rose sighed. "What does that mean where you're from, Elemental? It means you're out of here once we're underway. Head back to your base or whatever you're supposed to do."

"You're releasing me?"

"Yes."

"Am I that unworthy? You do not even deign to keep me as a prisoner?"

"Uh, no, or yes. No and yes." Rose was confused. It sounded like Thrace was hurt that he was setting her free.

"I would rather you kill me here than shame me by returning me to my Clan without a ransom."

"Your choice," said Rose as he turned to Leeza. "Waste her," he said with a slight shake of his head. Thrace simply closed her eyes and waited for the expected hail of lead.

"All right, all right, we're not going to shoot you," Rose said, "but you're not a prisoner. We don't have room."

Thrace opened her eyes. "Among my people there is little more you can do to completely shame a warrior than to capture him and set him free. It is an act of complete disrespect. It tells the warrior's Clan, 'here is one of such little value we cannot set a price.' I had heard you were barbarians, but I did not believe it until this moment."

Rose rolled his eyes and shook his head. Without another word we walked over to the *Masakari* and began the climb up the hanging ladder.

"What about her?" yelled Leeza.

"Cut her loose," he called into the darkness as he continued the climb. Rose reached the top and hit the recoil on the *Masakari's* ladder. As the winch lifted the ladder, he climbed into the cockpit and sealed the door. By the time the ladder was fully retracted, he was on the move.

"Recon Lance, move out. Battle Lance form on me. This is it, Thorns. If we want off this rock, we've only got one chance." Rose tightened the straps of the command couch and followed the rest of the company into battle. Behind him Kitten, Riannon, and Leeza awaited the outcome.

The task before them was daunting, but Rose was optimistic. He felt the plan was solid, but the trick lay in the execution. If all went well, Ajax and the rest of the recon lance would charge the crash site, shooting everything that moved. Rose was careful to remind them that the DropShip was non-moving. The rest of the Thorns would move at their best speed to support the attack. He had little doubt the Thorns could overcome the Battle Mechs defending the DropShip, even though they were OmniMechs. His primary concern was the big guns of the *Tracy K* herself. If the Clans managed to activate the DropShip guns before the Black Thorns could rush under their arc, it would be a short battle indeed.

Once the enemy 'Mechs were down, Cantrell and Danes would arrive at the DropShip. Each would pilot a Savannah Master packed with almost a ton of military explosives controlled by a radio detonator. Rose, Danes, and Cantrell each had controls to detonate the explosives. The plan was to get as close as possible to the DropShip, shut the fans down, and bail out. Although the explosives were rather small when compared to the overall size of the DropShip, Rose knew they would totally destroy the drive engines and probably set off a chain reaction that would destroy the entire ship. He was prepared to give Denard one chance to evacuate the ship or else have it blasted out from under him. Denard's life for the Black Thorns' freedom.

Of course, thought Rose, as the *Masakari* broke into a lumbering run, the plan depended on two things. First, the *Tracy K* had to still be there when the Thorns arrived. Rose was sure he had that covered, so his mind worked on problem two. The Cavaliers aboard ship were probably prepared for launching. That meant they'd be strapped into place and powered down. The fate of the ship would have been long since decided by the time they were ready to fight. If, on the other hand, the Cavaliers were ready for action, the DropShip could suddenly provide its own reinforcements. As Rose ran past the trees that had so recently provided cover, he wondered if perhaps there was something else, but in the distance he heard the alarms of the Clan camp, and suddenly it didn't matter.

The throttle was all the way forward, pushing every ounce of speed from the *Masakari*. Rose sighted on the camp and targeted a Clan *Gladiator*. As he centered the cross hairs, the Nova Cats launched the first volley. A flight of long-range missiles screeched across the plains toward the *Grand Dragon*, which was lagging just behind the much smaller 'Mechs of the recon lance. Myoto's 'Mech shuddered under the impact of the twin missile flights and stumbled to the ground. Rushing at top speed, the *Dragon* dug nose-first into the ground, ripping a gash in the plains. The left arm snapped off and cartwheeled through the air as the 'Mech ground to a halt. Rose caught the hint of movement as Myoto struggled to rise, but just then his indicator lights went green.

Snapping his attention to the *Gladiator*, Rose launched his own missiles and prepared to follow up with the PPCs. Guided by the targeting laser, the missiles flew true, but lights began winking on the *Gladiator* and suddenly Rose's missiles flew astray. He's got an antimissile system, thought Rose with a touch of dread. He slapped the commline.

"Battle One, I'm going to need some help with this one."

Rose watched Esmeralda adjust her course and head toward the *Gladiator*. Rose checked the main view screen. The *Gladiator* was humanoid, its head designed to look human. The 'Mech's arms were rather boxy, but the right one ended in a hand, adding more to the human appearance. Slung underneath the hand was a weapon barrel with energy coils and power feeds. The left arm was short and stubby, as though the limb had been removed below the elbow. The half-limb ended in a broad gun barrel of some type. Probably a Gauss rifle or autocannon, Rose thought.

The *Gladiator* fired at Rose just as he was pressing his own trigger. Each shot struck the other 'Mech squarely in the chest, but in a match of titans such as these, the opening salvo was little more than a challenge to engage in real combat. Rose snarled and raced forward.

A Nova Cat *Thor* stepped from around the *Tracy K* to support the *Gladiator.* "Command Three and Four, take the *Thor,*" Rose barked into the commline. He didn't wait for acknowledgment, but stabbed on the secondary TIC and sent two more PPC bolts on the way. Esmeralda followed with lasers, and the *Gladiator* staggered under the onslaught. The Clan pilot was skilled, however, and wrestled his 'Mech back under control as the beams gouged ferro-fibrous armor.

Rose released the fourth PPC as the range dropped, but his shot passed wide to the right. The seconds dragged by in agonizing slowness as Rose waited for his PPCs to recharge. Esmeralda launched her long-range missiles, but by now the range was so short the missiles didn't have time to properly activate. Between the short-range and the anti-missile system, less than a quarter of the missiles actually struck their target.

Rose roared in his cockpit. What was she thinking? That was an amateur's mistake. She was a veteran, not some wet-nosed kid straight from the academy. If Rose was angry, however, the *Gladiator* pilot was furious. Adjusting his aim, the Clan warrior pointed at Esmeralda with his left arm. Then came a flash of muzzle fire and a stream of empty shell casings ejecting out the back of the *Gladiator's* arm. Rose had never seen such a sustained rate of fire. For endless seconds he watched as the *Gladiator* fired shell after shell after shell into the *Mad Cat*. The shells sliced through the right-torso armor like so much paper, burrowing into the missile launcher and ammunition bay.

When one of his PPCs cycled back on line, Rose fired, but completely missed his target. To his right, Esmeralda's *Mad Cat* exploded as the long-range missiles of the right torso ignited. The cellular ammunition storage system saved the OmniMech, if not the torso. The force of the exploding missiles was channeled out the blow-out panels on the back of the *Mad Cat*. The blast ruined every component in the right torso, instantly cutting power to the right arm, but the rest of the 'Mech was still safe.

The *Mad Cat* hop-skipped under the rain of shells and the blast of the exploding ammunition, but Esmeralda refused to fall. Raising the *Mad Cat*'s left arm, she fired its two lasers, then staggered forward. As she did so, the right arm fell away, and Rose could see flames from within the *Mad Cat*'s torso.

"Battle One, punch out." If Esmeralda heard, she didn't answer. Two more PPCs came on line, and Rose fired at the *Gladiator*. The shots cored through the 'Mech's left thigh, and Rose saw the limb stiffen. The *Gladiator* pointed the right arm at Rose, but then swung the underslung PPC toward Esmeralda.

"Battle One ..." The blue lightning bolt leapt from the *Gladiator* to the *Mad Cat* as if it had eyes. It passed through the gaping hole in the right side and slammed into the engine, adding fuel to the raging fire. The *Mad Cat* slipped onto its right side and crashed into the dirt. The whole 'Mech spasmed once, then lay still as the engine failed completely. Fire crackled through the holes, sending thick smoke into the air. "... punch out," Rose finished with a whisper.

The *Gladiator* turned to Rose and began to aim the deadly left arm. Fear and anger gripped Rose as the barrel swung into line. He rushed forward and closed the distance between the two 'Mechs in five steps. As he planted his right foot on the final step, Rose slammed the throttle down.

The *Masakari* reared back, and Rose drove its right foot

forward. The metal foot struck the *Gladiator* squarely in the shin, driving the metal inward and shivering the entire leg. The *Gladiator's* thigh, already damaged by the *Masakari's* PPC, snapped in half. The lower spar jagged through the 'Mech's armor as the *Gladiator* fell. Rose could hear the scream of tortured metal as the spar ripped through the metal skin of the 'Mech. He caught his balance and was getting ready to kick the fallen 'Mech again when the left arm fired once more.

The shells ripped up the *Masakari's* right leg, peeling away armor and worming their way inside. To Rose the hammer of the giant gun was less threatening now that he was on the receiving end of the attack. He checked the status lights, amazed to discover them yellow inside of red. Although the armor had been breached, the leg had held under the withering fire.

Rose didn't trust the leg to another kick, but it supported him fine when he squared the *Masakari's* shoulders and pointed both arms at the fallen *Gladiator*. The head would have been an easy shot, but instead Rose pointed all four PPCs at the center of the 'Mech's chest. He triggered the primary interlock and burned a hole completely through the fallen OmniMech. The 'Mech died without a sound.

31

Courcheval
Nova Cat Occupation Zone
4 August 3057

Rose turned in a swift circle, careful to place as much of the *Masakari*'s weight as possible on the good leg. A Nova Cat *Thor* was already down, as was a *Loki*. Another 'Mech lay near the *Loki*. It was impossible to tell without moving in for a closer look, but he guessed it was the remains of Myoto's *Grand Dragon*. Rose could see firing from the other side of the DropShip and rushed around the side.

On the far side of the *Tracy K,* a Nova Cat *Vulture* stood in the middle of a killing field. As its feet lay another OmniMech. Despite the damage it had suffered, Rose easily identified it as another *Vulture*. Leeza's *Mercury* was partially entangled with the dead *Vulture,* a gaping hole over the heart of the Black Thorn BattleMech. In the distance Rose saw Hawg's *Battlemaster* struggling to rise, a vain attempt considering both legs had been shot off from the knees down. The *Raven* and the *Dasher* continued to move and fire, but the *Vulture* had its own agenda.

As Rose aimed at its back, the Cavalier OmniMech fired at Bell, who was approaching with Jamshid from the other side. Twin Gauss rifles struck down the damaged *Banshee* as Rose triggered four PPCs, which blistered the *Vulture*'s armor before burning their way through. The heavy 'Mech never knew what hit it as every component failed simultaneously. The joints locked in place as the engine died. Rose moved forward and pushed the *Vulture* over. Only the Black Thorns remained on the battlefield.

"Danes, move up." Rose scanned the field. "Ajax, round up the survivors and give me a status report." If Ajax acknowledged the order, Rose never heard it. He simply put his mind on automatic and continued with their mission. Their mission to get home. As if that mission mattered after such a price.

Rose watched as Danes and Cantrell roared across the plains toward the ruin of the Clan camp. Rose half-expected the *Tracy K* to open fire at the two hovercraft, but within seconds the two Savannah Masters were parked beneath the DropShip's massive engines.

"Commander, this is Recon One. Jamshid has the north cargo door covered. Yuri and I can take the east and west if you'll take the south."

"Affirmative, Recon One. What's the bill?" Rose asked as he moved into position. Ajax flinched at the expression, but responded immediately. He and Rose were professionals.

"We're down to five mobile 'Mechs, if you count the *Panther*. One immobile, but weapons ready."

"The people, Ajax."

Ajax had known that was Rose's request, but he wasn't prepared to answer. Without individually checking the cockpits, the report could be very inaccurate.

"Report, Recon One," Rose ordered.

"Besides the functional 'Mechs, I have reports from Command Three and Battle Five." Ajax dropped his voice. "Nothing from Battle One, Battle Three, or Recon Three."

"I understand." Rose paused for breath from a chest suddenly tight. "Prepare for phase two." He toggled the communications channel to an open frequency and cranked the volume.

"Star Colonel Denard Devereaux, this is Captain Jeremiah Rose of the Black Thorns. I'm sitting outside your DropShip, and I'm about to blow you and your whole damn outfit straight to hell. You've got ten seconds to respond or else kiss the ship goodbye."

Rose checked the chronometer, for a moment not really caring whether Denard answered or not. The channel crackled to life at eight seconds.

"This is Star Colonel Devereaux. I suggest you surrender immediately, Captain Rose, otherwise I will be forced to kill you," Denard said coolly.

"Cut the bull, Denard. I've got two tons of high-grade explosives sitting under your butt and I'd love to use it, so here's the plan. You and your troops haul it off the *Tracy K* immediately and clear a path to our JumpShip."

"And if I refuse?" Denard asked in a condescending tone.

"Pucker up, drekhead." The emergency light went off on the communications channel and Rose hit the toggle. With Ajax overseeing everything but the conversation with Denard, he knew there was a good reason for the emergency call.

"What?"

"Binary of BattleMechs approaching from the south. Kitten just called it in. I guess those garrison troops from the hills finally caught up with us."

It was only with herculean effort that Rose suppressed a scream. That was what had been nagging at him before the battle. The underground had warned him of a binary of BattleMechs prowling the hills looking for the Black Thorns. They were only second-line garrison 'Mechs, but more than a match for the Black Thorns after the mauling the unit had received at the hands of the Nova Cat Cavaliers. In the rush to get to the *Tracy K*, Rose had forgotten all about them. Now they would pay the price.

"Tell Kitten to close up. Bring Leeza with her." Rose flipped the toggle after taking a deep breath.

". . . another option," finished Denard.

"I'm sorry, Star Colonel. Could you repeat that? I must have dozed off." Rose adjusted the long-range scanner. Ten BattleMechs popped onto the screen at extreme sensor range. Between the approaching binary and the Black Thorns raced a lone *Panther*.

"A sudden change in attitude, Captain Rose? Perhaps you

have noted the arrival of my reinforcements. Maybe you should reconsider my offer."

Rose licked his suddenly dry lips. "Tell you what I'm going to do, Denard. I'm going to call you out."

"A batchall? You are joking."

Rose checked the scanner. "At a time like this? I don't think so."

"The terms?"

Rose knew it had to be something Denard would accept, and accept with confidence. "Man to man. No BattleMechs, no Elemental armor, no nothing. Just you and me."

"A Circle of Equals? I admit it would be a pleasure to kill you with my bare hands. The prize?"

"The DropShip. If I win, the Black Thorns take their wounded and leave with clear passage back to Wolcott, along with everything on board." Might as well go for some salvage, thought Rose. This was bound to be the final fight. "If you win, the Black Thorns surrender and you can have the DropShip with our blessings."

"No. I will take my chances with your explosion. Assuming, of course, that you actually have the means to cause an explosion."

"All right," said Rose, thinking furiously, "I'll sweeten the deal. You win and I'll give you the approach code to link with the JumpShip."

"Approach code. Your bluff is unworthy of you. There is no approach code. If there was, I would have found it when Captain Danes accessed the computer files. I can assure you, our technicians are very efficient."

"The code is new," said Rose in a rush. Kitten was almost to camp, and the binary was closing fast. Once they arrived, Rose knew he would be forced to play his hand the hard way and he didn't want that. "That was why your flyboys found two of our 'Mechs alone in the prairie earlier today. They were sending a message to the JumpShip. A new approach code."

Rose waited in agonizing silence as Denard must have been checking the information. It would be easy enough to verify the outbound message, and the downing of a Cavalier fighter should be all the proof necessary. But still there was no answer. Rose checked the scanner. Kitten crossed behind Rose and took up a position next to Ajax. The binary was almost in visual range.

"Agreed," came the simply reply. "Where shall we fight?" asked Denard.

Rose didn't need to think about that one. "The DropShip. I assume you're on the bridge."

"I am."

"Open the service door of the south cargo bay. When I close the door, you can leave the bridge. The entire DropShip will be the battleground. We meet, we tussle, we decide who gets to leave this place."

"What is to stop me from simply shooting you the moment you enter the cargo hold—or better yet, having several of my men kill you in the depths of the ship?"

"Honor."

"Ah, yes. You know about Clan honor."

"I know about Devereaux honor and Clan Nova Cat."

"I agree to the terms. You may exit your 'Mech as soon as you are ready."

Rose killed the connection and toggled to the Black Thorns' company channel. He filled in the conscious warriors on the change in plans, and ordered the Black Thorns to power down their 'Mechs while awaiting the outcome. The surviving mercenaries were unanimously opposed to the plan, but that was hardly a shock to Rose. In their place, he'd doubtless have felt the same way. They had trusted him before and they'd have to do so again.

The garrison binary joined the Black Thorns, but they stopped short and began to power down. Just as Rose had prayed, Devereaux was going to approach the duel fairly. One OmniMech walked around the DropShip, scratching a rough circle around the vessel, telling Rose that Denard was serious about the term "circle" in the phrase Circle of Equals. One of the access doors to the *Tracy K* popped open, and Elementals began to leave the craft. They were quickly followed by Clan MechWarriors who crossed the short distance to stand with the debarking garrison pilots.

Rose tapped out commands on the *Masakari*'s computer and slapped the system locks. He then ordered his people out of their 'Mechs. Removing his neurohelmet, he unfastened the couch restraints and left the BattleMech. The other Clan 'Mechs had arrived by the time he was on the ground, but Rose paid them no attention. He had already begun to focus his ki as he descended the ramp. Breathing deeply, he crossed the short distance to the *Tracy K*, feeling himself in perfect harmony by the time he stood before the service door. He was not surprised to discover it was already open.

Rose climbed the short ladder and passed through the doorway to the cargo bay beyond. A final deep breath and he closed the door behind him. Looking around the room he saw that the Clan technicians had been very busy since the DropShip's crash. The bay, which had previously held only Hawg's *Battlemaster*, now held two *Fenris* OmniMechs. As he crossed the bay, Rose ran a hand along the giant foot of the nearest BattleMech.

Rose moved to the bay's work bench and selected several tools from the rack. Going back through the bay, he went to the side door on the main level and jammed the lock into place. Using a hammer as a wedge, he locked the door shut. Now the only way into the cargo bay was through the access door on the gantry level, halfway up the bay. He returned to the workbench and selected a second hammer and a battered screwdriver. Examining the point of the latter, he smiled and continued working.

Thirty minutes later he heard the door on the gantry level slowly open. Rose shifted his weight and moved behind the protection of the *Fenris*' leg. From his vantage point on the 'Mech's foot he could see Denard step swiftly through the opening and fully onto the gantry. For a moment Rose envied the man's grace and strength. When Denard stepped fully into view, Rose could see that both of the man's hands were empty.

"I guess you took me literally," Rose called from below.

Nerves on edge, Denard spun on the catwalk before he fully realized the distance to Rose. When he saw how far away was his opponent, Denard wanted to laugh. This was the Black Thorn warrior? This was the man who had destroyed his command?

"You should not have called out, Captain Rose. An ambush was your only hope of success. Now you will die." Denard moved along the catwalk at a casual pace.

"And you should have made a weapon, Star Colonel. That was my only real worry. Now you'll die."

Denard laughed, a harsh, forced sound. "Your audacity is amazing. Under different circumstances . . ."

"We could have been friends?" asked Rose.

Denard shook his head. "You could have been my bondsman."

Rose watched as Denard walked forward along the gantry. Near the head of the steps he paused and extended a foot down onto the gantry floor, which promptly fell away. Denard looked down the hole to the array of screwdrivers and picks below. Had he fallen, he would surely have been impaled on the devices Rose had set up below. "Very clever, Captain Rose, but you failed to conceal your trap." Rose flashed a nervous smile and glanced around the room. Denard laughed and stepped over the gap. He paused at the top of the steps. "You can't beat me, Captain Rose."

"That's exactly what Ajax said," Rose replied.

"You're about to die, MechWarrior."

"And that's what Hawg said."

Denard began walking slowly down to the main level lightly balanced on the balls of his feet. "I should thank you before you die, Captain Rose. You taught me a valuable lesson. Or retaught me a lesson." Rose arced an eyebrow, but did not respond. He concentrated on his breathing and refocusing his ki. It should have been much easier this time because he had focused himself only moments before, but the presence of an enemy so lethal made it more difficult.

"You caught me unaware. Nobody has ever done that before. I was still several minutes away from being able to release the OmniMechs in the hold, but your call arrived just as I was about to release two points of Elementals out of the west cargo door." Denard shook his head. "I got lazy and failed to have my men ready." The Star Captain looked coldly at Rose. "It will not happen again."

He continued to ease down the steps, still moving casually. "Tell me, Captain Rose, do you really have two tons of explosives beneath this ship? Not that it matters now, but I would like to know."

Rose simply nodded.

"I thought as much." Denard stepped off the stairs and onto the wet floor of the cargo bay. The floors of most repair facilities were notoriously dirty, but if the Clansman thought anything of the puddle of water, he didn't show it. Rose reached into a back pocket as Denard stepped forward. With Rose still on the foot of the BattleMech and Denard down on the bay floor, Rose was a significant height advantage, but the Elemental didn't seem to mind. He continued to walk confidently forward as Rose brandished his weapon.

Denard stopped in mid-stride. "A gun?" he asked, staring at the weapon.

Rose shook his head and dropped the device into the water near Denard's feet. "Electric torch."

The small device was little more than two metal prongs, an insulated handle, and a high-capacity lithium battery. When turned on, the electric current passed between the two prongs. The device was powerful enough to cut through ferro-fibrous armor as fast as a man could pull the torch across the armor's surface.

The torch hit the water as Denard realized what was happening. He tried to jump clear of the water, but it was too late. The lithium battery burned out after only six seconds of life, but that was more than enough to reduce Denard to a quivering mass of flesh.

Rose jumped down from the *Fenris'* foot and pulled the battered screwdriver from his back pocket. Every muscle in Denard's body twitched and jerked as it suffered the aftereffects of the electrocution. Rose reversed the grip of the screwdriver and grabbed a handful of Denard's hair. Setting his jaw and tightening his grip, he thrust the screwdriver into the Elemental's right eye.

As he stepped away from the body, Rose could no longer

think of it as anything living or as something with a name. He dragged the Elemental's heavy form across the floor to the exterior door, and threw the door open. Pausing for an instant, he scanned the dawn sky, then dumped Denard's body out of the open door. After making sure none of the Elementals had reached for a weapon, he jumped the short distance to the ground below.

Without a word to the assembled Nova Cat MechWarriors, Rose walked to the *Masakari* and began the climb to the cockpit. Once inside the head of the massive 'Mech, he snapped off three toggles and killed the chronometer. The countdown timer to the explosives winked off with just under five minutes to spare.

32

DropShip **Tracy K**
Courcheval System, Nova Cat Occupation Zone
4 August 3057

Rose sat in the mess room of the *Tracy K* and slowly swirled the dregs of his coffee in the bottom of the cup. The DropShip was five hours out of Courcheval and closing on the Kurita JumpShip at top speed. Rose downed the last of the coffee and stretched across the table for the decanter. Savoring the aroma, he poured another cup and reflected upon the silence. With the ship under full acceleration, there was no need to use the dispenser bulbs.

After Danes had given the all-clear signal several hours earlier, Rose had come to the mess room, which he'd found empty. After checking several of the crew cabins and discovering that they too were empty, he was sure he knew where everybody was headed—the cargo bays.

Part of him wanted to be surprised that the Nova Cats at the DropShip site were honoring their dead commander's arrangement, but deep down he'd known exactly how they would react. They were warriors raised to live by a code of honor. Even though they would likely never attain their society's highest goal, they tried to live up to the ideal in all ways.

While two Elementals were carrying away the body of their commander, the garrison binary turned away. Led by Star Captain Thrace, they began the long march back to their base, leaving the Black Thorns with a clear path to leave.

While Rose sat drinking his coffee, Bell sat down across the table and also poured himself a cup. Rose wiped his mouth on his sleeve while Bell reached across to top off Rose's half-empty cup. "Everybody in the cargo bays?" Rose asked between sips. Bell nodded and smiled at his commander. There was a full binary of OmniMechs in the cargo bays below and enough repair and replacement equipment to keep a raiding force in the field for months.

"I thought I'd head to the med bay and check on our patients," said Rose. "Want to come along?"

"Sure."

Rose picked up his cup and led the way through the twisting corridors of the DropShip until they came to a set of double doors with the symbol for the ship's medical service. He slapped the entrance switch and stepped through.

On the other side of the door, the DropShip seemed transformed. There were still telltale indications that this was the *Tracy K,* but the Clansmen had updated some of the medical equipment in preparation for their planned raid. There was nothing here that didn't exist in a well-stocked field hospital, though the *Tracy K* could hardly be considered fully equipped by Clan standards. The room contained four beds and one critical care unit. Happily, the enclosed care unit was empty.

Three of the four beds were occupied, but only one of the patients was awake. Rose looked around for the cargomaster, who was also serving as the impromptu medical technician, but he was nowhere in sight. Rose crossed to his sister's bed and took her hand, receiving a reassuring smile in return.

"Glad to see you're finally feeling better, sis," he said, giving her his warmest smile. Ria tried to sit up in bed, but then slumped back down.

"I'm not sure this is what I'd call better, but it's nice to be awake. On second thought, scratch that." Rose began to rub her cheek with one hand. "It's nice to know I'm still alive, but I could do without the awake part."

Bell stepped up to the bed and smiled. "It's good to have you back." Ria tried to smile and nod in return, but even that simple effort turned her pale.

"Is there an echo in here?" she asked in a whisper. Rose and Bell shook their heads in unison.

"That's your inner ear," explained Rose. "It sometimes goes haywire after an ammo explosion. It will be normal again in a day or two. Till then you'll think you're listening under water."

"So that wasn't a dream," she said after several moments. Rose gave Bell an anxious look and turned back to his sister. She had closed her eyes, but Rose knew she was still awake.

"No dream, sis," he replied.

"Then it's gone." Rose didn't have to wonder what "it" was.

"Yes, it's gone."

"I'm dispossessed," she said as tears slipped from the corners of her eyes.

Rose gave her hand another gentle squeeze. "Not exactly. We, that is, the Black Thorns, still have the *Marauder II* and the *Shadow Hawk* on Outreach. You might like one of those."

Tears flowed freely now. "Jeremiah, those 'Mechs are up for sale. We need the money for McCloud and the OmniMech maintenance."

"Well, maybe not," said Rose. "Besides, while you were asleep, we had a slight reversal in fortune." Riannon opened one eye to see whether her brother was lying, but her eyes were too tear-filled to tell. She blinked away the tears and silently cursed the pain in her head.

"He's serious," offered Bell, as if independent confirmation of Rose's news would settle the matter for Riannon.

Rose squeezed her hand tighter. "Get some rest, and make it peaceful." Behind him Rose heard the door to the lab open. "There will be time enough for explanations later." Ria didn't respond, but Rose was sure she'd heard. The cargomaster tapped him on the back and motioned Rose and Bell to the other side of the room. Rose released his sister's hand reluctantly.

"You have to leave," the man said in a harsh whisper. "They all need rest." Rose nodded and placed his hand on the man's shoulder. All three men wanted what was best for the patients.

"Just tell me how they're doing and we're gone." The cargomaster paused, as if even a small delay was unacceptable, but he couldn't ignore the look Rose gave him.

"Your sister will be fine. I expect she'll be out of here by this time tomorrow." Rose's heart leapt with joy to know that Ria was going to be all right.

"MechWarrior Hawg has a broken hip and femur, assorted lacerations, and second-degree burns along the arms and face. The scanners indicate some corneal damage to the right eye, but we won't know more for a couple of hours at least. The machines are keeping him sedated because of the hip, but that should end in another twelve or fourteen hours."

"And Rippiticue?" asked Rose.

"Her left foot has been severed just above the ankle," the cargo master said calmly. Rose looked over at he sleeping MechWarrior in the amazement. She looked so peaceful. "I've got a preserving sleeve on it, but . . ."

"Does she know?" asked Bell.

The cargomaster nodded. "I've always heard you MechWarriors were tough, but that lady there might take the prize. She just laughed like it was no big deal when that other woman told her the news. Now she's sleeping peaceful as a baby. Not a care in the world." The man continued shaking his head.

"I'll tell them you were in," the cargomaster said as he opened the door. "And one more thing, ask the others to stay away for another few hours. These people need their rest."

"We'll tell them," Rose assured him as he and Bell left the room.

The two men walked back the way they'd come from the mess hall, neither speaking as they reflected on the sights in the medical bay. Rose couldn't help also thinking about Esmeralda and Badicus, who, unlike Ria and Leeza, would never rejoin their comrades. He suddenly felt their loss very deeply and painfully.

"Leeza can still pilot a 'Mech," Bell offered as they

reached the mess hall. Rose grunted agreement, unsure whether she would want to or if he should even let her.

"Captain Rose, there you are," said a voice. Rose turned and smiled at the woman who'd spoken. Her left arm was in a sling and she moved with a slight limp, but Rose knew the wounds were not serious and she would be as good as new in a matter of days.

"*Chu-i* Myoto, it's good to see you up and around," said Rose with forced cheerfulness.

"Thank you, Captain Rose." If Myoto caught his mood, she gave no indication.

"Sit down, *Chu-i*," he said.

"Please, call me Reiza." Bell poured a third cup of coffee as the woman slid carefully into the bench. The three sat sipping their coffee in silence, listening to the odd sounds of the DropShip. Rose allowed his mood to darken with no attempt to stop the emotions he felt. He looked across the table at Myoto, who was watching him intently.

"I'm sorry about your 'Mech," said Rose finally.

Myoto shrugged, then winced in pain from her wounds. "There is no need for apologies, Captain. The 'Mech was destroyed in the performance of its duties." Rose nodded.

"You fought well," offered Bell. Myoto looked across at him, searching for any traces of mockery. Then she glanced at Rose, who nodded agreement.

"I'm not given to idle praise, but your contribution to our escape will be duly noted in my report," said Rose earnestly. Myoto smiled and blushed at the compliment. "You've come a long way from the warrior I first met on Wolcott."

"Thank you, Captain, but there is no need to include me in your report. I have all the praise I need."

Rose saluted her with his cup as he recalled one of their previous conversations. "So you proved something to yourself, did you?"

"Hai."

"And what did you discover?" asked Rose.

"Perspective, Captain. I discovered that everything must be viewed in its proper perspective to be accurately judged. I have, at last, gained the first glimpse of that perspective which I had sought for so long." The three lapsed into silence as Rose considered Myoto's revelation.

"Excellent point, Reiza. Perspective is the key to viewing any situation." Rose rapped his hand on the table and suddenly stood. His dark mood began to evaporate as he, too, began to alter his own perspective of the situation. He still felt the losses of his comrades keenly, but the sadness was slowly being replaced with a new sense of purpose. Esmeralda and Badicus had not died in vain. Rose would make sure of that.

Without a look backward, Rose stood and headed toward his cabin. The Black Thorns had been mauled on Courcheval and he had lost near and dear companions, but Jeremiah Rose knew the Black Thorns could rise from that beating stronger than before. The veterans would be missed, but there was new blood ready to take their place. The Black Thorns were coming back, and everybody from the Kuritas to the Clans had better be ready.

Epilogue

Mercenary Garrison District
Wolcott, Draconis Combine
6 November 3057

Rose sat in the hospital room with a small bundle in each arm. It was well past visiting hours, but hospital security was laughable, especially to someone with the money, skills, and determination to get inside. Rose had all three.

Across the room Rachel Rose began to stir. Glancing up at the monitor, Rose saw by her vital signs that she was awake.

"Are you going to sleep forever, Mrs. Rose?" he asked. Rachel nodded in the darkness, then suddenly rolled over as fast as her sore body would allow when she realized who was speaking.

"What are you doing here?" she hissed in the dark. "And how did you get the twins in here?"

Rose smiled but doubted Rachel could see it in the darkness. "Well," he began slowly, "I'm here because of the twins, and they are here through careful planning and a rather large bribe."

"Are they all right?" she asked with sudden worry.

"They're fine, Rachel," Rose answered with a smile. "I just thought they should spend some more time with their mother and father, that's all." He stood and walked across the private room. From the hall he could hear the hospital staff going about their nightly routine.

"Let me hold them," said Rachel, reaching out both arms.

"You can hold one," answered Rose, bending over the bed to release the bundle in his right arm. "The nurse will be back in ten minutes to take the babies to the nursery. We have until then."

He eased down to the edge of the bed and cradled the small bundle in both arms. So small and utterly trusting, the boy had not awakened the entire time Rose held him.

"We should consider names," whispered Rachel.

"There will be plenty of time for that," Rose said quietly. For now it was enough to know that the twins were here. Names seemed so unnecessary.

"We should consider . . ."

"Not now, Rachel. Tomorrow we can consider anything you want, but tonight I just want to wrap myself in emotion and simply experience."

Rose waited for a response, but she made none. Emotion was enough for Rachel as well.

For the next ten minutes Rose sat in the darkened room with his wife and his children and reveled in his feelings. There were no wars, no killings, no painful loss. Everything was exactly as it should be. In his heart he was still a warrior, but now he was something more. Something stronger. Something better.

It made all the difference in the world.

BANSHEE

BATTLEMASTER

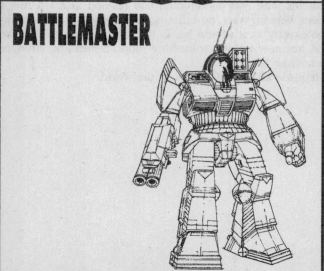

CHARGER

DASHER
OMNI MECH

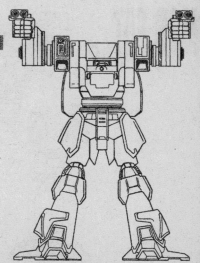

GRAND DRAGON

MAD CAT
OMNI MECH

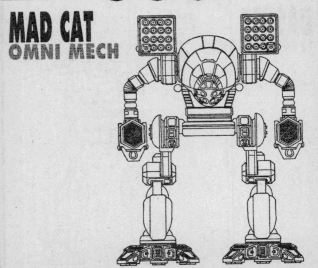

MASAKARI
OMNI MECH

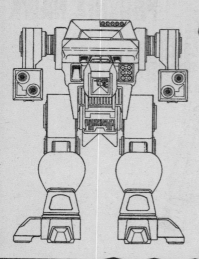

MERCURY

PHOENIX HAWK

RAVEN

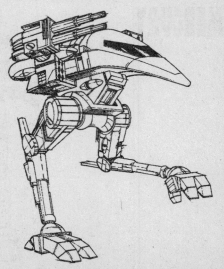

SHADOW HAWK

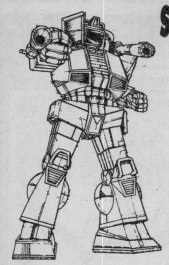

WARHAMMER

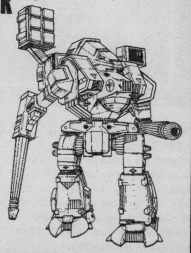

YOU'VE READ THE FICTION, NOW PLAY THE GAME!

Third Edition • 1604

BATTLETECH
A GAME OF ARMORED COMBAT

IN THE 30TH CENTURY LIFE IS CHEAP, BUT BATTLEMECHS AREN'T.

A Dark Age has befallen mankind. Where the United Star League once reigned, five successor states now battle for control. War has ravaged once-flourishing worlds and left them in ruins. Technology has ceased to advance, the machines and equipment of the past cannot be produced by present-day worlds. War is waged over water, ancient machinery, and spare parts factories. Control of these elements leads not only to victory but to the domination of known space.

FASA CORPORATION